The Chihuahua Affair

A Dog Lady Mystery

By Ellen Carlsen

TABLE OF CONTENTS

PROLOGUE

A tree-frog chorus rose through the evening air around them, as if sounding an alarm alerting others to the criminals in their midst.

Later, the two would blame the unfamiliar, small-town noises for what went wrong. Sirens, gunshots, growling trash haulers—those were the sounds they understood, the music that lulled them asleep in the city. The foreign chirps and croaks of the Missouri spring night left them unsettled and nervous as they crept around the house, hoping to catch their target in an unaware, unsupervised moment.

They'd been without work—their kind of work—for more than a decade. Then someone offered them big money for a seemingly simple task. They might be over-the-hill for their line of work, just a couple of old thugs, but they'd faced down dangerous men in the past and come out alive and, often, well compensated. This time, their target was a Chihuahua, protected only by a middle-aged woman living alone

They almost turned the job down. Too embarrassing.

Their instructions were to recover the Chihuahua and return it to the person who hired them, a retired drug lord. The two thugs couldn't imagine why anyone would pay so much for them to retrieve a yappy little dog. That was the question they'd asked each other all the way from Chicago. Why was this dog worth so much?

They'd stalked the woman and Chihuahua for several days, trying to learn when the dog was likely to be unsupervised. But it seemed it never was. They were running out of time and patience.

"Doesn't she ever nap? Doesn't she ever leave it alone in the yard for a few minutes?" Mel muttered.

Apparently not. Dog and woman seemed always to be together.

"I'll bet she lets the little monster sleep on her bed," responded Mort.

"Maybe even on the pillow."

Tonight was the night. If they couldn't snatch the dog away during its potty break, they'd break in, snatch the dog and run. If the woman gave them any trouble, they'd tie her up and shove her into a closet. No muss, no fuss. That was how they figured it would go.

Unfortunately, things went very wrong.

After waiting an hour past the expected potty break, they realized that the woman had probably retired early. The house was dark, something in their younger days they might have noticed and reached the logical conclusion.

Stretching their legs after spending too much time crouched by the back door, they easily mastered the door's lock and tiptoed into the house and up the stairs. They slid the bedroom door open, slowly.

At that moment, the dog began yipping and growling, waking the woman. She reached into a drawer in her bedside table, pulled out a small handgun and racked the slide.

Cha-chik.

A woman's gun, to be sure, but Mel and Mort saw it pointed at them. They wondered if she knew how to shoot. They were beginning to back away when the woman stepped out of bed and moved toward them. Then she made a fatal mistake. She fired a warning shot over their heads. Instincts kicked in, and Mel charged.

Mort rushed in to grab her arm holding the gun. The woman fought back, trying to keep hold of the gun. In the struggle, the gun went off and the woman fell to the ground, blood blossoming on the front of her nightgown.

After several moments of profanity and blaming each other for what happened, they remembered the Chihuahua who darted between them and toward the back door.

Mort caught up with the dog at the door and tucked her under one arm like a football. Mel soon joined them and opened the door.

Then Mort screamed.

The Chihuahua had bit into his arm, drawing a spiral of blood. He swatted at the dog as he would a mosquito, and the Chihuahua leaped free and raced across the yard and down the street.

Mel and Mort chased after it as best they could. Lumbering might better describe their movements. Time had not been kind to their physiques or their endurance.

Dawn was approaching quickly. Lights began blinking on in houses nearby. They abandoned the dog chase and instead stumbled and panted toward their car, hoisted their exhausted bodies inside and sped off.

An hour later, Police Officer Jim Butler found the Chihuahua as he searched the yard. He was on his knees looking at a footprint when the dog appeared from behind a bush, blood matted into her little face and coat. He recognized the dog as belonging to the victim.

"Oh, Mia, I'm so sorry. What am I going to do with you?"

Jim was an animal lover, so he decided to take it on himself to get the dog to a safe place.

But first, he recovered samples of the blood the dog had collected earlier.

CHAPTER 1

On the day before Sylvia Ritter disappears, she adopts a four-pound Chihuahua from the Redbud Area Dog Rescue.

After looking past all the other dogs at the adoption event in Omaha, Sylvia spots Mia the Chihuahua. Soon she has the tiny winner nestled snugly in her arms. She presses the dog softly against her right cheek, as if to feel Mia's warmth and fluttering heartbeat.

Audrey Nevins, head of the dog rescue group, knows Sylvia and her husband by sight because they live in or near Redbud, Nebraska, a town of about five-thousand located only forty-five minutes from the city.

Even in her late fifties, Sylvia is an attractive woman with what people describe as an energetic personality. Vivacious. Witty. Talkative. Some might also add that Sylvia is also a mystery. Everyone in Redbud knows about Sylvia Ritter, but, ironically, no one in Redbud can claim to know her well.

She'd grown up in Redbud but left the town not long after graduating from high school, where she'd been the most popular girl in her class. After staying away for more than twenty-five years, she returned home and in short order married the most forgettable boy in her former high school class: Carlton Ritter.

Carlton is thin, bald and quiet. Dependable. He had been a confirmed bachelor living at home when Sylvia returned to Nebraska. People still talk about their unlikely match. But for the most part, people see Sylvia and Carlton as just another Redbud couple, good, decent folk.

Audrey leans in to ask Sylvia a few questions about her history with dogs, trying to determine if Sylvia will provide a good home for Mia.

Sylvia pulls Mia away from her cheek and holds her out in front of her face, then pulls Mia toward her again to rub noses.

"I just love her. I love her," she coos, then looks up to Audrey and winks, "but my husband would kill me if I brought home a Chihuahua."

"We can't have that," murmurs Audrey, smiling and wondering how many times she's heard someone say their husband or wife would kill them (or divorce them) if they brought home a dog or another dog or a certain breed of dog. Audrey holds out her hands for Mia, but Sylvia resists and instead envelops the Chihuahua in a gentle hug, tucking her close to her heart.

"We can't adopt Mia to you unless everyone in the family is in favor of the adoption. It's just you and your husband, right? No children at home?"

Sylvia, pouting, slowly hands Mia back to Audrey.

"I'll talk him into it. I'll be back."

Sylvia stalks away, pulling her cellphone out of her purse as she heads toward the door.

Audrey hears laughter behind her and turns to see that two of her volunteers had been listening in.

Lois James, one of the Redbud women who fostered dogs for the Redbud Rescue, is wearing a straw hat with dog decals dangling from the brim.

"She'll talk him into it. She can talk Carlton into anything."

"Oh, Lois. That hat, really."

Audrey, unsentimental by nature, constantly ribs Lois and her friend Barbara Hansen about their over-the-top cute dog-adorned hats, sweaters and jewelry.

"I know them, Audrey. She'll be back."

As if on cue, Sylvia bursts back through the door, beaming widely and waving her cellphone.

"He says it's okay. Here, do you want to talk to him?"

Sylvia thrusts her arm in Audrey's direction, wagging the phone back and forth as if daring her to grab it.

Lois reaches in front of Audrey's face to snatch the phone. Holding the phone like a microphone, she speaks as if her audience is everyone else in the room.

"Hey, Carlton. Looks like you're about to meet the most adorable little Chihuahua I've ever seen. This is Lois, by the way."

She nods at the phone a few times.

"Uh-huh. Uh-huh. I can tell you're pretty excited."

She rolls her eyes and laughs as she closes the phone and hands it back to Sylvia.

"Give him some time. He'll be a Chihuahua lover before you know it."

And so Sylvia adopts Mia. After a leisurely run through the pet supply store sponsoring the adoption day, she heads home with the little dog and a cartload of dog treats, dog food, a padded dog bed, dog toys, a wardrobe of dresses and sweaters just Mia's size and a sparkly collar with matching leash.

Audrey and several others with Redbud Area Dog Rescue stand shoulder to shoulder, watching the new "mom" and dog leave the store.

Ellen Carlsen

"A good adoption," Audrey declares. "I don't think we'll need to worry about that one."

She will feel the same way the next morning, but not for long.

CHAPTER 2

Morning creeps up on the citizens of Redbud, tickling or teasing some and threatening others.

Audrey Nevins knows that with more than a dozen dogs in the house, she can't just pull the blanket up over her head. And yet, the dogs remain silent. Maybe she can stretch and yawn a few minutes more. Mornings come early enough at Redbud Area Dog Rescue.

Tired. Tired. I'm getting old.

Yesterday, she'd placed nine dogs during the adoption event in Omaha. That means there's room for more at her rescue. Today she can think of rescuing a few more from local shelters or from the list of owners who, for reasons good or bad, want to surrender their dogs. A couple of her foster parents are already asking her about new rescue dogs, reminding her that they now have vacancies.

Tired. Tired. How old am I?

As sensible as she usually is, Audrey always peels a few years off her actual age. But she's also well aware she receives regular mailings from organizations targeting retired persons, and even the occasional flyer discussing burial arrangements.

Oh, to be fifty-five again.

In spite of her age, Audrey walks with the comfortable stride of a much younger person. She is tall and stands straight as a drill sergeant, neither thin nor fat, more what people would call sturdy. She has an angular face defined by lines rather than curves and bright eyes that attract almost as much attention as the corkscrew curls bouncing almost horizontally from her face.

As a young woman, Audrey was the type men described as interesting rather than beautiful, but nevertheless she always caught their eyes. Even today, she still catches some admiring glances and a few indulgent stares.

But now she faces another day. And sometimes in the morning, Audrey feels the memories of the past year smacking her in the face without mercy. This year she lost several friends, other women who ran dog rescue organizations. She very nearly lost her own life.

She pushes herself up and drops her legs over the side of the bed. Sitting there for a while, she reminds herself that she is still alive and so is Judy. Redbud Area Dog Rescue continues to do well. Her daughter and family thrive. Audrey is happy living in Redbud.

Who would have thought a transplanted Californian would fit so comfortably into a small Nebraska town?

But that had happened. Audrey had retired early and moved to the town where her great-grandparents had settled in the 1870s. She'd been curious about those ancestors and about the old stories her grandmother had told her, hinting at family secrets and hidden treasures.

When she settled in Redbud, Audrey had followed one of her passions by founding a not-for-profit dog rescue organization. She'd bought property, modified it to make it more conducive to housing dogs as well as people. She even put in a swimming pool for the good of dogs and humans alike. In time, she recruited a small regiment of volunteers, most of whom fostered dogs in their homes until those dogs find homes.

Audrey's home is located in the countryside only about fifteen minutes from the center of Redbud. And soon, Redbud Area Dog Rescue will create a new center on the property once owned by her forebears, also a rural property not far from town.

Thanks to the discovery of a few gold coins.

Audrey fingers the coin she keeps on her bedside table and holds it up so that it glows from the morning light.

For all the pain you've caused, will you now stand for hope and courage?

***

Down the hall from Audrey, Judy Barnes wakes up with six dogs stretched out like petals around a flower. With eyes still closed, she feels a couple of Lab mixes, a pair of Chihuahuas, an elderly corgi mix and a young thirty-pound dog that doesn't look like any identifiable breed.

She opens her eyes and looks for a moment at the picture on her bedside table of a couple holding a baby between them. For most of the past year, she'd kept the picture hidden away and talked to no one about the two deaths that had left her in despair, untethered from her former life. Now she touches the photo every morning and evening.

You deserve to be remembered, even if it hurts. I'll never forget you.

Her tragedy had put her in a spotlight, the subject of both pity and criticism. Unable to tolerate her life in St. Louis, she'd decided to find a new path and purpose for herself. Inspiration came from stories about her great-great-grandparents who'd settled as immigrants near Redbud, Nebraska.

Soon after arriving in Redbud, Judy moved in with Audrey and her houseful of dogs. Audrey's empathy was not limited to dogs, and the rescue could always use as many hands as it could get. Stranger still, Judy learned that she and Audrey both claimed the same Nebraska settlers as ancestors.

Although she'd never thought of herself as a dog person, Judy took naturally to the dog rescue life and followed the dog-centered philosophy Audrey dished out: *Don't worry about being happy. Don't worry about interpreting dreams. It's all about dogs. Just take care of the dogs and everything else will take care of itself.*

Wise as those words seemed, they didn't always prove true. Soon after arriving in Redbud, Judy found out that peace and safety are illusive anywhere—even in small Nebraska towns. Soon she was not just reading murder mysteries, she was living one. Several murder victims throughout the country all had two things in common: they were all Dog Ladies, women who ran dog rescue organizations. And they all knew Audrey.

As Judy and the local police chief searched for answers to both the Dog Lady murders and the mysteries left behind by her ancestors, Judy and Audrey both nearly joined the list of murder victims.

That all happened almost a year ago. Judy had stayed with Audrey and by spring had decided to remain in Redbud. She reached her decision the day she first saw the Redbud trees in bloom, also the day she celebrated her thirty-eighth birthday.

Now she listens to the sounds of Audrey clattering about in the kitchen and knows it's time to get up. She'll help with the feeding, exercising, mopping, cleaning, answering of emails, updating of website and generally doing whatever needed doing. Maybe she'll even find time to blog about one of the dogs.

As she rises, she rubs a couple of grateful dog bellies and kisses the head of one.

Let's head for the yard, kids. Time to start our day.

***

Carl and Bella Warner work together shaking out a tablecloth and dropping it slowly around one of the tables in their café/bed-and-breakfast.

"Flowers, Carl. Hurry. Our guests will be waking up soon."

The two former New Yorkers had stumbled into Redbud a few years ago on their way to a new life on the West Coast. Instead, they stayed and opened Bella's Bed & Breakfast. It didn't take long before Bella's became the place to be—not only for Redbud citizens but also for travelers who sought it out because of word that the food and the atmosphere were worth the drive.

On the way to the backyard garden, Carl glances at his metal detector propped against the outside wall. He smiles. People laugh at his hobby. A few have even photographed him out in the fields, waving the metal detector back and forth across one Nebraska farmland after another. But that metal detector had done its job finally by pointing the way to a cache of gold coins worth more than five million dollars.

The money was doing good things now—providing college scholarships for young people whose relatives had been among Redbud's earliest settlers. Some of the money was providing low-cost spay/neuter surgeries for dogs and cats. And some would help build the new facility for Redbud Area Dog Rescue.

A brilliant solution, if I do say so.

"Did you say something, Carl? Where are my flowers?"

Carl returns with a few wild daisies and black-eyed Susans. He holds them out to Bella with a satisfied grin.

Bella tucks the flowers into vases on the two tables that will soon welcome guests. She heads for the kitchen, hands flying as she talks about the day's plans. Bella is incapable of talking without moving her hands, as if writing in the air the words that she speaks and then rearranging them.

Carl smiles at his wife. They're already dressed in matching shirts, something the community has come to expect of them. He runs his hand over the drooping mustache that some people say makes it hard to tell whether he is smiling or frowning. He thinks that his eyes give him away. He's aware that Judy Barnes calls him "The Walrus," a title he doesn't mind at all. Judy calls Bella "The Words," for obvious reasons.

Ah, Judy. How are you doing, really?

"Did you say something, Carl?"

He looks around the room, straightening a few chairs and tables and stepping back to see that all is in order. He follows Bella into the kitchen.

"I was just wondering about Judy—well, and Audrey too, of course. They both seem to be charging ahead with their lives, so strong and alive."

"Yes. Alive. Emphasis on alive."

Carl pulls Bella's hands down from the air and holds them awhile.

"We survived. Even when we thought we couldn't."

Carl and Bella had left New York after their two children died in a school bus accident. They'd been unable to bear the sad eyes of their friends, magnifying their own grief.

Carl lets her hands go and grabs a skillet. He knows they'll be busy all morning. After the guests eat, the morning coffee clubs will start arriving. He speaks softly, almost to himself.

"People always say you can't run from your sorrows. But sometimes you can. Sometimes it's the right thing to do. At least if you land in a place like Redbud."

What a strange town this is, to take in and heal so many wounded.

***

Randy Sorensen, Redbud's Chief of Police, checks the time and knows he should put down his knitting. Yes, although Chief Sorensen has a distinguished and unquestionably macho history as a former homicide detective from Chicago, his not-so-secret life as a proficient knitter is now common knowledge in Redbud. While once he knitted behind closed doors, he now takes his latest knitting project along to Bella's whenever he stops there for a meal or just coffee and socializing.

Randy had taken up knitting to help him stay sober. A friend from Alcoholics Anonymous had suggested knitting as a way to keep his hands and his mind away from alcohol. For him, the trick worked. He went from a serious drinker to a serious knitter. One addiction replaced another.

Today, he's beginning work on a sweater he is piecing together from leftover yarn from previous projects.

A sweater of many colors.

He arranges some of the yarn in rows, deciding which colors should follow which.

I like the orange next to the yellow, but should I follow the yellow with red, white... or maybe green?

He'd been knitting for almost two hours after waking early, something that happened often since the recent death of his 110-year-old grandfather. He'd been living with and caring for the elderly man for the past fifteen years.

He should be thinking of how much easier his life is now, but the empty house bothers him. He'd moved back to his hometown of Redbud in part because of his grandfather, but also because he needed a new start after burning out in Chicago. He likes Redbud and its people and feels responsible for their safety.

His eyes turn to the door that hides the room with all his historical files. He isn't just the police chief here; he's also the closest thing to the county's historian. Almost daily, he receives inquiries from people wanting to know more about relatives who once lived in or near Redbud.

It was his historian hat that had first brought some of the town's residents his way. First Audrey the Dog Lady, then Carl and Bella, and most recently, Judy. And he can't forget Lydia Harrison. Each of them had been researching the same ancestors, following similar family stories and myths. Randy's grandfather, with his long memory, had helped Judy imagine the past with its tendrils reaching into the present.

Then the family intrigue made a dire shift from fascination to fatalities. Judy had found a dead body. And deaths elsewhere began to connect and lead back to Redbud. Ultimately, Audrey and Judy nearly lost their lives.

My peaceful little town turned dangerous.

He tucks away his knitting into a plastic bin and snaps on the lid. Looking at the time on his cellphone, he figures he still may have time for coffee and a couple of Bella's famous muffins.

***

Lois James put her feet up on the deck's railing and figures it's almost time to get dressed and head to Bella's for breakfast with a few of her friends.

Her fingers tap on the laptop balanced on her thighs.

Why not? What would it hurt?

She stares at the Facebook page of a man she hadn't seen in thirty years.

One tap and I can just write "Remember Me?"

But she closes the laptop and stands up.

Don't be ridiculous. You are too old for this. Suppose we get together. We'll first need to get over the shock of what time has done to us.

She pinches some of the extra flesh at her waist and reminds herself that she no longer recognizes the face in her bathroom mirror.

Not pretty.

Lois leans back for just a moment and closes her eyes. At her feet are two miniature pinschers who'd survived two surgeries apiece to bring them to the point where they are ready for adoption.

She'd been fostering dogs for Redbud Area Dog Rescue since shortly after her husband's death three years ago. With her college-aged sons away from home most of the year, she needed the activity.

She still does some substitute teaching and in fact is Redbud High School's favorite substitute, known for her reliably upbeat moods. She also fills in with some of the younger grades.

Maybe this is enough. It's not bad. I'm doing something worth doing. What if I do meet this man from my past? What will he think of me?

She hasn't always favored t-shirts with dog slogans and jewelry that prominently displays her interest in dogs.

I've become eccentric. Eccentric and overly sentimental.

She knows she isn't any more eccentric than Audrey, but Lois is comfortable with sentimentality, something Audrey groans about regularly.

What was I thinking yesterday, wearing that straw hat with dog decals dangling from the brim? It's not bad enough getting old? I also need to be a public embarrassment? Ah, well. At least little Mia found a good home yesterday. I'll have to call Sylvia and Carlton later today to see how things are working out. Time to get my cheerful on!

***

Twelve-year-old Daisy Jensen focuses her binoculars on a trio of goldfinches on the neighbors' birdfeeder. While her parents sleep in on this Sunday morning, Daisy can't wait to start her day. She sits on the deck with a guidebook to backyard birds by her side and looks away from the finches for a moment.

Something catches her attention beyond the feeder, something small emerging from the tall grass near the back of the neighbors' yard. She steps closer to the railing and looks over at what is obviously a small dog racing in and out of the grass, yipping hysterically.

"What's the trouble, little dog?"

Almost as good at identifying dog breeds as birds, Daisy studies the dog through her binoculars and pronounces it a Chihuahua—a tan and white longhaired Chihuahua. The dog seems to be looking up at Daisy, barking toward her as if to say, "Come here!"

"Are you trying to tell me something?"

Daisy looks behind her into her own house. Still no sign that her parents are awake. She decides to go to the dog. Still in pajamas and slippers, she plods down the steps to her backyard and crosses over into the neighbors.'

Spotting Daisy, the little dog runs in her direction and then abruptly turns, as if inviting Daisy to follow her into the grassy area that separates the homes on Daisy's street from those on the next street over. Most of the grass here is long, probably just weeds, a natural barrier.

Looking up and beyond the grassy divide, Daisy can see through to the house directly across from where she stands. Raising her binoculars to her eyes, she sees a man looking in her direction. She wonders if he is looking for the Chihuahua, or maybe something else.

"Here, little one. Here, little one."

Daisy bends from the waist, making herself smaller and less intimidating. She even tries talking in a high, squeaky voice because she'd read that dogs are sometimes afraid of low, loud voices.

The Chihuahua looks back, tilts its head and leads Daisy to a spot just inside the grassy area. Daisy can see that someone has flattened a path through the tall grasses, a path that leads up to the house where the man stands on the deck.

The little dog places its front legs on Daisy, begging to be picked up.

"What do you think, little one? You want to come with me?"

Daisy picks up the dog in one hand and lets her binoculars swung slowly like a pendulum from her other hand.

"Maybe my parents will let me keep you."

She kisses the Chihuahua on its head.

"I'm lonely in Redbud, being the new kid in town. I don't know anyone. We've only lived here a couple of weeks. I need a dog."

She hurries across to her yard and up the steps to the deck.

"Mom! Dad! Look what I found!"

***

Dr. Shirley Thomas, Redbud's only veterinarian, arrives early at her clinic on Redbud's main street. She doesn't have Sunday hours, but she does have a couple of hospitalized pets who need attention.

First, she checks Olive, a cocker spaniel who needed nearly fifteen stitches after an encounter with a raccoon. A quick walk around the backyard gives Olive a little exercise and the chance to take care of business. Back inside, Olive ducks her face into a dish of kibble while Dr. Thomas strokes an elderly shepherd mix who's lost his appetite. She tempts him with a few slices of turkey meat and feels encouraged when Buster lifts his head enough to sniff the offering and nibble part of it. She offers him water and pinches his coat to make sure he isn't dehydrated.

Poor boy. It's probably just your time.

She knows, though, that Buster's owners aren't ready to put their old friend to sleep. They want to make sure they've done everything they can for him.

And who knows? Maybe you will perk up enough for a little more time with your people.

Later this afternoon, Dr. Thomas will return to check on the dogs again and to meet with Buster's adoptive parents, who want to visit him.

During the next hour, Dr. Thomas cleans the two dogs' cages and takes both outside. She carries Buster and sets him gently in a warm spot he'll enjoy in the center of the yard.

She sits in a lawn chair near the door, closes her eyes and thinks of the coffee and muffins waiting for her at Bella's.

CHAPTER 3

Chief Randy Sorensen strides quickly to his favorite table at Bella's. It's off in a far corner where he can sit with his back against the wall while keeping watch on those who come through the door.

He has more than one reason for visiting Bella's almost daily. Sure, the food is excellent, the coffee strong and the atmosphere as comfortable as a good friend's living room, but Bella's is also where he can take the temperature of his town. Everyone comes to Bella's.

He chuckles to himself.

What a change from my life as a homicide detective in Chicago. Here in Redbud, I feel like I'm what every police officer should be— everyone's friend and everyone's protector. I know his town and its people. I know their problems and I keep their secrets. And most of the time, Redbud is a peaceful place.

Just not all the time. Last year—the year he helped investigate several Dog Lady murders across the country—he had to remind himself that no community was ever immune from danger and crime.

The bell over the front door jangles as Audrey and Judy step inside. Both spot him and wave.

Last year, at different times, he'd sat by both of their hospital beds. Audrey had almost become one of the murdered Dog Ladies when she had drunk wine tainted with phenobarbital. Later, Judy had nearly died from stab and gunshot wounds after she stumbled onto a crime scene. It all seemed so long ago but was barely a year past.

Thank God that's over. I'll be fine if I never need my homicide detective skills again.

Something about Audrey always makes him comfortable. Randy surprises himself realizing how much he enjoys seeing her, talking with her, teasing her.

And Judy?

He'll let Judy tag along with him on some of his investigations, in part to keep an eye on her, but also because she reminds him of the daughter he seldom sees anymore. Judy arrived in Redbud, lost and bedraggled, allegedly to research her ancestors but mainly to escape two tragic family losses. With a little research, Randy learned all the facts related to both deaths shortly after Judy's arrival. But Judy needed many months and a brush with death herself before she could talk about what had happened.

He looks at the two women. Audrey is bustling toward her favorite table, her brown and gray curls bouncing away from her face. The much shorter Judy hustles to keep up, needing at least two extra steps for every one of Audrey's. Judy ties her blonde hair back securely in a stubby ponytail. She is wearing khaki pants and an ironed t-shirt, a contrast to the billowing sundresses Audrey favors when she isn't in dirty overalls.

A year ago, Judy would have been in the same shorts and t-shirt she'd worn the day before. Her feet would be shuffling in cheap flip-flops, her hair flying recklessly, her face without a trace of makeup. Randy admires the changes.

She's feeling better. She's going to be okay.

"Hey Randy," Audrey calls, turning in her chair to catch his eye. "You can join us. We just need a bigger table."

"Thanks, but I need to get moving. Duty calls."

As if to show he has work to do, Randy pulls out his phone and dials the station. The patrolman going off duty fills him in on what sounds like an uneventful night.

He's just getting to his feet when several other Redbud citizens join the growing breakfast crowd. Lois spots Audrey and Judy and heads to their table. Randy nods at her and she smiles back. Her hair falls part way across her face, almost as if she's trying to hide. Lois is an attractive middle-aged woman, but Randy suspects that she feels insecure about her looks and thinks she should lose weight. Everyone knows Lois for her jovial good humor and willingness to help anyone who needs help.

Arriving a few steps after Lois is the town's veterinarian, Dr. Shirley Thomas. She spots Audrey's table and heads that way. Also joining Audrey's table is Barbara Hansen, another of Audrey's foster parents and Lois James's closest friend.

Then when Randy is almost to the door, a man opens the door and stands still in the doorway, scanning the room.

Randy recognizes him as Carlton Ritter, a man who commutes to Omaha for his job with Union Pacific Railroad. Carlton seems confused. Randy stops next to the other man and speaks softly.

"Is everything okay?"

Carlton looks at the chief briefly, then walks toward Audrey's table.

His voice is a little too loud as he monotones, "Has anyone seen Sylvia? She's gone."

Lois looks up at Carlton, whose arms cross firmly in front of him as if he feels cold.

"Why Carlton, what did you say? Why aren't you home with that cute little dog Sylvia adopted yesterday?"

Carlton's voice seems to go higher with every word.

"I said, Sylvia's gone. I don't know where she is. The dog's gone too."

The chief turns from the door and touches Carlton's back.

"Maybe I can help. Let's talk."

He leads the seemingly confused man out of the café and away from the startled faces staring up at both of them.

Neither man hears the hushed remarks passing around the table.

"Remember what Sylvia said?"

"About how her husband would kill her?"

"If she adopted a Chihuahua?"

"But she was just being silly."

"She talked him into it. He said it was okay."

"How well do we know Carlton and Sylvia?"

"Don't be silly. They are both lovely people."

"Are we sure of that?"

"Of course we are."

"Should we tell the chief?"

And, of course, they will.

***

Is it happening again?

Or is this only what it appears? A simple domestic quarrel. Probably about the Chihuahua. Carlton may not have been all that happy about Sylvia adopting the dog. Maybe the little dog peed on the rug and Carlton blamed Sylvia. Maybe they fought and she stomped out to cool off alone somewhere. She'll probably be back with the dog before the day is gone.

That's the most likely scenario. In Chicago, he wouldn't have wasted any time on a case like this. Not this early, anyway. But this is his town and his people, and he operates differently here.

Chief Sorensen knows the couple. He'd known them from the time he'd moved in with his grandfather as a boy. They'd been teenagers together, had attended the same high school.

Then Sylvia left for California the day after graduating from high school. Carlton signed on with Union Pacific. Randy moved to Chicago and become a police officer and later a homicide detective. A lot of living good and living bad passed before Randy returned to Redbud and became the town's new police chief. Then he learned that the vivacious and outspoken Sylvia had returned from California and married Carlton. If there was a "most likely" category that best applied to Carlton, it was "most likely to be forgotten."

Poor Carlton. And yet, he won the most popular girl in the class. How did that happen?

The chief had been surprised to even find Sylvia back living in Redbud. In high school, she let everyone know she was moving on, leaving boring little Redbud for someplace with spice and verve and most of all, excitement.

And yet, she returned to Redbud and settled down with the boy from high school that everyone forgot. So where is she now?

"When did you last see her?"

Chief Sorensen and Carlton sit across from each other at the Ritters' dining room table.

27

"I went up to bed about nine. I always like to read in bed for a while. That's why I retire so early."

"No need to apologize for that."

"Sylvia said she was taking the little dog Mia for a walk. I must have fallen asleep. I don't remember her coming to bed. She wasn't here when I woke up. I panicked then, and ran about the house and the lawn calling her name. The neighbors must really think I'm crazy now."

Carlton looks at the chief, his eyes begging for an answer.

"Where could she be? Could someone have grabbed her?"

Chief Sorensen knows to tread carefully. He suspects Carlton is leaving something out.

"Any chance she just got up early and took the dog for a ride?"

"Her car's still here. And she's never awake before I am"

The chief looks into the eyes of a man who is twisting in his chair, thumping fingers on the table, biting on his lower lip, a man obviously upset and uncomfortable.

Is he telling the truth? He behaves like someone who is either hiding something or flat out lying.

"Then I decided to check out Bella's. Everyone goes to Bella's. Well, except for me, maybe. I'd rather drink my coffee alone on my deck. Bella's is a little too popular for me. Too busy."

That's the exact opposite of what Chief Sorensen might have said. He would have said Bella's was comfortable, friendly, his favorite place to sip a cup of coffee or enjoy a meal. But then, Carlton has always been uncomfortable in social situations. He was that way in high school. Maybe his current discomfort is natural for him, his normal reaction to stress. The chief nods, encouraging him to talk on.

"But Sylvia liked that place. She said she always saw someone she knew there. I thought that maybe she walked there with the dog. Maybe she fell asleep downstairs and then woke up before me and decided to walk to Bella's with the dog."

Carlton's speech grows faster as he works through the possibilities, studying his drumming fingers at the same time.

Then he stops and looks up.

"But she wasn't there."

Chief Sorensen wants to reassure the man, tell him everything will be okay, but he knows there are several ways things might not turn out okay for Carlton. At the least, his marriage might be in trouble. Worst case, and most unlikely, someone kidnapped or even killed Sylvia. Then there was always the possibility that Carlton himself is responsible for Sylvia's absence.

Isn't that usually the case? The husband is the number one suspect.

The chief stands, inviting Carlton to follow.

"Let's take a look around the house and yard. Tell me if you see anything out of place."

The Ritters live in a thirty-year-old, split-level home with a large deck on the back looking over a common area that separates their block from the next block over. The walk through the house shows nothing out of place, nothing missing from Sylvia's closet. As the two men step out onto the deck, the chief asks if Carlton has called any of the neighbors yet this morning.

The chief tries to sound reassuring, "Maybe she walked over to show off the new pup."

"Not yet...although they might have heard me calling." Carlton seems to look across the common ground. "Earlier, I thought I saw something over that way. But I didn't have my glasses on yet. I went and got them, but when I looked again, I didn't see anything unusual."

"Are you friendly with your neighbors?"

"Oh, yes. You know Sylvia. She meets everyone. Of course, we don't know the new people yet." He points at a house across the common area and to the left. "They moved in a couple of weeks ago."

Chief Sorensen knows about the Jensens, but he hasn't yet stopped by to introduce himself. This might be a good time to meet them and, at the same time, ask if they'd noticed anything.

But it's still so early in the investigation. Too early to assume the worst.

Chief Sorensen squeezes Carlton's upper arm.

"Maybe you could make some calls. Chances are, she'll be home in no time. I'll check back in a few hours." He adds, "Try not to worry."

Why did I say that? If he wasn't worrying before, I'm sure he will now. But Sylvia probably is fine. She might be sharing morning coffee with a neighbor. Maybe she decided the new dog needed a long walk. The two of them might even now be in the park getting to know each other better. I'll drive around town and look through the park on my way back to the office.

Then he thinks of something.

"Have you tried her cellphone?"

"It's still on the kitchen counter, being charged."

As the chief leaves, he touches one finger to his brow, a slight salute toward Carlton.

"Get started on those calls. That's the best thing you can do now."

In other words, keep busy.

Chief Sorensen never lets go of his game face. But the face behind the face is beginning to twitch.

Something feels wrong.

After leaving Carlton, Chief Sorensen drives methodically up and down streets in the neighborhood. He stops at the nearby park and steps out of his vehicle, seeing nothing but unoccupied benches and playground equipment.

He returns to his office and finds Audrey, Judy and Lois all waiting for him.

CHAPTER 4

"We thought you should know," starts Lois.

"But we really don't think it means anything," interrupts Audrey.

The two women stop long enough to look at each other. Judy just smiles, seemingly ready to laugh.

"Something happened at yesterday's adoption event," Lois continues.

Chief Sorensen holds up his hand as if to stop traffic. He leads the three women into his office and drops into the chair behind his desk. He points at three chairs for the women. Before he speaks, he begins rubbing his forehead as if he's trying to carve an additional worry line.

"I know Sylvia adopted a Chihuahua, if that's what you're trying to say. I also know the Chihuahua is missing along with Sylvia. I'm assuming they're both together somewhere, bonding."

"But that's not all that happened at the adoption event," Audrey insists.

The chief smiles at Audrey.

"OK. Spill it. What happened, and how will it solve the mystery of the disappearing new pet owner?"

He knows both Audrey and Judy think of themselves as amateur sleuths.

The chief raises his arms in surrender. "I'm not too proud to accept some help."

Audrey nods, as if to say: "That's why we're here, and we know you need our help."

Then she goes on, "Sylvia fell in love with Mia the Chihuahua. But then she said her husband would *kill* her if she brought home a Chihuahua… or maybe she just said 'dog.' I told her we couldn't let her adopt Mia if her husband didn't want the dog too. I think I joked a bit about how I didn't want to be responsible for anyone's murder."

Lois lifts a hand, as if asking permission to talk. "So Sylvia stomped out and said she'd call her husband and talk him into it. And I told Audrey that Sylvia could talk Carlton into anything."

Audrey takes over again, "And a few minutes later, Sylvia came back in, waving her cellphone and saying Carlton was fine with the idea. Lois talked to him a bit and told him he'd be a Chihuahua lover in no time. Then Sylvia shopped for supplies and left with a shopping cart full of dog food, treats, dog bed, toys and even a wardrobe in Mia's size."

"A wardrobe?"

Chief Sorensen likes dogs, but he doesn't quite see the charm in providing a dog with its own clothing. Neither, apparently, does Audrey, because she rolls her eyes before adding that she felt confident then that the adoption would work out.

"But now I'm worried. This is no time for Sylvia to take off in a huff because Carlton didn't fuss over Mia long enough."

"Is that something Sylvia might do? Take off in a huff?"

Lois smiles. "We all love Sylvia, but as you should remember from high school, Randy, Sylvia was always a drama queen."

The chief does remember that about Sylvia.

Always center stage. The highest highs and the lowest lows. Laughter and tears. Hot and cold. No temperature control at all.

34

He wonders, "What was it about her that made her so popular then? Why did we all put up with the drama?"

Lois, the only other one in the room who'd gone to high school with both Randy and Sylvia, pushes out her lower lip and squints, as if remembering something important. She punches one finger in the air as she talks.

"There was just something about her. She was pretty and smart. And charming. All she had to do was talk to you and you felt special. She could make your day."

Judy leans forward in her chair.

"But what about Carlton? Does she still 'make his day'? And what does he do when she doesn't? I'm betting he was the class president and star football player. Right?"

Both Chief Sorensen and Lois break into peals of laughter.

"Carlton?" The chief explains, "When Sylvia introduced me to Carlton as her husband—that was shortly after she moved back here from California—I asked where she'd met him. I didn't even remember going to school with him."

Judy smiles. "Hard accounting for love. Maybe he was the one who made her feel special."

Lois adds, "And he's probably the least aggressive man I've ever met. He's really a sweetheart, in a bland sort of way."

Audrey twists the long silk scarf draped around her neck.

"But sometimes those quiet men surprise you. They hold their emotions in for so long. Then one day, they just snap."

She snaps her fingers to illustrate the point.

Judy leans forward and looks straight at the chief. "Over a Chihuahua?"

The chief responds with a grunt, "I have yet to investigate a murder where the motive had anything to do with a Chihuahua."

Audrey stands up as if ready to leave.

"Judy, we've got some dogs who need our attention. And maybe we should consider rescuing a few dogs from death row."

She pauses and turns to Chief Sorensen.

"But I'll sure feel better when I know both Sylvia and Mia are safe. I felt so good about that adoption. And now I'm not sure what to feel."

Just then, Blanche Olson, the department's office manager, pokes her head in the door. She is a fortyish woman who favors floral dresses and wears her blonde hair short and curly.

"There's someone here you might want to see."

Blanche steps back from the door as a plump woman in black slacks and a long purple tunic steps into the room. Behind her is a young girl, wiping away tears and sniffing loudly. In the young girl's arms is a tan and white Chihuahua.

"Mia!" the three women gasp at once.

And in that moment, everything changes.

Sylvia is not out for a long walk with her new dog. She's not anywhere with Mia.

She is missing.

In Chief Sorensen's mind, Sylvia's disappearance is now an official police matter. He steps out from behind his desk and introduces himself to the woman and her daughter. Audrey, Judy and Lois look back and forth between Mia and the chief.

What now?

Audrey reaches for the Chihuahua, but the girl holding her turns away and holds the little dog protectively against her chest.

"I'm Chief Sorensen." He sticks out his right hand for a quick shake. "You must be Redbud's newest residents."

"I'm Margaret Jensen, and this is my daughter Daisy. I wasn't sure if this was where we should come. At first I thought we'd just put up some Found Dog signs, except that…"

She gently pushes her daughter forward.

"Tell him, Daisy. Tell him everything."

Daisy looks straight into the chief's eyes and tells her story about spotting the little dog while she was looking through binoculars at the neighbors' bird feeder. She describes leaving her deck to follow the Chihuahua into the tall grass.

"And the grass was all smooshed up in that area."

The chief asks Margaret and Daisy to show him the area where Daisy found Mia.

"Not Mia. I named her Birdy because I was looking at birds when I found her. I want to keep her if my folks will let me. I think she needs me."

Audrey looks at Daisy and recognizes that it's Daisy who needs a dog.

What should I do?

She steps up to Daisy, "Well, you see, Birdy already has a home."

"Where?" asks Daisy. "And how did she end up all alone?"

Good question—one going through all their minds: how did Birdy end up all alone?

"Maybe you could foster Birdy while we try to sort things out," Audrey suggests, starting to explain to mother and daughter about Rosebud Area Dog Rescue and the duties of foster parents. "I'll need to follow you home and tell you more about how things work."

Margaret nods, and Daisy looks from Audrey to her mother with hopeful glances.

"Does that mean I can keep her?"

Audrey looks at Daisy, whose bony shoulders poke against her t-shirt. Looking at this preteen with the piercing green eyes, Audrey wonders how she'll ever be able to separate this skinny girl from this tiny dog—even if Sylvia does return home safely.

And did I just say "if"?

***

For Daisy, it has been one of the most exciting days of her life. Oh yes, she knows something terrible might have happened to the lady who adopted Birdy the day before. But she doesn't know the lady. So far, it's like a television show running live in her neighborhood.

Something is happening! Something is happening, and I'm an important part of it!

She watches carefully as Chief Sorensen and a couple of crime scene investigators tiptoe around the area where she found Birdy. The chief walks back to her several times to ask other questions.

What time did this happen? Had she seen anyone else?

Yes, she had seen the man on the deck over there. She points across the grassy common ground.

"I think he was looking this way, too."

The chief makes some sort of humming noise.

Daisy knows she's smart, all As in school. She also watches all those crime shows on television and isn't surprised to see the police taking soil and grass samples and sealing them into bags. After tonight, she'll be even smarter because she'll go online and learn everything she can about solving crimes with both science and brains.

Maybe I can be a junior detective!

"What do you think, Birdy? Maybe we can both be detectives."

Birdy dances at the end of the leash that the lady with the crazy hair and long scarf had given Daisy. Whenever Daisy talks, Birdy looks up at her.

"Hey, Birdy. You might be a key witness. I wonder if a dog has ever testified in court. Could you finger the bad guy?"

Daisy picks Birdy up and holds her in her arms.

"Whatever happened, it must have been scary."

Daisy stays back as far as Chief Sorensen tells her to, but whenever he isn't watching, she inches a little closer and stands up on her toes.

A little later, a man from across the grassy common area crashes toward them.

"Is she there? Is she there?"

The man stumbles and almost falls. Chief Sorensen marches toward him and puts an arm around his shoulders. A few minutes later, the man returns to his house.

Daisy notices another police officer knocking on doors down the street. He's probably asking people the same question Chief Sorensen had asked her and her parents: "Did you hear or notice anything unusual last night or early this morning."

Daisy's parents had looked at each other first and then at the chief. They shook their heads. No. Nothing. Daisy hadn't heard anything either.

Best of all, I'm now Birdy's foster mom. It's an important job.

She and her parents had sat around their kitchen table while the lady—her name was Audrey—told them all about the responsibilities (yes, responsibilities) involved. Daisy knows she's a responsible young person. All her teachers tell her that.

Before they'd gone to the police station, Daisy's mom had said they'd need to return the Chihuahua to its proper owner. Someone was probably frantic and looking everywhere. But both mom and dad agreed she could foster Birdy. They all signed papers making it official. Daisy did most of the talking. Her parents didn't seem to know what to think of all these Redbud people. Her mom and dad stayed quiet most of the time, sneaking looks at each other and even holding hands under the table. They're acting as if they're afraid of something. But in the end, they agreed Daisy could be a dog's foster mom.

I'm a foster mom for a dog. How about that? And I thought things were going to be dull here. And that isn't all. One of the women. Her name is Judy. She said this Redbud Dog Rescue needs more young volunteers. Whoopee! Of course, I volunteered. Maybe I'll even make new friends.

Daisy can see that Audrey and Judy want to be detectives too. They act mad when the chief asks them to leave.

"I know you have other things to do," he offers, politely.

Audrey stands still next to Daisy for a few minutes, before slowly turning to leave. She and Judy amble across the yard to the van with Redbud Area Dog Rescue stenciled across the side. They turn and look back every couple of steps or two, and one of them, Daisy isn't sure which one, calls, "You'll need our help."

Then the other one says, "If you have time for dinner tonight, come by Bella's. She's introducing her vegetarian menu."

The chief turns when he hears that and rubs a hand across his balding head.

"A vegetarian menu? In Nebraska?"

He shakes his head.

Then he calls after them, "What happened to Lois?"

"She went to console Carlton."

"Great," Daisy hears him mutter, but she knows he doesn't mean he is happy about it.

Daisy pulls a little notebook out of her pocket and writes down a few things. She doesn't want to forget anything she sees or hears. Not if she's going to be a detective.

When she sees the chief and the others preparing to leave, Daisy walks back to her house, walking Birdy next to her on her left side. Once inside, she sits down on one of the still-unpacked moving boxes and lifts Birdy up next to her. She makes a few more notes as she thinks about what has happened.

How does someone just disappear? She takes her dog out for a walk and the next minute she's gone, snatched away, maybe, but by whom? Maybe the dog got away from her and ran after something into the tall grass. But what? There's no real walking path through the grassy area. Except for that flattened area, it's just tall, scratchy, buggy grass and weeds. No one would walk a dog through that area on purpose. So what did the dog see? Or smell? Or was it the lady who saw something and wanted to investigate an area that was a lot closer to Daisy's house than her own? Or were lady and dog running from someone? Or to someone?

Daisy stuffs her mini-notebook into a side pocket on her shorts and contemplates for a while. She pulls her feet up on the box and rests her chin on her knees while scratching Birdy behind the ears.

And why didn't anyone hear anything? Redbud is a small town, not a city with all its night noises. People watch out for each other. That's what she'd always heard. That's what her parents told her before they moved. They'd be safe in Redbud.

Or will they?

***

When you're law enforcement in Redbud, the police footwork doesn't take long. Chief Sorensen and two young officers canvass the neighborhood near Sylvia and Carlton's home, finding most of the residents at home on a Sunday afternoon.

No one had seen anything. No one had heard anything.

Lot of sound sleepers around here. Early to bed.

They miss a few neighbors, though. One young couple lives only two houses down from the Ritters. Chief Sorensen leaves a message on their door. He also hopes to hear back from a few teenagers who might have been out last night and were not home during the canvass.

The chief looks up at the clouds now rolling across the sky. He hopes this isn't a bad sign. He sorts through the events of the morning as he ducks into his car. His phone rings and he sees that it's Carlton calling.

Maybe Sylvia's back home with a hilarious explanation of what happened, something to make us all laugh with relief.

But that isn't the case. Carlton asks if the chief has learned anything.

Could Sylvia really be a victim? Could Carlton really be a suspect?

He knows he'll need to press Carlton for more details, but his memories of the quiet, nearly invisible high school classmate keep surfacing as if warning him to consider alternatives.

Sure, the husband is the first suspect, but… Carlton?

The chief shakes his head, remembering times in Chicago when guilty husbands had sobbed and quivered when reporting the terrible news that their wives were missing or dead; or, in other cases, when police had notified the husband of his wife's misfortune.

If Carlton faked his confusion and fear, he's a master performer.

Chief Sorensen rolls down his window as one of his officers pulls up next to him.

"Let's check out all gas stations, fast food places and motels within thirty miles either way. See if anyone's seen anything unusual."

The chief heads west, his officer east.

By late afternoon, they meet back at the station, ducking inside in the midst of a rainstorm that slices diagonally through the Nebraska sky. Of possible interest is the sighting of a car with California plates filling up just outside of town. Unfortunately, the attendant doesn't remember more than a couple of numbers on the plate and a sketchy description of the driver—young, tall, dark hair.

Sylvia had spent time in California. Maybe.

Chief Sorensen has already sent out a Be On the Lookout (BOLO) alert including Sylvia's picture to law enforcement agencies. If Sylvia isn't home by tomorrow, he might talk some of the television stations into a story about the missing Redbud lady.

For now, he'll end his day with a more serious conversation with Carlton, digging a little deeper into the details of their marriage and any secrets Carlton may be hiding. Somewhere in the past—in Sylvia's or Carlton's or both of theirs—he'll find the clues he needs.

Then he might actually head to Bella's and check out the new vegetarian menu. Although the new dishes aren't much of a lure for a red meat man, Randy knows that, at the very least, he'll catch an earful from Audrey and Judy. Both, in their minds, will have nearly solved the mystery of Sylvia's disappearance by now.

He also hopes Lois will be there since she seems to know Sylvia and Carlton.

Someone knows something. And since everyone goes to Bella's, that someone might be there tonight.

CHAPTER 5

Audrey and Judy spend part of their day taking care of dogs, cleaning out crates, mopping floors and answering calls and emails from people either interested in adopting dogs from Redbud Area Dog Rescue or hoping the rescue group will take the dogs they no longer want.

Both women are in silent moods. Too many calls from people wanting to dump their dogs will do that to them. Plus, Audrey scowls over a pile of bills and reviews plans for the shelter on the new property. Judy paces from one window to another grumbling about the endless rain.

The off-and-on rain the past week has knocked out the possibility of taking a swim break. Dogs and pools always make for fun and, sometimes, trouble. Which dogs enjoy a swim? Labs? Almost always. Others surprise her either with their aversion to water or their delight. She remembers the Jack Russell terrier who'd splashed through the pool snapping at the bubbles sprouting in front of her.

Both of them worry about the missing Sylvia. Only twenty-four hours ago, they'd smiled at Sylvia as she waved back at them, little Birdy tucked under one arm. A perfect home for the young Chihuahua, they all thought. Now, Sylvia is gone—possibly abducted or even killed. Fortunately, Birdy is safe. But knowing Birdy is safe makes Sylvia's disappearance all the more sinister. Sylvia would not have left home without Birdy no matter how angry she may have been at Carlton. Or would she? Neither of them know Sylvia that well.

At one point Judy sighs, and Audrey looks up from her paperwork.

"What if Sylvia hadn't adopted a dog yesterday?" Audrey asks. "Would Randy be worried about her if that little girl hadn't found Birdy running loose? Hardly. We would all have just figured she finally got tired of him. Birdy's the only reason we all think otherwise. I don't think Sylvia would have left that little dog behind while taking off for a new life."

"But she didn't take her car," Judy points out.

"Who said she needed a car? Maybe someone picked her up— some old lover… or a new lover."

Judy rolls her eyes. She still has trouble listening to women in their fifties, sixties and beyond talking about old or new lovers—but especially new lovers. But she's listened to plenty of such chatter since moving in with Audrey. Redbud seems well stocked with older women with active libidos, or at least active longings and even more active imaginations. Judy's personal loss has left her bereft of such feelings. Well, maybe a few longings, but she's never sure for what.

"Could Carlton have killed her? Does he have a temper?"

Audrey considers Judy's question.

"I don't know either of them more than to say hello. But Redbud is full of people who grew up with them, including Lois and Barbara, not to mention Randy. And I'd sure like to hear more about how the most popular girl in her class married the most forgettable boy."

"Hmm, yes." But Judy has seen stranger things. "There must have been something that drew her to him."

"Or maybe she was running from something, or someone, and found a safe hiding place with Carlton. How much do we know about her time in California? And why did she return to Redbud?"

They both chew on those thoughts awhile.

Audrey checks the time and suggests they visit one of the nearby shelters that has been leaving messages about dogs in need. Maybe there's time to save a few lives today.

A rescue run is enough to take their minds off the chilling question of what might have happened to Sylvia. But first, they need to lead the dogs they already have outside for a bathroom break. Judy opens the side door and grabs a broom propped against the wall. Holding the broom high, she acts the role of a high-stepping drum major, hoping to lead a parade of dogs into the rain.

"Who's afraid of a little rain?" she calls. "Hut, two, three, four."

When she turns her head to look behind her, she sees six dogs still crowded together in the doorway marveling at her foolishness.

"Come on! I'm not afraid of rain. Follow me! Rain is nice. Rain doesn't hurt." She marches farther. "Hut, two, three."

Still no movement at the door.

With a sigh, Judy steps back inside and decides that, if she can't lead them outside, maybe she can sweep them out. This maneuver proves more successful. The dogs, realizing her serious intent, step reluctantly a few feet into the rain, squat and pee in unison, then turn and nearly knock Judy over in the rush to come back indoors. They're more than willing to crawl into their dry and comfortable kennels for naptime.

After Audrey controls her laughter, she beckons, "How about the county pound? They've been begging us all week to pull a couple of their dogs."

The county pound is a "kill" shelter, also known as "open intake." Staff there picks up stray dogs and takes in any dogs people dropped off. Staff and volunteers try to find new homes for as many of the dogs as possible, either through adoption or rescue. They contact groups such as Redbud Area Dog Rescue whenever they reach the point where they will need to start euthanizing dogs for lack of space.

"No-kill" shelters and rescues never face the need to euthanize healthy, adoptable dogs. If they don't have room, they stop taking in new dogs. But today, Redbud Rescue has room. Audrey and Judy share an umbrella, trying to stay in step as they hunch shoulders and bump heads on the quick sprint to the Redbud Rescue van. Judy still finds the wide-open Nebraska sky frightening at times, the way it slips down around her knees, making stormy days all the more menacing.

"Give me a tiny room any day," she mutters. "I feel safer when I'm closed inside."

"Don't be silly, Judy. The sky is what Nebraska is all about. Freedom and space and horizons that go on forever."

"Well, I do love Redbud and the Redbud trees and Bella's and all the people I've met here who've been so good to me."

"Do I hear a 'but' coming?"

Audrey holds the umbrella high as Judy ducks into the passenger side of the van. Then she hurries around, backs into the driver's seat and fights with the umbrella awhile as it tries to fly loose from her grasp. Finally, Audrey closes the reluctant umbrella, pulls it after her and tucks it between the two of them.

She starts the van and looks at Audrey. "But what?"

Judy sighs, "Oh, I don't know. It's just that I want Redbud to be a safe place, a refuge from the rest of the world. Sometimes it seems like I brought something with me when I showed up here a year ago. Look at everything that's happened."

She doesn't need to mention the dead body she'd found or the murders of several Dog Ladies, women who knew Audrey and ran dog rescue groups in other states. And she certainly doesn't need to mention that both she and Audrey had nearly been murder victims themselves.

"It seems like I brought with me an evil infection, a disease that wasn't here before. Now we have a missing woman, and not just any woman, a woman who'd just adopted one of our dogs."

Audrey doesn't say anything for a while. When she does, she reaches across the seat and pats Judy's leg.

"And last week someone killed seven people during a church prayer meeting. And other killers have targeted children in classrooms."

"And in some parts of the world, people are beheading people in the name of their god. I guess the whole world has gone crazy." Judy cracks a halfway smile. "Ah, for the good old days."

"Not for this old gal. As far as I'm concerned, the good old days were never that good. The life of a typical dog today is a lot better than it would have been a hundred years ago. In fact, the life of a typical dog today is probably better than that of most people a hundred years ago. And as far as violent crime goes, in America violent crime is the lowest it's been in more than fifty years. Ask Randy. He has all the FBI statistics."

Judy smiles whenever Audrey calls Chief Sorensen by his first name. She is the only one who does, a reflection perhaps of their growing closeness.

Judy looks out her window and sighs, "I guess sometimes our world just doesn't seem safer than it once was. Like today."

"Cheer up. Sylvia might be back home by now." Audrey doesn't sound like she believes her own words, but she adds, "If anyone brought trouble to Redbud, I did."

"But you also brought good things. You brought Redbud Area Dog Rescue."

"And Redbud is still one of the safest, most congenial places on earth."

They both smile and drive on to the county animal shelter in silence.

As they walk into the shelter, Audrey and Judy head for the squarely built blonde woman behind a ten-foot-long counter. Jane Olson, all five feet of her, beams back at them and claps her hands together twice.

"Have I got some dogs for you!" She bends over and picks up a scowling red and white Pekingese. "This is Ruby. She can be a little opinionated, but she's still a love."

As if to demonstrate, Jane kisses Ruby on the head. Ruby scowls into Jane's face but reluctantly (it seems) licks the woman's dimpled chin.

"Her owner entered a nursing home yesterday. Now Ruby's alone. Yesterday, she was sleeping on cushions. Today she doesn't know what happened."

Audrey nods her acceptance and Jane beams.

"Now come and see some others."

A few minutes later, Audrey and Judy load up a thirty pound white American Eskimo mix named Snowball whose owner had died; a bulldog mix with a bad back leg due to a gunshot wound; a dachshund/beagle mix girl who'd been picked up as a stray; a seven-year-old cattle dog mix with a beautiful blue-ticked coat; and an eighty pound black Lab/Rottweiler mix, also a stray. And, of course, Ruby the Pekingese.

Jane Olson claps her hands together several more times and bounces on her heels.

"We've cleared out enough cages. I won't need to euthanize tomorrow."

50

The rain has stopped and the sun is now peeking around a shelf of clouds.

Jane continues jumping and clapping, and occasionally hugging, both Audrey and Judy until everyone breaks into silly laughter.

With all new dogs safely locked into crates in the back of the van, Audrey and Judy back up the Redbud Area Dog Rescue van, turn it around in the parking lot, and head home.

"Now don't we feel better?" Audrey smiles at Judy and reaches across the seat to slip Judy's cellphone from her purse. "Now start calling those fosters who said they were ready for new dogs. Maybe some of them can even meet us at home."

Monday morning, Audrey will set up vet appointments with Dr. Thomas. Within days, most will be spayed or neutered, microchipped, up to date with shots, and well checked over to make sure they're in good health. Within a couple of weeks, most will be ready for adoption. Judy will photograph and post their photos online with cute descriptions. The new dogs will start coming to adoption events, and all will eventually find forever homes.

That's how they hope it will work, and it usually does.

Audrey checks the time on her own phone.

"We should be able to settle these dogs in, take care of our other dogs, get cleaned up and still make it to Bella's to see if she can sell vegetarian dishes to Nebraskans."

Judy laughs again as she punches in the first of several phone numbers on her list.

"Vegetarians and Nebraskans. Two words I never thought I'd hear in the same sentence."

CHAPTER 6

By late afternoon, Sylvia is still missing.

Chief Sorensen stops back at a few of the neighbors' homes and catches up with seventeen-year-old Al Johnson. Finally, someone has something to offer.

"Sure. I saw her just after 1:00 a.m. walking a little dog down the sidewalk that way."

He points left from his home, the way Sylvia might have walked if she were on the way home from circling the block. Al is a lanky teen, the type whose hands, feet and knees all seem several sizes too large for the rest of him. He is excited to be part of a police investigation.

"You never see anyone out walking around here that late. I couldn't believe she was still awake. My parents were asleep and Mrs. Ritter is older than they are."

"And did you notice anything unusual?"

Al seems to be thinking it over, trying to remember some detail.

"Not really. She was just walking along at a pretty good clip. I was a lot more interested in the car."

"A car?"

"I guess I'm more interested in cars than old ladies walking dogs. I'd just gotten home and the thing that really got my attention was the sports car that passed by about the same time. I didn't recognize it as from around here. It was low and smooth. Maybe a Jaguar."

He stops himself short. "Hey, could that be a clue?"

Chief Sorensen wants to sigh loudly. Instead, he smiles.

"I don't suppose you got a license plate?"

Al bows his head apologetically.

"No. Sorry." He looks up. "But I did see who was in the car. He was an old guy, maybe my parents' age or older. He had gray hair and a lot of it and he wore gloves, you know, driving gloves."

He nods his head, proud that he had noticed the gloves.

Chief Sorensen grimaces. "Gloves in the summer?"

"Right. Driving gloves can give you more control. If you're serious about your driving."

Again, Al nods, as if he were part of a brotherhood of serious sports car drivers.

The chief remains still. "After the car passed, did you happen to notice Mrs. Ritter again?"

Al scratches his head.

"That is funny." He thinks for a moment. "When I looked that way again, she was gone. Maybe she cut through the weeds to get to her house."

The chief looks off in that direction.

"Maybe she did. And did you see what happened to the car that might have been a Jaguar?"

Al shrugs and shakes his head slowly.

"No, but I'll look around town and let you know if I see it."

He stands straighter as he promises action.

"You do that," the chief answers and hands Al a card.

Next stop is another visit with the worried husband. Chief Sorensen arrives at the Ritters' home just as Lois is leaving.

"He's terribly upset," she whispers, holding the door open. "Maybe we could talk later."

Later probably meant "later, at Bella's."

Chief Sorensen finds Carlton slouching on the living room sofa, his head in his hands. He looks up when the chief sits down in the chair opposite him.

"Is there something you're not telling me?"

Carlton seems calmer now, sad but not as twitchy.

"Did I kill her? No, of course not. Were we happy? I was. But I never understood why a girl like Sylvia would marry a guy like me. You knew me in high school. I was nobody. Sylvia was the most popular girl in the school." He looks up and searches the chief's face for understanding. "Sylvia had traveled all over the world before she came back to Redbud. I'd never traveled farther than Iowa and once to Colorado."

"What was it that brought you two together, then?" Chief Sorensen asks the question quietly, hoping Carlton will talk freely.

Carlton seems free, almost eager to talk about the marriage that some found unbelievable. He looks up and smiles, then scans around the room, pointing out the photographs on one wall—all whales.

"Those are her pictures. When she was in California, she worked one summer on a whale-watching boat. She still travels all over the world to watch whales."

"And you, too? Do you share her passion for whales?"

Carlton looks up, startled.

"Oh no. I'm afraid of flying. I'm just not as adventurous as Sylvia. I'd rather stay in Redbud. She travels with friends from her California days. She's tried to talk me into a few trips, but I just can't do it. That's one thing about me she's always found a little disappointing, I'm afraid."

He looks down and studies his hands.

"But otherwise? Are there other interests you share?"

"Sylvia has so many interests. I could never keep up. Did you know she even went sky diving? And sailed her own boat? And once ever drove a race car?"

Chief Sorensen doesn't respond. The more Carlton speaks, the more unlikely it seems that he and Sylvia could possibly be happily married.

"She's also an expert on Native American culture and organic gardening. She loves camping and hiking in the mountains."

Carlton beams more like a proud parent than a devoted husband.

"Ah!" the chief exclaims. "So it's the camping and hiking you enjoy together?"

"No. I don't like insects. I'm more of an indoor boy." He smiles shyly. "She has other friends she shares those activities with."

Why did she stay with him? That's the question. Not why did she marry him. Maybe she was tired. Maybe she was scared, and dull Carlton promised something safe. But how long before she chaffed under all that security?

The more the chief thinks about it, the more he believes that a sudden and mysterious disappearance might well appeal to the sparkling but sometimes overly dramatic girl he remembers from high school.

"What did Sylvia do in California? She was there for what, twenty years, twenty-five?"

"At first she was trying to become an actress, be discovered and all that. I guess that didn't work out. I know she traveled around a bit while working for a travel agency and later with her own travel agency. She told me she just got tired of California and wanted to move back home. She never told me much about those days, said they were all in the past and best forgotten."

"Best forgotten?"

"Yes. That's what she said. California wasn't the answer to all her prayers, I guess."

"When she returned to Redbud, were her parents still alive?"

"They'd both died the year before. She took it hard, felt guilty about not spending more time with them."

"So she moved back here and the two of you met."

Carlton smiles, "I signed up for ballroom dancing lessons. That's where we met."

"Ah. You were both taking lessons."

"Oh no. I was taking lessons. She was teaching. Sylvia is a wonderful dancer. I'm not bad. She's a good teacher, but no one could be as graceful as Sylvia." Carlton leans forward. "Funny thing was, she didn't even remember me from high school. I had to remind her. But before long, we were a pair; six months later, we were married."

Chief Sorensen smiles, "You must have swept her off her feet."

Carlton looks down.

"It was really more the other way around. I was pretty much a confirmed bachelor by then. She swept me off my feet." He chuckles softly, then wipes a tear from one eye. "I couldn't believe it."

Chief Sorensen lowers his voice, "And nothing has been different lately? Has she acted worried? Scared? Has she had a lot of unusual phone calls?"

Carlton seems almost not to understand the questions.

"I don't know what she does when I'm at work. But when I get home she always seems the same."

The chief knows Carlton works for the railroad as some sort of administrative assistant.

He's probably very dependable. Never misspells a word or forgets an appointment. One of those who keep things going without ever drawing attention. You want people like that working for you, but how much do you enjoy knowing them?

Chief Sorensen pushes himself out of his chair. He hands over his card.

"Let me know if you hear anything. Call even if it's late. And I'll be back in touch tomorrow. Oh, and do you know anyone who drives a Jaguar or a car that might be mistaken for one?"

"A Jaguar?" Carlton acts surprised. "Not for me."

"But anyone you know?"

"Drive a sports car? I don't think so."

Well, it's not such a shocking idea, is it? Even people in Nebraska sometimes buy fancy sports cars.

As he walks to his car, the chief mentally lists the steps he plans to take next, steps that will include going through Sylvia's phone records and, if possible, her emails. He'll make a few inquiries about the sports car Al Johnson had seen.

I also want to learn more about Sylvia's other friends, the ones she traveled with, watched whales with, hiked and camped with. Who are they?

And why did Sylvia really leave California and return home to marry the most forgettable boy in her high school class?

Right now I'd put money on Sylvia leaving Redbud and Carlton willingly.

But he wonders what Carlton might have done if he'd known she was leaving.

And what, he wonders, might he learn tonight at Bella's?

***

Daisy's bedroom looks out over the back yard. From her window, she can see the Ritters' home, and that's where she focuses her binoculars. She'd moved her desk to place it in front of the window, so that she could sit and take notes while keeping an eye on any suspicious activity.

An amateur detective must be observant. An amateur detective must notice details.

She'd spent time online reading up on detective work and was already planning her investigation. She is in a perfect position to watch the husband.

She notices him pacing back and forth in the living room. Once, he steps out onto the deck but then immediately turns back around. Shortly after Chief Sorensen leaves, Daisy sees Carlton pick up a phone and then throw it back on the sofa. In Daisy's opinion, the husband's behavior has changed. When the chief was there, Carlton sat hunched on the sofa. Now he seems tall and straight, active, maybe even angry. She writes that observation down in her notebook.

Birdy the Chihuahua lounges lazily on the corner of the desk. Daisy reaches over to scratch Birdy behind her ears.

This might be important. His behavior is different now. A detective notices changes in behavior.

Daisy sets her binoculars aside and purses her lips, thinking.

"We'll solve this, Birdy, you and me."

She fingers the magnifying glass her father used with his stamp collection.

"We'll study every blade of grass, every clump of dirt, every spot on the sidewalk. We'll find the clues we need."

The tan and white Chihuahua wags her body across the desktop and drops onto Daisy's lap. Daisy's hand reaches down to stroke the dog, who responds by tilting her head for a quick peek at Daisy.

"Wish we could bug his house or hack into his computer. I just bet he knows where she is or where her body is."

The Chihuahua adds nothing, but rearranges herself on Daisy's lap. Daisy picks up the binoculars again but sees no one moving in the house.

She thinks she hears the sound of a car starting up.

He must be on the move. Oh, why am I not old enough to drive?

Daisy writes down the time in a notebook and the words "drove off." She pulls her long hair to one side and catches it in a rubber band.

"Come on, Birdy. Let's go for a walk."

She snatches Birdy's leash and picks up the magnifying glass, sticking the notebook in the back pocket of her shorts. She wants to look for clues while Mr. Ritter is away.

A few minutes later, she is on her hands and knees in the Ritters' back yard, hunching over the magnifying glass as she creeps inch by inch toward the house.

If Daisy had known a single other girl her age in Redbud, she might have been singing in a musical production or playing on a soccer team. She might have been shopping for new clothes or challenging someone to a video game. She might have been begging her parents to drop her and her friends at the movie theater. She might have been swimming in someone's pool.

Instead, she is crawling through the yard of a home where the wife has gone missing and the husband is still a suspect.

CHAPTER 7

Bella and Carl stand like sentries on either side of their café's front door, welcoming those brave enough or curious enough to show up for vegetarian night. They hand out menus and greet most of the arrivals by name.

"Sit wherever you want," Bella sings out every few minutes.

With her ever-busy hands, she sometimes has trouble handing out the menus and, several times, drops a few. Carl, by contrast, stands solidly in one place, eyes twinkling as he welcomes guests and firmly places menus into outreached hands.

"If this catches on, we'll have a vegetarian night every Sunday and a vegetarian selection or two available every day we're open," Carl repeats to any who linger long enough to listen.

Randy steps carefully around a clutch of arrivals and looks around the room. The room includes not only tables but also several sofas and armchairs. He heads for his favorite table, then changes his mind and selects a large, empty table almost dead center in the room. He makes sure his table has plenty of chairs, then parks himself on the far side and carefully places a bag full of knitting supplies next to his chair.

I might be the only man on the continent going out to dinner with both a gun and knitting needles.

He watches the door, ready to beckon over as many diners as possible. He wants a full table tonight, a talkative table. He doesn't plan to ask questions. He knows what the main topic of conversation will be. Tonight he will listen and, he hopes, learn more about Sylvia and Carlton.

Randy reaches down to pull up his latest project, which someday will be a many-colored sweater. As he lifts his head up and looks toward the door again, he sees a few startled Redbud residents backing away when they hear there will be no meat dishes tonight. But then he sees Audrey and Judy edge through a group near the door, spot him and beeline his way. He stands up, one hand wrapped in his knitting, and greets both. Audrey slips into the chair next to him and reaches for the knitting as he sits back down.

She turns his work in several directions, not sure what to say. "What now?"

"It will be a sweater made of yarn leftover from other projects."

"Hmm. I see." She pats his arm and smiles up at him. "But more important, what's the latest on Sylvia? Is she back home?"

The chief shakes his head.

"No. And she's the main reason I'm here tonight. I want to hear what others know about this couple, but I don't want to interrogate anyone. Maybe you could steer the conversation and ask leading questions?"

Audrey rubs her hands together, obviously willing and delighted.

"We have a job to do," she cheers to Judy.

With heads together, the two seem to be deciding on their path to discovery. The chief, meanwhile, beckons several other new arrivals to the table: Lois, Barbara, and the town veterinarian, Dr. Shirley Thomas. To his surprise, he spots Redbud's newest residents, the Jensens, parents of Daisy, the girl who found Birdy the Chihuahua. He halfway sprints toward them and points them toward two empty chairs. The Jensens seem uncertain of the invitation at first, but then readily agree to sit with these friendly Redbud people.

Randy introduces them around. "Meet Margaret and Martin Jensen."

"Oh!" Audrey looks up at the Jensens. "And how is our little Birdy? And where is that amazing daughter of yours? Didn't she want to try out a vegetarian meal?"

Margaret takes a deep breath as if she's about to speak to a large audience.

"Well," she begins, looking at all the faces looking back at her, "Birdy is doing great. The two are quite the pair. I tried to bring Daisy along, but she preferred staying home with a bologna sandwich. She's too busy playing amateur detective to go out for dinner."

Randy looks up from his knitting and drops a stitch.

Margaret continues, "She said she has to keep an eye on the Ritters' place. When we left, she was sitting in her room looking out her window with binoculars to her eyes. Earlier, I found her out crawling through the grass with a magnifying glass. Looking for clues, she said."

Randy forces a chuckle, "Looks like I might need to have another chat with that young detective of yours."

The chief tries to sound unconcerned, but all his internal alarms ring. He doesn't want a young girl putting herself at risk. Until he's satisfied that Sylvia's disappearance was her decision, he wants to remain on alert. That means no little girls crawling through the grass with magnifying glasses.

Then, as if just noticing Shirley at the table, Audrey begins telling the veterinarian about the dogs she and Judy rescued earlier from the county shelter.

"I'm afraid three of them have pretty bad cases of kennel cough. We'll need to bring them by tomorrow."

"Maybe it would be better if I made a home visit. I'd rather not bring kennel cough into the clinic. Expect me for lunch tomorrow. You'll have my PB&J waiting?"

"Of course. And who knows, you might even find some peanut butter and jelly on this vegetarian menu."

Audrey runs a finger down the menu and frowns.

"Well, I don't see peanut butter, but here's something with pine nuts, spinach and couscous."

"What's couscous?" Randy asks.

Audrey punches him lightly on the shoulder but doesn't answer.

"And this might be good—cashews with rice, green beans, carrots and raisins."

"I'll try that," Shirley agrees, turning her menu over on the table.

Lois votes for a salad with apples, walnuts and wild rice.

"Dieting," she explains.

Lois's friend Barbara opts for baked tomatoes stuffed with peas, cheese and couscous.

Randy points at one menu item. "This one has barley, mushrooms and onions. That sounds almost Nebraskan. I might try that."

He shakes his head almost sadly.

If the guys on the Chicago force could only see me now, I don't know what they'd think. I'm knitting, ordering from a vegetarian menu and sitting thigh-to-thigh with a Dog Lady whose hair looks like bouncing corkscrews. Actually, I do know what they'd think.

Judy decides on a fettuccine with asparagus in lemon sauce. The Jensens both decide on a vegetable lasagna. When Bella comes by to take orders, Audrey just asks for "whatever you think is your best dish."

And then the conversation turns to the topic of the day.

"How well do either of you know Sylvia and Carlton?" Judy asks, looking at Lois and Barbara, who both lived most of their lives in Redbud.

As expected, they both agree all the girls in their high school wanted to be Sylvia, and all the boys wanted to date her. Randy, who'd also gone to the Redbud High School at the same time, nods.

They all remember that no one paid much attention to Carlton then.

Barbara adds, "He was almost a shadow, nearby but only watching, not a part of things. I don't remember if he was smart or dumb. I can't remember a thing he ever said. Nobody teased him or made fun of him, though. It wasn't like that at all. People don't tease or bully the one they never even notice."

"I remember him a little," Randy joins in. "He sat across from me in chemistry. I just remember that he always looked very intense, determined, focused. He just never talked much. I wonder now if he would have welcomed a little teasing or mistreatment. It would have made him more visible."

"And Sylvia? How well did you know her," Audrey asks Randy.

"Only to admire from the distance. I was not in her league."

"Well who was?" Judy looks from face to face. "Who was in her league? Who did she date? And why didn't she marry him or someone like him?"

Lois and Barbara both seem to be clicking through mental lists.

Barbara starts, "Well, there was Ron Boyes. He was class president. And Morley Ames. He was captain of the football team."

"And let's not forget Greg Long," adds Barbara. "He starred in every play and musical all during high school. He and Sylvia were an item when we graduated. I think they both moved to California not

65

long after graduation. But they may have gone their separate ways there. Sylvia wasn't much for staying with any one boyfriend for long."

The chief pulls out a pen and writes the three names on a napkin, then adds a few more from his own memory.

"But does anyone know much about her time in California?" Audrey asks.

Lois says that Sylvia didn't stay in touch with anyone in Redbud except for her parents.

"They were always bragging about how successful she was and how much money she was making."

"Doing what?" Judy asks.

After a lot of shoulder shrugging from Barbara and Lois, the chief says Carlton had told him Sylvia owned her own business, maybe a travel agency. He also mentioned the various activities Sylvia enjoyed but didn't share with Carlton, but rather with friends that Carlton had never met.

Lois lifts both hands, palms-up. "Who knows? She never talks about her California days."

Lois explains that Sylvia just showed up in Redbud one day. Her parents had died the year before.

"There she was. An unmarried woman in her forties, no children. She was still attractive but I wasn't embarrassed standing next to her for fear people would ask, 'Who's that dowdy thing next to the pretty girl?' By this time we both looked like nice Nebraska women of a certain age."

She smiles at her own words.

Conversation stops for a few minutes when their dinners arrive. Everyone tastes, nods, reaches with forks to sample from each other's plates and murmurs their pleasure at each bite.

"Is couscous really a food?" Randy asks again.

Again, everyone ignores his question.

Lois continues her story, "Only a few months after she arrived here, she married Carlton. He was still living at his parents' house and working in Omaha. Once we got over the surprise, they seemed like an ordinary Nebraska couple. They looked like they belonged together. Of course, she did most of the talking, but Nebraska men—especially those with Scandinavian ancestors—are known for their long periods of silence, right, Barbara?"

Margaret laughs and squeezes the arm of her own husband, who hasn't yet contributed a word to the conversation. Martin grins and nods, nothing more.

"I guess we'll fit right in here as a couple," Margaret confirms.

Barbara nods.

"Right. I have one of those quiet types at home too," she shakes her head and heaves an exaggerated sigh, "but I love him, anyway. Quiet, but dependable. But can I get him to come to vegetarian night at Bella's?"

She shakes her head, then smiles at Margaret, "At least yours isn't afraid of a vegetarian menu."

Lois nods. "So you see, after a while Sylvia and Carlton didn't seem like an odd couple at all."

The chief continues, "Did she have any close friends here?"

Lois shakes her head.

"Everybody knew her; but if she had a best friend or someone she was especially close to, I don't know who that would be. I'd see her at the Lutheran church. She did some substitute teaching for a while, usually in business classes. She was a pretty regular breakfaster here at Bella's, joining any table where she recognized people. She'd tell funny stories about Carlton, usually about his fear of anything adventurous. But it never sounded like she was unhappy with him. She did take a lot of trips on her own, though, and sometimes she'd talk about them but never anything about her traveling companions. I was always hoping she'd invite me along sometime, but she never did—not me or anyone else in Redbud as far as I know."

Judy asks, "What about Carlton? Did he have any close friends?"

Randy thinks he should know the answer to that one but doesn't comment. As he scrolls through his memory, he can't remember ever seeing Carlton with anyone but Sylvia. Carlton doesn't golf, hunt, bowl, run, belong to the health club, swim, play tennis or share home remodeling stories with other men at the hardware store. He certainly doesn't knit or participate in any arts or crafts... not that Randy knows.

Maybe he has work friends, people he shares lunch with. I'll explore that possibility. I still have no idea what Carlton might be capable of doing under stress. Nothing? Too much? Could that quiet, well-mannered man be dangerous? Could Sylvia?

For a while, they all enjoy their meals silently. Randy is soon soaking up the last remnants of his meal with a piece of bread. As he looks around the table, he sees others scooping up whatever remains on their plates.

"I guess we all liked our vegetarian meals," he confesses, sucking in a well-soaked crust of bread.

Audrey turns around in her chair and waves at Carl and Bella, who are both standing, arms crossed, near the double doors to the kitchen.

"Hey Carl. Hey Bella. Everyone loves it!"

They all look around and notice several other tables with apparently satisfied diners. The crowd is smaller than a typical Sunday night, though.

"Don't worry," Audrey calls. "Word will get out. In a few weeks, you'll have a line outside the door."

Bella is now standing behind Audrey. "Hope so."

"And what did I just enjoy so much?"

"I call that Bella's Surprise. It's got a lot of everything: tomatoes, wild rice, raisins, cashews, corn, green beans, asparagus and anything else I could get my hands on."

"Bella's Surprise. Everyone! Next time, try Bella's Surprise."

As Audrey and Judy grab for their purses and get to their feet, the Jensens also say they should get back home.

"We need to make sure our junior detective hasn't arrested anyone yet," Margaret laughs.

The chief grimaces and asks the new couple what brought them to Redbud.

"Oh," Margaret answers, "we were both offered teaching position at Midland College. We were curious about Redbud since my husband's ancestors settled here in the 1870s. We thought we might learn more about them and about some of the family stories."

Audrey and Judy drop their purses on the floor and sit back down. Bella says she'll go get Carl.

"You aren't, by any chance, talking about Johannes and Karen Jensen, are you?" asks Judy.

"Well, yes."

"Well, prepare for a few surprises. You're talking to a couple of distant cousins right now, and another is on his way from the kitchen."

The new Redbud residents look at each other and then at the others around the table.

Martin speaks up for the first time.

"Do you know about the rubies?"

CHAPTER 8

Shirley sits for a few minutes in her car, wondering if she's made a serious mistake.

I should have said something. Eventually, it will all come out and everyone will wonder why I remained silent.

She is surprised that no one had asked her directly about Sylvia. It had been no coincidence that she set up her veterinary clinic in Redbud shortly after Sylvia moved back from California.

Does no one remember that?

From the evening's conversation, she realizes that she knows things about Sylvia the others don't.

Why didn't I just speak up? I know why. Do I really want the world to know about the life I lived in California? Can I still hide it?

She and Sylvia had promised to keep each other's secrets. Shirley will not break that promise easily. She owes her career to Sylvia. Without Sylvia, Shirley would never have found a way to pay for veterinary school, helping her achieve her childhood dream. Sylvia had urged, no, insisted that Shirley set up a practice in Redbud, a practice she cherishes. In many ways, Shirley owes her life to Sylvia.

But no one in Redbud connects the two women. They never socialize together other than at a breakfast table at Bella's. Shirley and Sylvia never mention their earlier connection. Maybe she shouldn't be surprised that no one thought to ask her about Sylvia.

Although Shirley thinks of Sylvia as a friend, there is a distance to their friendship now. They stay in touch the way old friends who live in distant cities might stay in touch—with occasional calls to catch up. Sylvia travels with other friends, only once inviting Shirley to join her.

Once they had been close, sharing their triumphs and failures. But those days faded away, and eventually all they shared were the dangerous secrets from their shared past.

Shirley was surprised to hear about Sylvia's high school days, surprised to hear that Sylvia had been so popular, so admired, so envied. To hear the others talk about Sylvia, anyone would think the entire world loved her. Shirley knows that isn't the case.

Shirley replays in her mind the last phone call they shared a couple of nights ago.

And now what? Sylvia, where are you? What have you done?

***

"Can you believe that?!" Audrey hoots as she and Judy begin their ride home. "Yet another descendant of Karen and Johannes shows up in Redbud."

"But this one knew something the rest of us didn't. Rubies! I guess we're not done with all our family mysteries yet."

"Martin sure came alive once Carl came out of the kitchen, didn't he? Not a word all evening, and then he couldn't stop talking. I'm betting he and Carl are about to be best buddies. They'll both be out on the farm waving metal detectors around."

"Are rubies a metal?"

Audrey shrugs.

"I think they liked knowing that Daisy will receive a college scholarship because of their ancestry here in Nebraska."

"But I wonder if Martin wasn't wishing they'd arrived a year earlier. They could have been here when we found all the gold coins and realized their value."

"Maybe, but their heads must be spinning tonight. They still have boxes to unpack, and they've got a missing neighbor and a handful of new relatives. And they've already had a run in with the police chief."

"I wouldn't call it a run in. The chief didn't accuse them of anything."

"He might accuse them of forcing him to do more research on Johannes and Karen Jensen."

Judy and Audrey had provided the Jensens with a quick summary of the past year, how they learned some of their family history and discovered some of the family treasures. They had decided to put some of their newly discovered wealth in a scholarship fund for Jensen family descendants. As Judy and Audrey excused themselves and headed out the door, they noticed Carl and Martin deep in conversation. The chief was taking notes, either planning further historical research or mapping out plans for finding the missing Sylvia. The Jensens had been surprised to learn that Chief Sorensen was also the county historian.

After a few minutes traveling in silence, Audrey turns back to the topic of the missing Sylvia.

"If we knew why she moved back to Redbud, we'd know where to look," Audrey proposes.

"And if we knew why she married the boy nobody remembers from high school, we'd know even more."

***

Lois yawns as she drives past the Ritters' home.

I wonder if he needs company. Maybe I should stop.

But she notices only one light in an upstairs window.

Perhaps he's already gone to bed. Poor man. I hope he can get some sleep.

Lois drives on past and thinks instead of Randy and Audrey, the way they leaned toward each other. The casual touching, the smiles. Even when the subject was crime, or a possible crime, they seemed pleased to sit next to each other.

"I wonder if they even know they're in love. Silly old fools."

***

As they take one last look around their café before heading for bed, Carl and Bella agree the night was at least a partial success. They had hoped for a better turnout, but they're pleased with the reactions of those who did show up for their first vegetarian night.

"We might need to include one or two meat meals next Sunday," Bella warns, frowning. "Some husbands, especially, just won't step in the door if they can't order a hamburger."

Carl places a hand over his mouth and smooths his walrus mustache.

"Or maybe we should pick a different night for the vegetarian only menu. Maybe Tuesday—always a slow night anyway."

"Maybe. Let's consider Vegetarian Tuesday. I like that."

Both in agreement, Carl changes the topic.

"Isn't that something about the new folks in town? I'm meeting Martin tomorrow out at the farm. I'll show him around and fill him in on everything that's already happened. I know we told him almost everything, but I'd like him to see it all, including where we found the coins."

Bella smiles at Carl's enthusiasm.

"Back with the old metal detector, huh? What was it Martin said about rubies?"

"Martin, it seemed, had learned about his ancestors through a grandfather who'd told him Johannes hid a fortune around the house and farm. He never really believed the stories, but like the rest of us, he couldn't let them go either. But he had a story the rest of us didn't have."

"About rubies."

"Yes."

Carl puts an arm across Bella's shoulders.

"A gift to Karen," he explains.

"Another gift from the Queen of Denmark?"

Bella chuckles at the memory of the string of pearls Karen had received when the Queen of Denmark visited Danes living in America. Redbud, where many Danes had settled, was one of the stops. But the pearls had been fakes, lovely but inexpensive gifts bestowed on delighted housewives during that historic visit.

"The rubies are probably fakes too—but pretty fakes."

"Martin said he has some notes and some old correspondence he'll bring with him tomorrow. Who knows what we'll find?"

"Speaking of finding something, I wonder if we'll find Sylvia any time soon. Maybe she was hard to know well, but she was also hard to ignore. She was always so full of fizz and sparkle."

***

Something itches inside Randy's memory. He feels sure something from the past is struggling to break free.

Is it about Sylvia or Carlton? Does it go back to our high school days?

If Sylvia hasn't returned home by morning, he knows what he'll be doing. He'll be looking through Sylvia's phone records, checking to see who she contacted recently. He'll also be looking up Sylvia's old boyfriends from high school. He hopes to find out more about her time in California, including what she did there and why she returned to Redbud. Maybe he'll send a press release and photo to local media asking for help in locating the missing Redbud woman.

He rubs his forehead as he enters his quiet home.

What secrets are they hiding? Is Sylvia running from something? Or is someone dragging her away—from something? Or to something?

He realizes his neglected knitting project remains in his car and turns around to claim it.

Maybe an hour or so of knitting will let other ideas settle into place. It's worked before. Once I stop thinking about a case and concentrate instead on knitting needles and following a pattern, other ideas slip in behind the earlier ones.

Before he finally retires for the night, Randy decides he should look into police reports from years past—the years when he'd attended high school with Sylvia and Carlton, and with Barbara and Lois.

What happened then that might be important now?

And with all that talk about silent Nebraska men, isn't it odd that the only person who barely talked at all this evening was a woman, the usually garrulous Dr. Shirley Thomas, Redbud's veterinarian.

CHAPTER 9

Thomas Hardin arrives at the wildlife sanctuary just before 9:00 a.m. It is his job to open the sanctuary located ten miles outside of Redbud. As a retired teacher, he appreciates the unpaid job. He enjoys the peace of the sanctuary where Canada geese and other waterfowl rest during their annual migrations. He feels privileged to share this slice of nature with American bald eagles as well as the songbirds and animals that include deer, fox, squirrels and raccoons.

Tom's work includes resupplying the bird feeders just outside the viewing area. Retirees enjoy sitting and watching the birds at the feeders. Some bring their coffee with them in the mornings, settling into the chairs arranged in a semicircle just inside the window overlooking the feeders. When they tire of the birds at the feeders, they'll stroll through the small museum with its displays and telescopes aimed at the lake. Parents bring children here, and people of all ages enjoy the trails that cross through the sanctuary. Tom expects to welcome a few hikers on a Monday like today, although not as many as on weekends. He knows today's schedule includes a visit from a class of fourth graders on a field trip.

Tom is a lean, hard-muscled man, looking more like someone who'd spent his life in physical labor than in combat with high school students struggling through chemistry. He stands only about five foot six. His white hair, thick as ever, blows slightly as he opens the gate blocking the entrance. After parking his car, he walks to the museum with a stride that belies his nearly eighty years. He whistles softly, studying the sky, alert for changes in the weather.

He'd heard about Sylvia's disappearance through the Redbud grapevine and figures his former student had a "Sylvia moment," a phrase he'd used during Sylvia's high school days. Others were surprised when Sylvia returned to Redbud and married Carlton. Tom welcomed the news. Carlton had qualities others missed. Carlton could steady Sylvia, something she needed. She could comfort him, something Carlton needed. Others might disagree, but that is how Tom saw the couple.

As he turns the key in the museum door, Tom hears what he first thinks is an animal scrambling in his direction. He turns to see a barefoot woman with arms stretched toward him stumbling through the gate, her mouth wide open in a soundless scream. Sticks and dirt clogs festoon her hair. She collapses at his feet, and he sees the rips and mud spatters on her sweatpants and sleeveless top. Otherwise, she seems unharmed.

"Sylvia? Is that you?"

"Help me," she whispers.

Always the dramatic one. Why do I feel like we're back at Redbud High and I'm watching another play starring Sylvia?

He shakes his head, scattering the image of Sylvia on the stage.

"Sylvia? Oh, thank God. You're okay. We need to call Carlton. We need to call Chief Sorensen."

"No!" She sits up abruptly. "We can't call anyone yet. I need your help."

"Well of course, I'll help you, Sylvia. But what's the problem? Why can't you just go home?"

78

He sees something hard in her eyes, something that tells him arguing with her won't change anything. Sylvia has a plan, and Thomas Hardin is about to be part of it.

***

Chief Sorensen's first call in the morning is to Carlton, who says he is on his way to work, and no, he hasn't heard from Sylvia.

His wife is missing and he goes to work as usual!

The chief calls several television stations but is told to call back in a couple of days if Sylvia is still missing. To most, this disappearance sounds like a domestic incident that will resolve itself in a day or so.

The chief isn't so sure.

Sylvia hasn't just walked away from her home. She hasn't driven herself away either. Shouldn't she have called Carlton by now to either apologize or insist he apologize? What happened here? What secrets are they hiding?

Chief Sorensen understands these Redbud citizens because he is one of them. He guesses that every one of them would describe himself or herself as a very private person. By that, they mean they don't share their secrets. Their mistakes, their missteps, their accidents all remain tight inside their chests, leading some to early strokes or heart attacks. But most would prefer death to revealing their embarrassing moments—no matter how insignificant.

And the significant ones? The arrests? The accusations? Illegitimate children? Lost savings? Lost jobs? Lost loves? Bad decisions? Bad enough that it happened. Not as bad if kept secret from the rest of the world. Redbud citizens don't wait for their seven minutes of fame. They fear it. Better to pass through life unnoticed than to become the source of too much note.

So different from Chicago, he recalls, where people sometimes told you too much, more than you wanted to know about them. In Redbud, his biggest struggle is reaching into the hearts and minds of people who aren't sure they can trust you with even their middle name. He prefers the Redbud way but hates it when trying to solve a crime.

How does no one know more about Sylvia, other than what she wanted them to know? Why are the ones most willing to talk to me a preteen girl and a few Dog Ladies?

With that thought, he reminds himself that he needs to check on Daisy. He also wants to drive out to see Audrey although for the life of him he can't think of why he needs to do that.

Maybe she can help. Maybe she knows something.

Chief Sorensen has located two of Sylvia's high school boyfriends. Ron Boyes is now an advertising executive in Omaha. Morley Ames is the football coach in one of the Omaha suburbs. Greg Long is still on the missing list, but Chief Sorensen hopes to run down information on him through California agencies.

Shortly after arriving at his office, Chief Sorensen learns that the owner of the car spotted at a service station is a Californian in town to interview for a teaching position in the Redbud School District. One of the night officers had caught up with him at his motel room outside of Redbud. The young man was surprised and somewhat amused at being part of a police investigation.

No word on the mysterious sports car spotted at the time Sylvia was out walking her new Chihuahua.

The Chihuahua Affair

Both Ron Boyes and Morley Ames have agreed to come by later in the afternoon. As Redbud High graduates, they probably relish the opportunity to be part of something newsy in their hometown. Randy had been better friends with Ron than Morley during high school, but he remembers both of them as decent sorts, although a little too full of themselves.

I wonder how they turned out. Did success in high school lead to success as an adult? Or did they both turn out to be the type who peaked in high school and then slid sadly through the rest of their days?

He turns his attention to the box of files he'd requested from the years when he, Sylvia and Carlton had all been high school students. Fingering quickly through the files, he finds two records involving calls to Sylvia's childhood home. Both came from a neighbor complaining about noise and fighting next door. The woman, though quite elderly now, is still alive and living in the same home. He'll visit her later.

Then he notices a penciled note at the bottom of one page: "See Child Protective Services: Sylvia Sawyer."

In the few minutes he needs to reach his destination, the hot wind leaves him red-faced and sweating.

"A scorcher," he mutters to himself, as he steps into the sudden chill inside the air-conditioned building.

He shivers involuntarily, stops to compose himself and asks to see Louise Feldt, the social worker he hopes will be helpful.

Louise, two-hundred-plus pounds on a five-foot frame, walks his way almost as soon as he mentions her name. She steps lightly for a woman of her dimensions, seeming to almost bounce with each step. Her flowing tent dress whirls around her as she moves.

"Chief Sorensen. We are honored." She grins at him, tilting her head to one side. "Follow me."

She leads him down the hall to a tiny office with a desk nearly buried in files and stacks of papers. Several diplomas tilt awkwardly on the wall behind her desk.

He quickly tells her of his need to know why Child Protective Services has a file on Sylvia Sawyer, who is now Sylvia Ritter.

Louise frowns and jabs at her head, shaking loose several curls from a bun resting precariously on the top of her head.

"Well, shoot. We have a lot of files on a lot of children. I'm sure we have one on you. I understand quite a few people wondered if your grandfather was qualified to raise a young boy."

The chief smiles and nods but pushes on.

"I'm sure that's true, but today I'm investigating the disappearance of Sylvia Ritter, which I'm sure your radar has picked up by now."

Louise nods. "But how could a couple of reports from more than thirty years ago help you find Sylvia today?"

"You'd be surprised how often the past points the way."

Louise wiggles in her chair.

"Some people are just too snoopy," she complains. "They think they see a possible problem with a child and they say things maybe they shouldn't say. It isn't enough that a child acts up in class but some teacher will think the bad behavior is because of abuse at home. Sometimes the child is just going through a phase, sometimes the child is just undisciplined or immature."

As she speaks, Louise pats her desk, as if to make her point.

The chief hears echoes of the old Redbud "private person" refrain. He realizes how horrifying it would feel for a parent subjected to an investigation into their parenting practices. He holds up both hands to halt Louise's speech.

Louise stops talking, as if in mid-vowel, leaving her mouth open for a few seconds.

"I understand, Louise. You want to protect people from embarrassment. You think people are too quick with accusations. But I really need your help with this."

Louise bends down and disappears behind her desk, reemerging with a file pulled from a pile next to her chair.

"I was curious myself."

She doesn't use the word snoopy, the chief notes. He watches as she opens the file. She pauses to look at him without blinking.

"I'm sharing this because I trust you. I was actually surprised to find this, but like I said, everyone has a file somewhere."

The chief is relieved that he won't need to subpoena the records.

"It's probably not important," he speculates, trying to reassure Louise.

"That was my opinion, at first. And I'll always believe people should be careful what they say about their neighbors, but sometimes those accusations have teeth."

"And those in Sylvia's file? Did they have teeth?"

Louise sighs.

"Maybe. But those who looked into it then didn't think so. Today, if I'd been looking into charges like these, I'd have been a little more suspicious."

She looks up from the file she's studying. "I just don't want this to be public knowledge. Sylvia would just die if people knew about this."

She flushes suddenly, obviously wishing she hadn't used that phrase.

Chief Sorensen stands up and moves behind the desk, looking over Louise's shoulder.

Louise speaks as the chief scans through the reports.

"Sylvia's fourth-grade teacher was the first to report something. She said Sylvia constantly wiggled in her chair and was in the habit of hugging and kissing some of her classmates a little too enthusiastically. The teacher found Sylvia hard to handle, someone who wanted to be the center of attention all the time."

"And what did your people think? Just a hyperactive child? Or a disturbed child? Did they suspect abuse?"

"Those who investigated talked to the parents and Sylvia and decided Sylvia was just a challenging child with more intelligence and energy than a typical parent or teacher could manage easily."

"And what do you think?"

"We know more now. We know abuse happens even in seemingly respectable families. But this was before my time, so I can't speak from any personal experience or knowledge. Maybe Sylvia was just a high-strung kid with too much imagination."

The chief taps at a second report. "What's this about?"

"One of her high school teachers talked to the school counselor, who talked to someone in this office."

"I went to high school with Sylvia. She was beautiful, vivacious, the most popular girl in our class. She certainly didn't look like she had a care in the world. She was always having fun. Everyone loved her."

"Maybe she was trying a bit too hard?"

Louise taps an index finger at a name on the report.

"The high school teacher thought Sylvia was trying a bit too hard, putting on an act, hiding her true feelings behind a lot of charm and drama. Looks like she confided in him and he didn't know whether to believe what she was telling him or not. He marched straight to the counselor's office, and the counselor contacted this office."

"But again, nothing happened?"

"And again, Sylvia said Mr. Hardin must have misunderstood. When contacted, Hardin said Sylvia might have been playing with him. That was the phrase he used."

Chief Sorensen nods. He remembers the word "drama" attached to Sylvia throughout high school. Maybe she just liked to stir the pot, keep life interesting. And maybe sometimes she carried it a little too far. But then Sylvia left town the day after graduation and stayed away until both her parents were dead.

Chief Sorensen rubs his forehead and looks at Louise.

"Hardin? Are we talking about Tom Hardin, the chemistry teacher?"

"One and the same. Still alive and still living in Redbud. Maybe you should visit him."

"Maybe I should."

Chief Sorensen thanks Louise and ventures back into the heat and the short walk back to the police station.

As he walks past Blanche Olson's desk, she hands him several pages covered with phone numbers. It's a list of all phone calls to and from Sylvia's home and cell phones.

Chief Sorensen stops next to her desk as he leafs through the pages, settling on the last few calls. One on the day before Sylvia's disappearance catches his attention because it lasted twenty minutes.

Ellen Carlsen

Once in his office, he dials the number and hears a recording: "You have reached the Redbud Veterinary Clinic. I'm out making house calls. Please leave a message. If this is an emergency—"

The chief hangs up his phone.

My dance card is filling up fast. But will they dance or dance around.

He contemplates Ron Boyes, Morley Ames, Tom Hardin, the elderly woman who'd lived next door to Sylvia's childhood home, Greg Long, if he can find a number for him. And now Dr. Shirley Thomas, the town veterinarian. He also needs to check back with Daisy and pay a call on Audrey.

Chief Sorensen realizes he hasn't finished looking through files in the boxes his officer had dropped on the desk. He finds the name he was looking for, pulls out a thick file and learns why Carlton avoids attention.

***

Daisy writes in her notepad the time that Carlton leaves his home, wearing a suit and tie.

He looks like he's going to work.

Even a twelve-year-old knows that's odd behavior for a man whose wife is missing and maybe kidnapped or even murdered. She considers the behavior for a while, scratching the tan and white Chihuahua yawning on her lap. Then as she is about to call Chief Sorensen with her report, she sees a car turning into the Ritters' driveway. From her perch by her bedroom window, Daisy can't see much of the car. She keeps her binoculars trained on one of the home's back windows, hoping to catch a glimpse of someone inside

86

the home. She isn't disappointed. Someone has entered the house. Sylvia catches a quick glimpse of a woman climbing up the stairs.

I know I'm not supposed to go onto their yard, but I'll be careful. I'll just walk around the block and try to take a picture of the car. I won't even step onto their yard.

Daisy pulls out the cellphone her parents had given her on her previous birthday and charges out the door. At the last minute, she notices Birdy racing after her.

"Birdy! Good idea."

She steps back inside and snatches the Chihuahua's leash.

Now it'll look like I'm just out walking my dog.

Once outside, Daisy and Birdy walk quickly around the corner and slow down only once they're two houses away from the Ritters' home. Daisy lifts her cellphone and snaps a few quick pictures of the car, maroon with four doors. She doesn't notice the man in the driver's seat. Her thoughts are on getting a picture of the license plate.

Pretending she's bored, Daisy whistles softly and stops just long enough behind the car in the Ritters' driveway to snap a picture of the license plate.

"We did it, Birdy," she whispers to the little dog as they quicken their pace past the house.

They're three houses past the Ritters' home when Daisy dares look back. She sees a tall woman coming out of the house, opening the back door on the passenger side and tossing in a suitcase.

Could that be the missing woman?!

The woman slams the back door and backs into the front passenger seat. As she lifts first one and then a second leg inside, the woman notices Daisy and Birdy and makes a sound, something like a crow's caw.

With her last ounce of courage, Daisy snaps another picture, then forgets about her earlier plan to walk slowly around the block. Instead, she grabs Birdy and ducks between two houses and stumbles toward the grassy divide that separates the backyards.

Aiming for home, Daisy races through several yards, stretching out her legs and leaping over a series of bushes the way she'd learned to jump hurtles in last year's gym class. She races up the steps to the back deck and bursts into her home.

"Mom. Dad. Call Chief Sorensen!"

CHAPTER 10

Audrey and Judy can't help meddling into the mystery of Sylvia's disappearance. Both read murder mysteries to the point of addiction. Both figure they can solve the mystery themselves but grudgingly admit that it might be a job for the police, in particular, Chief Sorensen.

Audrey brushes a few more burrs from Snowball's coat.

"We do need to be careful. You know how sensitive men are."

Judy is trying to wrestle Elvira, the Lab/Rottweiler mix, into a so-called no pull harness. In the process, Elvira slobbers joyfully as she knocks Judy over and proceeds to pin her down and wash her face.

"Let me go, Elvira. Get off me."

Judy rights herself and manages to snap the harness shut under Elvira's chest. The big dog laps at Judy's face again.

"This one needs some work." Judy looks back at Audrey. "Do you really think Chief Sorensen needs our help? Maybe we'll just make him mad if we interfere."

"He's used to my interference. I think he enjoys it."

Audrey's corkscrew curls bounce as she brushes Snowball's coat vigorously. The little white dog yelps and turns to look at Audrey, pleading for understanding.

"Maybe. But maybe he's reached his limits. I know he likes you, Audrey, maybe more than likes you. As we used to say, I think he likes you likes you."

"Don't be silly," Audrey interrupts, laughing at the thought. "I'm collecting social security and he's old enough to know better."

Now it's Judy's turn to laugh.

"As you suggested yourself, we need to consider his feelings. I guess what I was trying to say is that we should be careful not to take advantage of his tolerance toward our interference or his affection for you. And just think how he'd feel—big homicide detective—if a couple of Dog Ladies proved to be the better detectives?"

This time they both laugh.

Audrey, wearing her work overalls, brushes through Snowball's coat one more time, then looks at the collection of white dog hair floating around the room.

"Why isn't dog hair valuable? We have so much of it."

"It's valuable to the dogs. I think Snowball's given up enough."

Judy tucks a loose blonde hair back into her stubby ponytail.

At least I have enough hair to pull into a ponytail. But I wish it would grow a little faster.

A year earlier, doctors had shaved her head so they could stitch up wounds caused by a bullet that grazed one side of her head. Slowly, Judy's hair grew long enough that she no longer needed any of the many hats that had decorated her head for much of the past year. She was still quite fond of those that Chief Sorensen had knitted for her.

Judy gets to her feet, brushes hair and dust from her shorts, and points Elvira and Snowball toward the door.

"Outside, hounds. Leave us in peace."

She opens the door to the fenced yard and watches the two dogs bolt into the shimmering heat.

"Now, how are we going to solve the mystery of the disappearing Sylvia?"

Audrey presses her fingers together, making a teepee. As she considers Judy's question, Audrey taps her finger teepee against her mouth.

"First, we need to get to know Carlton better. I'll start by calling a few people I know at the railroad. They might know him. Then maybe we should pay a courtesy call tonight to see if he needs anything."

"He might not welcome that."

Judy watches out the window at the dogs racing in wide circles just inside the fence line. She turns to smile at Audrey.

"Or maybe he would welcome our help. Our first step should be some internet research. I'll take on that job. We know when Sylvia graduated from high school. We know when she returned to Redbud. Now we just need to fill in the space between those two events. I'm pretty good at that. I dug up a lot of info on people during my reporter days."

Judy pretends to be cracking her knuckles as she pulls out the chair next to the computer and sits down.

Audrey takes up a position behind Judy and watches as the computer screen comes to life.

"I guess I'll work on Carlton. And I'll call my daughter in California. Her husband's a lawyer. Maybe he'll have a few suggestions. And I'll also talk some more with Lois and see if she knows more than she thinks she does about Sylvia."

She's on her way to her room to make a few phone calls when the doorbell rings.

Audrey calls to Judy, "I'll bet that's Dr. Thomas, here to check out our new dogs. I'd better get going on her peanut butter and jelly sandwiches."

The first thing Audrey notices is the tired way Shirley steps into the room. She looks like someone who hasn't slept in a week. Audrey notices dark smudges under the veterinarian's eyes and the limp hair drooping around her face. Gone is the smiling enthusiasm this woman usually brings to her work.

"Are you okay?" Audrey asks.

Judy also turns to take in Shirley's glum appearance.

Shirley responds with a slow nod, "I'm fine. Just tired. Let's look at those new dogs."

She drops into the closest chair and turns half of her mouth up into a partial smile.

"I'll get the dogs," Judy volunteers, rising from her chair.

"And I'll start the sandwiches," Audrey adds, looking back only briefly on her way to the kitchen.

She isn't going to let Shirley leave this house without learning what's bothering the veterinarian, and Audrey is pretty sure the problem has nothing to do with dogs or cats.

***

Carl and Martin sit shoulder to shoulder on the bench that overlooks the lake on the former Jensen farm. Anyone noticing them together might have guessed them to be brothers. Both are squarely built, sturdy and about the same height. They move in unison and sit in synch, legs spread, feet turned outward and heads slightly bowed. Carl points out various locations on the farm; Martin follows Carl's gestures, nodding to emphasize his understanding.

They'd met here early. Carl recounted the past year when he helped uncover a fortune in gold coins believed to have been Johannes Jensen's gambling wins. Carl also shared what ancestral details they had uncovered in their search.

After the Jensen family responded to a religious revival in the Danish community in the late nineteenth century, Johannes agreed to give up his talent for card games and disperse his ill-gotten wealth. But instead of giving the gold coins away, he hid them, most of them inside furniture he'd built himself.

Stories passed down through the generations had brought many curious descendants to this Nebraska site, but the discovery of a long-forgotten diary led the small group of distant cousins to the family fortune. Expecting that other descendants might yet appear in Redbud, the three had set aside some of the money to provide scholarships to children of early Redbud pioneers. Daisy Jensen would be one of the first beneficiaries.

But now Martin has another story—of rubies.

"Look at this," Martin hands over a yellowed letter, its writing faded and barely legible. "Here's where my granddad wrote down what he remembered about the rubies. He was the youngest child, so maybe he was still living at home when this happened."

Both men look at the letter that Martin holds up so they can read it together.

"But, why rubies?" Carl asks. "Where would they get rubies? Not from gambling, I wouldn't think."

"No. See what he writes there." Martin points at a line halfway down the letter.

"My granddad said an old man visited and gave his mother the rubies. He showed up at the farm one day unannounced and left after pushing a pouch full of rubies on the protesting Karen, who my granddad said seemed both sad and angry."

Carl strokes his mustache and explains the speculation that the father of Karen's first child might have been a Danish aristocrat.

"You think maybe he decided to look her up? And their child?"

"And found, I think, a stout and exhausted woman, one who'd borne eleven children. If there was such a meeting, I wonder if both might have regretted seeing each other one last time. They might have preferred their memories."

Martin nods, "He was probably quite frail by then too, hardly the handsome lord Karen might once have loved. Instead she finds herself looking at a tottering eighty-year-old."

"But one who came all the way from Denmark to Nebraska to see the girl he'd wronged. The guilt of a dying man."

"A dying man who brought rubies for his lover and her child."

Neither Carl nor Martin knows this for a fact, but their imaginations prod them on, and they imagine the scene:

Did the oldest child even know of her parentage? Was she loyal only to Johannes, the man who had raised her? Were the only people involved in this gift exchange an old, sick man, a timeworn pioneer woman and the small boy who listened and watched, unnoticed. What did they say to one another? What did they remember?

"According to my granddad, Karen accepted the rubies."

"But what did she do with them?"

Carl points out that since the rubies weren't gambling winnings, Karen would have had no reason to get rid of them.

Or would she?

"My granddad writes there that his mother noticed him then and shooed him away. He never heard their parting words, never learned what Karen did with the rubies."

"Maybe Karen didn't want her husband to know anything. Maybe she held on to the rubies, thinking she'd leave them to her daughters. Maybe she just liked looking at them, imagining the life she might have lived."

"Maybe she sold them to pay for things her family needed."

Carl stands up and stares out at the lake.

"Or maybe in anger she pitched them into this lake."

Martin stands and both men stare out at the lake, hands back in pockets, watching the sun paint white streaks across the surface.

Neither man believes Karen would have buried the rubies or hid them in furniture as her husband had with the gold coins.

Carl pulls a handkerchief from his pocket and runs it over his perspiring face. Martin does the same.

Carl offers to show Martin around, including outbuildings and the house construction, remodeling it into the future headquarters for the Redbud Area Dog Rescue. But the Nebraska heat smothers their enthusiasm and the two instead walk to their cars, both sighing about the humidity.

As Carl opens his car door, he looks up at the sound of a car barreling down the road, rattling noisily as gravel sprays in its wake. As the car races past them, Carl squints at the car's occupants and freezes in place.

"My God, that looks like Sylvia Ritter."

CHAPTER 11

Once again, everything changes. First, he had a simple domestic dispute. Then it escalated into a possible kidnapping. Now he's back to square one, with Sylvia leaving town willingly for unknown reasons.

Chief Sorensen watches Daisy as she bounces in front of him, chattering about her recent adventure photographing the car that delivered Sylvia to her home and then drove her away. He frowns to show his concern for the child's disregard for her own safety.

But there it is on Daisy's cellphone. Several pictures of the car, the license plate and a shot that definitely shows Sylvia getting back into the car after tossing a suitcase in the back. Daisy's surveillance has outdone his own.

The chief sits at the Jensens' kitchen table scrolling through the photos. He'd responded immediately after Mrs. Jensen's excited phone call to his office. He's studying the license plate when another call comes in on his cellphone. It's Carl, saying he's sure he's just seen Sylvia driving down a rural road in a maroon Ford going eighty miles an hour.

So, Sylvia's alive. And it's looking more and more like she left because she wanted to leave. She stopped home to pick up some belongings and left again. She's made no effort to call for help or let Carlton know she's safe. But is she safe? I wonder.

A quick call identifies the owner of the car as Thomas Hardin, the retired chemistry teacher who'd once told a counselor he was concerned about Sylvia and later backed away from his comments to suggest that maybe Sylvia was playing with him.

Mr. Hardin must be eighty by now. What is he doing with Sylvia? And why would a man his age race away from Redbud with Sylvia as if the devil himself were in pursuit? Good question. And is Mr. Hardin a willing participant in this escapade? Or has Sylvia kidnapped him?

Hah. My imagination is spinning out of control. Maybe Sylvia stole the sports car, kidnapped and then killed its driver, dumped the car and body somewhere, and then kidnapped Mr. Hardin. The man is probably even now trying to kick his way out of his own car's trunk, which Sylvia is now driving to destinations unknown for nefarious purposes, also unknown.

After running through all the most absurd turns this case might take next, the chief asks himself if this is even still a police matter.

Should I stand down now and let Sylvia and Carlton work out their own problems, or not work them out, whatever the case might be? Should I assume Mr. Hardin is just helping one of his favorite former students?

The chief turns his attention to the sprightly Daisy, thanks her for her service and suggests she return to activities that are more suitable for one her age.

"Maybe Audrey Nevins could use some help with the rescue dogs."

The chief looks up at Margaret, who smiles and nods. He looks back at Daisy.

"She might even introduce you to some other animal lovers your age."

"Don't you think I should still keep an eye on the house?" she asks. "Someone else might come by."

The chief stands and towers over the girl, making sure she notices his size. He points a finger at her.

"Do not go close to that house again. And stay off their yard!"

98

"Yes, sir!"

He shakes his head, wondering what more he can say.

He calls Carlton at work and tells him the news. Carlton seems pleased but confused.

"But where is she now?"

"Are you sure you don't know? Where would she go if she just wanted to get away? Does she have a favorite hiding place?"

Carlton doesn't answer, but the chief knows he's asked the right questions.

The chief's cellphone rings again, and he learns a couple of men are waiting for him at his office.

I'll tie up a few loose ends and then leave this mystery alone.

***

As Chief Sorensen walks into police headquarters, he sees two men in animated conversation punctuated with laughter and arm punches. The one in a suit and tie wears his thinning hair slicked back. Dark-rimmed glasses rest snugly on his nose. He is thin enough to give the impression that he watches his diet carefully and probably belongs to a gym. The other man wears sweatpants and t-shirt and looks like he's been carrying an extra fifty pounds for a long time. The chief immediately tags the first as the class president, the second as the football star.

Both men extend their arms at once. "Hey, Randy."

Suddenly they're all back in high school. All three men rock on the soles of their feet as they dredge up shared memories of the year they were all seventeen.

After a few sentences that begin with "Do you remember when—", Chief Sorensen finally turns to the business at hand.

"Things have changed since this morning. A couple of people have spotted Sylvia. We know she's okay."

"That's good news," affirms Ron Boyes, keeping his face serious.

Morley Ames nods, following Boyes' example with his own serious face.

"But I'd still appreciate a few words with each of you. I'm not sure it's time yet for me to be unconcerned. And if you don't mind, I'll take you one at a time. Ron?"

The chief points toward his office door and leads the way. Morley takes a seat in the lobby.

The chief takes one of the two visitor's chairs and Ron Boyes takes the other. The chief wants everything as casual as possible.

"Did you stay in touch with Sylvia after graduation?"

"No. As you might remember, she dumped me the day after prom. I was devastated. All along, I thought we were the perfect couple. Then all of a sudden, we weren't. She wouldn't give me any reason, said she just wanted to move on. Those were her exact words. She wanted to move on."

Chief Sorensen wonders—but just for a moment—if he should even be asking questions about Sylvia's high school days.

Am I just being snoopy now?

But then he reminds himself that Sylvia had last been seen speeding away from Redbud in a car driven by a retired high school science teacher.

What's that all about?

"What did you think when I told you Sylvia had disappeared?"

Ron bounces a forefinger off his nose before he answers.

"I was surprised, actually, and worried. The old Sylvia might have taken off in anger, but the new Sylvia wouldn't have left without a good reason."

He sits up a little straighter in his chair and rests his hands on his thighs.

"I ran into her a couple of years ago at a Christmas party in Redbud. She seemed to have it all together, still charming, but in charge of herself. I don't think she was ever happy in high school. Oh, she was fun. She was beautiful. She was exciting. But mainly she was faking it, creating herself as she went along. But get her alone and the shadows dropped around her. I tried to talk to her, to find out what was bothering her, but the more I tried, the farther she moved from me."

"Funny. I always thought she was the happiest, most confident girl in the whole school. Of course, I was only admiring her from a distance. She was way out of my league."

The chief writes something down on the notepad resting on his lap, then continues, "Do you know anything about what she did in California?"

"Nothing. We weren't in touch. I heard by the grapevine that she was making a lot of money doing something, but I didn't hear any details. Then one day she was back in Redbud. She married Carlton— a standup guy, by the way. I've met him a few times. I wonder where she found him."

The chief looks up. "You don't remember Carlton?"

"Should I?"

"He was in our high school class. He never left Redbud. Sylvia met him after she moved back."

"Is that right." Ron speaks those words softly as a statement, not a question.

A few minutes later, Chief Sorensen hears similar comments from Morley, although the former football star, now coach, talks more about how much fun Sylvia could be and not as much about any perceived unhappiness.

As Chief Sorensen shows Morley to the door, he finds Ron still waiting in the lobby.

"I just thought of something," Ron explains. "You should talk to Greg Long. He and Sylvia were pretty tight for a while and both of them thought they'd give Hollywood a try. They might still be in touch."

"Do you know where I can reach him?"

"I don't. I don't think anyone knows what happened to him except for maybe Sylvia. His parents died years ago. I don't think Greg even came back for the funerals. I just thought you might have a way to run him down."

"I'm working on it," Chief Sorensen replies as he walks both men to the door.

He checks the time and decides to drive out to see if, by some miracle, he'll find a note from Mr. Hardin explaining his absence. Then he'll stop by the elderly woman living next door to Sylvia's childhood home. He might still have time to see Shirley at her veterinary clinic before driving out to Audrey's place to see what Audrey and Judy might have uncovered.

That may be it for the investigation into Sylvia's disappearance.

Maybe we'll all be laughing about this later
Or maybe not.

CHAPTER 12

"That's it? You were afraid we'd find out about your life as a stripper?"

Audrey hoots and slaps her thigh after a tearful Shirley admitted she had met Sylvia in California where they had both danced in a popular Los Angeles nightclub.

"Exotic dancers. We were exotic dancers."

"OK. So you were strippers who once took ballet. Who cares? Honey, that's nothing to be all upset about. We've all done that."

Judy sits up straighter. "We've all done that?"

She stops talking as soon as she feels the sharp kick under the table that the three women are sitting around. They'd retired to the kitchen after Shirley finished checking out and vaccinating the dogs just rescued from the county shelter.

"Audrey? You?"

Shirley sets down the peanut butter and jelly sandwich she's been pulling apart.

Audrey waves one hand as if batting away flies.

"Sometimes a girl just needs to do what she needs to do."

She reaches across the table and pats one of Shirley's hands. Shirley wipes a tear.

"I doubt the ladies at the Lutheran church would see it that way. Or any of my clients. And I know Sylvia didn't want that story out. Oh, she'll be so upset if this gets out. We promised to keep each other's secrets."

Judy notices the "s" on the end of secret. Is there something else, she wonders, while guessing Shirley has already revealed more than she had wanted anyone to know.

It had taken Audrey all of fifteen minutes to convince Shirley she needed to unload whatever was burdening her so.

"The money was good, and you needed money," Audrey presses on, hoping to learn more.

Shirley nods.

"I was saving up for veterinary school. Sylvia was trying to make it as a Hollywood starlet but wasn't getting any call backs. We were both pretty cute back then. We had great figures if I do say so myself." She throws up both hands. "And we could dance."

Judy rubs her bruised ankle and asks Shirley if she earned enough money dancing to pay for vet school.

"I didn't have to. Meeting Sylvia turned out to be the solution to all my financial problems."

Both Audrey and Judy frown, not understanding. Shirley sees their confusion.

"Sylvia helped me come up with the money. Let's just leave it at that. She also helped me set up my practice here in Redbud. All she asked was that I not tell people here about her life in California. She didn't even want me to say we knew each other there. I guess that seems funny to both of you."

Shirley looks from Audrey to Judy and back to Audrey.

Both women nod. Audrey leans across the table and looks Shirley straight on.

"What I don't understand is how Sylvia went from someone supporting herself by dancing in a nightclub to someone with plenty of money. Did she inherit money? Did she win the lottery?"

Shirley smiles and shakes her head. Then she winks.

"Maybe she had a sugar daddy—the owner of the club."

They try not to laugh, but both Audrey and Judy break out in giggles.

"This just keeps getting better," Audrey chuckles, trying with limited success to control her amusement.

Sylvia with a sugar daddy. Nobody in Redbud has ever had a sugar daddy. This has to be a first.

Shirley covers her mouth with both hands, then removes them just long enough to say, "Now I've really told you too much. Sylvia would kill me if she knew I was telling you all this."

"If you help save her life, she'll be forever grateful. I'm sure of that."

Again, Audrey reaches across the table and pats the veterinarian's hands.

While Audrey believes she's just getting started with her questions, Shirley decides otherwise. She stands up, snatches her supply bag from her side and backs toward the door in a quick retreat.

"But—" starts Audrey.

"Wait," interrupts Judy.

But the veterinarian is out the door, tossing back a quick few words about "appointments. Must get back to the dogs and cats."

"I think she feels better," Audrey observes, as they watch the vet sprint to her car.

"A little, maybe. But I think she left a lot out."

Both women now have more questions than before.

Did Sylvia really have a sugar daddy? Is that where Sylvia found the money to set up her own business? Did she really own her own travel agency? Maybe Sylvia came by the money some other way, with some business she didn't care to share with Shirley or anyone else. And why did Shirley set up practice in Redbud if the two were going to keep their shared past a secret?

"There's so much more we need to know if we're going to find Sylvia," Audrey complains, turning to look through the window at some barking dogs outside.

Judy leaves the room to begin work on a blog post about several nearly perfect dogs overlooked during recent adoption events. Since the four she has in mind all weigh less than twenty pounds, she decides to title the blog "Small Perfections" and feature two Chihuahuas, April and Carlos; one Pomeranian, Victoria; and a Boston terrier/Chihuahua mix named Lulu.

She has one paragraph out of the way when the phone rings.

Audrey answers and immediately waves her hand at Judy.

"What? You said what? She's been found? Not found, but spotted? Doing what? Yes. Please come by later."

Listening to only one end of the conversation, Judy still knows that someone has spotted Sylvia. She is alive. But she doesn't understand what that means—spotted, but what?

Spotted where? Is she on her way home? And who is coming over later. That's easy. Probably Chief Sorensen.

Audrey ends the call and places one hand on her chest.

Judy waits silently for what's to come.

***

While Judy and Audrey are coaxing a few secrets from the town veterinarian, Chief Sorensen decides his investigation into Sylvia's disappearance is almost over. But first, he needs to cross a few things off his list.

His visit to Thomas Hardin's home reveals nothing. No one is at home and everything seems in order except for the absence of its resident. The chief leaves a note on the door and looks up Mr. Hardin's phone number, leaving a second message there asking that Mr. Hardin call him immediately.

I still need to be sure Mr. Hardin is a willing participant in Sylvia's adventure.

A visit to Eunida Heppelwhite proves only slightly more interesting. In her mid-eighties, Eunida hasn't forgotten Sylvia or her parents, and she still harbors a dislike for the entire family.

"That girl was trouble, and her parents were just as bad. Yelling. Always fighting. That girl was always sneaking around, thinking she was so special."

As she talks, the frail woman shakes a finger at Chief Sorensen, as if scolding him as well. The chief feels as if he just shrank several inches. He nods and tries to appear sympathetic, calling on the patience he'd acquired while caring for his ancient grandfather.

"You called the police a few times. Can you remember why? What happened that made you want to involve the police?"

She leans on her walker and purses her lips, "Well!"

For a moment, the chief thinks that's the end of the conversation, but she continues.

"Well! She was a thief, she was. She stole tomatoes from my garden and flowerpots from my porch. But did anyone believe me? No!"

Chief Sorensen wonders if someone her age should be getting all worked up over memories several decades past.

"I guess you were pretty surprised when she moved back to Redbud."

The old woman turns her walker around and walks away from Chief Sorensen.

Without looking back, she huffs, "She hasn't changed."

As she slowly retreats into another room, this seems to be the extent of the information the old woman is willing to provide.

"I'll show myself out," he mutters to her back.

As he walks to his car, the chief remembers someone telling him that people become more of what they've always been as they age. Eunida has aged from an angry young person into a sour old person, he guesses. He wonders how anyone can live that long with such anger boiling away inside.

He thinks of his own grandfather who'd lived to be 110 years old. Some might have described him as gruff or even crabby, but the grandfather Randy remembers was gentle and teasing, a talkative old coot who whined and complained at times but still approved of most Redbud residents, young and old. The chief looks back at Eunida's door and sees her scowling back at him.

She sure does give a different picture of the young Sylvia. Not one word about how charming, how popular or how good she made everyone feel. Eunida saw someone quite opposite. But maybe she never spared a good word for anyone.

The chief next stops at the Redbud Veterinary Clinic but finds Dr. Thomas in the midst of spaying a Labrador retriever, so decides to check back with her later.

He returns to his office and finds several messages. He quickly returns the call from California, where a state officer tells him that a person named Greg Long is on parole after serving almost fifteen years on drug charges.

"He fits your age and profile. I've got the number for his parole officer if you'd like it."

The chief jots down the number and redials as soon as he thanks the California officer.

The parole officer picks up after a couple of rings, listens to the chief's questions and puts the call on hold while he looks up the Greg Long file. The chief drums his fingers on his desk as he waits. Finally, the parole officer comes back on the line.

"I should have remembered this without looking it up. Greg Long failed to show up for his last appointment. There's a warrant out for him."

Chief Sorensen feels a tingle work its way up his spine. He grips the phone tighter.

"Any chance you know if he had a car?"

"Hmm. Let's see. Oh, yes. Interesting. Looks like he put a Jaguar in storage while he was away. According to my file, that's what he's driving."

"A Jaguar. An old Jaguar."

Suddenly one puzzle piece snaps into place.

Thank you to all car-loving teenagers everywhere.

After ending the call with Greg Long's parole officer, Chief Sorensen knows that Greg has been in Redbud looking for Sylvia. He'd snatched her or she'd hopped into his car willingly and they'd driven off together early Sunday morning. Sylvia had either left the

Chihuahua behind deliberately, or the Chihuahua had managed to hide in the weeds and avoid capture.

But then, what? How had Sylvia gone from Greg's Jaguar to Mr. Hardin's old Ford? And what had happened to Greg? And why would he risk going back to jail by coming to Redbud, Nebraska, to trail Sylvia while she was out walking her newly adopted dog? What was it Morley had said? That Greg and Sylvia were once pretty tight and had left Redbud at the same time for California. Had they stayed together? Had he come to Nebraska to reclaim his former love? Or was his reason to seek out Sylvia something other than love? Did Sylvia even know about Greg's imprisonment on drug charges?

Just when I'm ready to quit this case, it starts getting interesting.

His last call to return is from Carlton. He knows before Carlton answers what he'll say. He wants to call off the dogs.

"Sylvia will be back when she's ready to be back. You don't need to do anything more on my behalf."

"Are you sure of that, Carlton?"

"Absolutely."

There is finality in the way Carlton says the word. Firm. Certain.

"For now, we'll consider Sylvia's disappearance a closed case unless something changes."

What the chief doesn't share with Carlton is that something has already changed. An ex-con has appeared in Redbud, and not just any ex-con, but one who'd grown up here, attended high school here, dated Sylvia, moved to California with her, failed to become a successful actor but perhaps had become a successful drug dealer.

And there is that one other thing.

The chief again works on his forehead as if carving a new worry line. He feels a sudden urge to find his knitting supplies and dive into the project that will take his mind off the desire to pour himself a stiff drink.

He pulls over the file on the corner of his desk, the file that has revealed more about the Ritter family and why they moved to Redbud. He knows now that Carlton had not always been easy to forget. Quite the opposite. But in Redbud, he and his parents had carefully avoided attention.

Carlton had floated through years in Redbud, diaphanous as a ghost, quiet as night.

Intentionally so.

***

Lois pauses only a minute before opening her cellphone and calling Carlton. She's just heard the news from Audrey. Sylvia has been spotted alive and on the move in the company of a retired chemistry teacher.

"Carlton? This is Lois James. I just wanted to make sure you were okay. Maybe you'd like some company. I know I'd hate to be alone at a time like this."

As she speaks, she knows she's nothing like Carlton, so she really doesn't know if he'd like company or if he'd much rather be alone. She knows that his parents are long gone and that he doesn't have any siblings or close friends that she knows of.

So she is actually surprised when he takes her up on her offer.

"I really don't want to be alone right now. Thank you, Lois."

***

After leaving the old Jensen farm, Carl and Martin return to Bella's. Carl disappears into the kitchen for a few minutes and returns with a basket of warm fries topped with cheese and bacon.

"Since it's not a vegetarian night, bacon's allowed," Carl proclaims, plopping the basket in the middle of the table.

Martin's hand shoots quickly into the basket.

"My favorite appetizer," he admits.

He'd already called his wife and suggested she bring Daisy over for dinner.

They talk briefly about spotting Sylvia and wondering what's going on with her, but their conversation turns quickly back to rubies, a gem they know is more valuable than diamonds.

But where are these rubies?

Bella joins them for a while and says that if they'd been her rubies, she would have had them made into enough separate necklaces, bracelets or rings to give to all daughters and daughters-in-law. They would pass them down through the generations.

Carl scrunches up his face, causing his eyebrows to form a V on his forehead.

"I don't remember my grandmother ever wearing rubies, but I was a boy. I probably didn't pay attention to jewelry."

Martin shakes his head slowly.

"I don't remember any fancy jewelry in my family either. Maybe she planned to do it but never got around to it. Do we know when she died? And was it sudden? Maybe she'd hidden the rubies away, always planning to do just what Bella suggested. But maybe she died too soon."

Martin smiles. "Or maybe I'm just hoping that's the case."

Carl suggests they talk to Chief Sorensen to see if he knows more about Karen's death—was it sudden? The chief might also know if a Danish aristocrat had visited Redbud in the early twentieth century.

They all look up suddenly as a sextet of high school students burst into the café.

"Ah. It's the high school crowd," explains Bella, rising from her chair. "Soon to be followed by the seniors who like to beat the dinner crowd."

She laughs but doesn't lose her smile. She is proud that Bella's has so quickly become the favorite spot for Redbud residents of all ages.

And even a few who are just passing through.

She looks at the two older men sitting a couple of tables away. They'd spent the night in the B&B—an odd couple, she figures. Rough looking. Broad. She can imagine them in younger years as nightclub bouncers. Now they seem a little seedy.

Carl and Martin return to their discussion of rubies.

"If the rubies didn't stay in the family, then they're still out on the farm somewhere—probably buried. But where would Karen bury them? Was there a place on that property that was just hers?"

Carl nods politely at the two men who are staring at them. The men drop their eyes and return to their sandwiches.

***

Daisy is bored. She wants to continue being a junior detective. She and Birdy walk around the block again and slow down in front of the Ritters' house.

"Something funny is going on, Birdy. This house still needs watching."

She returns home and checks her Facebook page, hoping for news from the friends she'd left behind. She finds her mother working on lesson plans for her college classes.

"Will you take me out to the Redbud Rescue place tomorrow? Maybe I could help with the dogs."

Her mother smiles and agrees, "That's a good idea, Daisy."

Daisy runs her fingers across the piano in the living room and pokes through books still packed in a moving crate. Nothing interests her. She returns to her room, picks up her binoculars and aims them at the back of the Ritters' home.

Nothing.

Nothing yet.

CHAPTER 13

"Are Fern and Thistle ready for adoption?"

Judy looks up from her laptop.

"Someone wants to know if they'll be at our next adoption event."

"Soon," answers Audrey. "Soon. But not yet."

She sighs. It seems like forever since Redbud Area Dog Rescue took in the two pocket beagles, as some call them. It's actually only been a year. But the two sweet-tempered beagles had come with advanced cases of heartworm disease. Judy tagged them "the synchronized beagles" since they move in unison wherever they roam. Fern turns left. Thistle follows. Fern reverses direction. Thistle follows. Fern rolls in the grass. Thistle rolls in the glass.

Redbud Rescue has treated hundreds of dogs for heartworm disease, a mosquito-borne disease that is almost always fatal if left untreated. In rare cases, the treatment can be fatal.

Audrey had debated whether to treat them at all. They were already coughing and wheezing. Exams revealed what Dr. Thomas called the worst case she'd ever seen. She pointed out weakened arteries packed with worms, visible on x-rays.

"We can try."

With those words from Shirley, Audrey had given the go ahead.

"These two old ladies deserve a chance."

When Judy heard the decision, she'd nearly cheered. A Good Samaritan had found the beagles running together in the country and had transported them to Redbud.

Almost a year later, Fern is in complete recovery, but Thistle still needs a few more months before she'll be fit enough for spay surgery.

Judy looks out the window at the two beagles romping around the yard in step, moving at a brisk clip they could not have managed a year ago. Audrey stands behind Judy and they both watch the beagle performance.

"I just hope we don't take in too many dogs that stay with us for a year or more," says Audrey.

"Or cost us this much," Judy adds.

"But Fern and Thistle had survived. Shirley said their survival was almost miraculous."

"And they may have saved a few lives."

Redbud Rescue has used Fern and Thistle to help educate the public about heartworm disease, which is completely preventable with a once-a-month pill. Now they hope Fern and Thistle will soon be ready for a new home together.

The phone interrupts their beagle-watching break. Audrey picks it up.

Minutes later, she ends the call.

"You won't believe this. That was a policeman who wanted us to take a pair of Jack Russell terriers whose owner was murdered."

"Again?"

"This was a different officer and a different murder. The officer who brought us Mia was in Missouri. Remember, his wife drove Mia to us. That murder is still unsolved. The officer I just talked to is in Grand Island. He says the boyfriend murdered the dogs' owner."

"Poor things. They must be terrified."

Audrey flops onto the sofa and stretches out her legs. She sits silently wiping a finger up and down over her lips like a windshield wiper, then turns her head toward Judy.

"That little Mia, or Daisy's Birdy, certainly does find herself in the midst of trouble, doesn't she? First, her Missouri owner is murdered. Then Sylvia adopts her and immediately disappears under mysterious circumstances. And as I understand it, the Missouri woman had owned Mia for only a month or two. Who knows why Mia ended up there, maybe another murder?"

Judy deletes out several emails and closes her laptop. She looks over at the reclining Audrey.

"An interesting coincidence?"

"You know I don't believe in coincidences. Let's see what Randy thinks."

Audrey swings her legs off the sofa and boosts herself up with a quick grunt just as the doorbell rings and a chorus of previously napping dogs sounds the alarm.

"Quiet!" Judy tries to scream over the noise.

Randy slips sideways in the door, leading with his knitting bag, shoving a couple of dogs away as he guards against any escapes.

"They love you, Randy," Audrey insists. "They all love you. You have a way with dogs."

"Hah!" he responds.

Judy smiles, remembering how Audrey had told her she had a way with dogs even when Judy was still claiming not to be a dog person.

Audrey beckons Randy inside toward the sofa, "Have a seat while I pour you a tall ice tea."

Audrey barely returns with the tea and two glasses of wine when Randy announces that the Sylvia Ritter investigation has taken a few strange turns, but he is pulling back for the moment from a full-scale investigation.

Audrey sits down on the sofa next to Randy.

"But you haven't heard about the strange history of Birdy the Chihuahua."

Randy breathes in deeply and lets his breath out with a whoosh.

Here they go again. A Chihuahua with a history. What next?

"Before you begin the story, let me pull out my knitting."

I won't admit it, but I need the knitting to keep me from coveting their Merlots. I also might need the help holding back my laughter—or tears.

Randy soon finds the lower edge for his a multi-colored sweater project. He attaches yarn from a maroon ball of heavy wool and pulls through a loop for the first stitch in a knit row.

"Go ahead," he beckons to the two waiting women.

"You are amazing, so talented," Audrey grins, poking Randy's arm.

Much to his surprise, the chief finds Birdy's story interesting. He stops knitting and pulls his cellphone from his pocket.

"Give me the name and number for that police officer."

He dials and reaches the young officer immediately. A few minutes later, he's learned something Audrey hadn't known or mentioned.

"They haven't arrested anyone, but they have DNA. Birdy must have bitten the murderer because the officer was able to take a blood sample from her teeth. They also have witnesses saying they saw two men running from the scene."

Judy tilts her head to one side.

"But what does that have to do with what happened here. What's the connection?"

"Maybe nothing, but a Chihuahua at the middle of a crime wave is worth a few minutes of my time, don't you think?"

118

With that, they all laugh.

"Just like the old days in Chicago, right, Randy?" Audrey jokes.

"Good thing the old gang can't see me now."

Against his better judgment, the chief fills the two women in on the afternoon's developments. He describes his stop at Mr. Hardin's empty house and his conversation with the grumpy Eunida.

Audrey looks up, "Maybe Eunida needs a dog. A dog might improve her outlook."

"But what would it do to the poor dog?" The chief presents more intrigue when he reveals what he'd learned about Greg Long.

"Wait till Barbara and Lois hear this. They went to school with Greg."

Audrey is now sitting straight up. She slaps Randy's thigh.

"Ouch," he fakes a bit of pain. "I went to school with him, too. I can tell you I would not have picked Greg as someone who would end up in jail for any reason."

Judy jumps in, "And his car was here in Redbud? He violated parole to come here and find Sylvia? But where is he now?"

"Good question. Where is Greg now? And is Sylvia running from him?" Audrey wonders.

"Or maybe after him," Judy adds.

Randy and Audrey both look at Judy, considering her words. Randy sips his ice tea and puts the glass down on the coffee table before responding.

"Interesting as all this is, and as curious as I might be, I don't really have a case to pursue. Carlton wants to call off the search."

Both women have speculations to offer about Thomas Hardin.

Audrey suggests, "Maybe Sylvia kidnapped him. Maybe you should try to find him."

"Well, if I don't hear from him soon, I could consider that. But people are allowed to leave town now and then without checking in with the local police."

Judy rubs the ankle that was still smarting from Audrey's earlier kick.

"Still. This seems a little different." She remembers what Shirley had told them. "We learned something else interesting today. Dr. Thomas and Sylvia Ritter knew each other in California."

The chief nods. He'd wondered about that after seeing evidence of telephone calls between Shirley and Sylvia.

"I'd certainly like to know more about that. But, as I said, this case seems closed."

"Oh we know a lot more about that," Judy begins to blurt, but halts her remarks when Audrey catches her with a sharp look and a finger to her lips, her head carefully turned out of Randy's eyesight.

"But nothing all that important," Judy finishes, getting to her feet. "I'll feed the dogs and take care of their playtime. You two can just talk and take it easy for a while."

Some things will stay secret.

Specifically, Audrey had let her know that exotic dancing was the sort of thing to keep private.

We still keep our secrets. At least some of them.

Unknown to Judy or Audrey, Chief Randy Sorensen is keeping a few things secret too.

He says nothing about what he's learned about Carlton.

***

Judy plays to perfection the role of chaperone to Audrey and Randy. She stays out of the way but makes enough noise to let them know she's still there.

It's come to this. Not only am I sleeping with dogs and spending my days with no one under the age of fifty, now I'm acting like a proper parent to a pair of hormonal senior citizens. Of course, I don't really know about the hormonal part. Maybe they really are just friends.

She doubts the just friends part, although she suspects that both Audrey and Randy would use those words. She smiles that they might be the last to know what their friendship is really all about.

After feeding, watering and playing with a dozen dogs, Judy decides to recruit a Labrador retriever, Shenzi, for a late night swim. Ready for a bit of relaxation, Judy undresses and slips into a lightweight robe. She leashes up Shenzi and pads as softly as possible past the laughter in the living room and outside to the path leading to the pool. Once there, she drops her robe and eases her nude body into the cool water. Shenzi splashes in after her and begins swimming circles around her. After several laps, interrupted by collisions with Shenzi, Judy floats on her back, searching for the few constellations she can name.

One of life's simple pleasures. Sinking into a cool pool on a steamy night.

As Judy floats, the stars seem to be blinking out a message in an unknown code. Judy sighs.

Are you telling me what to do next? Why not make it easier? Don't make me work so hard.

Just over a year ago, she'd become a part of the Redbud Area Dog Rescue. Audrey had rescued her as if she were just another lost

121

dog, pulling her in her front door and offering her a place to live, plus work to fill her time.

I found my way back to earth thanks to the soft comfort of older women.

The thought surprises her, because Audrey especially seems anything but soft. Judy searches for the right words to describe Audrey but finally gives up.

Eccentric? Kind? Wounded? Survivor? Hearty? Resilient? Alive? Unsinkable? All seem right and all seem equally wrong. Nothing fits quite right. There's so much I still don't know about her. I wonder if I'll ever learn more of her secrets, Judy wonders. Is it possible to have too many secrets? Do we lose the comforts of intimacy when we hide too much from others? She remembers the relief she'd felt after finally opening up about the tragedies that had taken her family.

She thinks of Sylvia and Shirley, of their shared secrets. Judy suspects that the exotic dancing is only part of it.

And had Audrey once been a dancer? Or was she just trying to make Shirley more willing to talk?

Judy closes her eyes and lets herself sink below the surface. After enjoying the muffled noises in her submerged ears, she stretches her arms wide and flips over to swim a couple more laps, much to the delight of Shenzi, who crashes back into the water from where she'd been resting by the side of the pool. When she flips back over onto her back, Judy continues her questions.

But how long can I stay here following Audrey around? What's next? Is it time to step out from under the shelter of the people in this town, a town that includes a café with the best food I've ever sampled and a police chief who is also an historian and a knitter? But why leave Redbud? I like it here. Maybe I should concentrate on making a few younger friends, maybe join a gym. And I should think about a new career. I can't go on forever living rent free in exchange for helping with the dogs.

Before moving to Redbud, Judy had worked as a newspaper reporter, interviewing people and writing their stories. But newspaper jobs are hard to find and she isn't sure she wants to return to that world.

As if out of nowhere, she thinks of the Chihuahua who'd collected DNA from a murder suspect. She giggles loudly enough to alert Shenzi, who paddles toward her.

"What do you think, Shenzi? Maybe I could write a murder mystery."

Shenzi pushes her head against Judy's shoulder as if to say it's time to go inside and go to bed. Then the dog lifts up her head and stares beyond the pool.

A cracking and rustling near the pool prompts Judy to submerge her naked body up to her nose. Shenzi freezes and begins growling. Two shadows thump past, not three feet from the fence around the pool. Judy moves silently through the water, aiming for her robe discarded by the far end of the pool. Shenzi hoists herself out of the pool and barks after the shadows.

"Damn. Not another stupid dog."

Judy is wrapping her robe around her when the front door cracks open and Chief Sorensen bellows into the yard.

"Who's out there?!"

As the shadows head away from the house, accompanied by pants and grunts, one voice shouts back.

"No one. No one at all. Wrong house."

CHAPTER 14

TUESDAY

After staying too late at Audrey's and shouting a couple of trespassers off her property, Randy hopes for a quiet, crime-free day in Redbud, Nebraska.

He isn't comfortable shutting down the Sylvia Ritter case, but he doesn't really have a crime to investigate there. Sylvia has left Redbud on her own. Carlton, who probably isn't telling all he knows, has asked the chief to stand down.

But several inconsistencies leave the chief feeling unsettled.

Why did Sylvia leave town with an elderly, retired high school teacher instead of using her own car? She returned to her home long enough to pack a suitcase. Why not take her car? Why didn't she leave with her old boyfriend?

The chief sent out a bulletin asking the highway patrol to please stop Thomas Hardin's car, with a request that he call Chief Sorensen regarding an emergency at home. When he hears from Mr. Hardin, the chief will know whether he's really done with this case.

And then there's the strange case of Greg Long, who violated parole to visit Redbud. There is no doubt in the chief's mind that Greg had been the one who picked up Sylvia early Sunday morning as she walked her new Chihuahua.

Why then had Sylvia ended up in a car with Mr. Hardin? And where had Greg gone?

Fortunately, Greg's parole officer provided the license number for Greg's Jaguar. The chief turned that information over to other law enforcement, sure that most officers will gladly pick up a parole violator who's done time for drug charges.

Then again, the Jaguar might have a stolen plate. And let's not forget the Chihuahua, now with Daisy. Should a middle school girl be taking care of a dog that seems to attract trouble? First a murder in Missouri. And now, well, whatever set Sylvia off into the sunset—or wherever. And what should I think about the news that Sylvia and the town veterinarian had actually known each other in California and kept that secret from everyone in Redbud?

The chief rereads the information uncovered about Carlton's life before moving to Redbud with his family.

Is Carlton really the quiet, unassuming Nebraska husband he seems to be?

Randy leans back in his chair and props his feet on his desk. He'd enjoyed his evening with Audrey. She seems to have mastered the basic knit, purl stitches and is now working on a simple hat. The evening had ended with a cacophony of barking and the sight of two overweight men lumbering from the yard as Judy, wrapped in a thin robe, ran toward the house dripping pool water. Next to her trotted Shenzi, the chocolate Lab, who alternated between keeping up with Judy and stopping to bark at the retreating men.

The men probably were trying to locate some other home and Audrey's dogs scared them away, along with a little help from my own outraged shouting. That would figure, anyway.

He rubs his forehead.

He'd told both Audrey and Judy that the men had probably just stumbled into the wrong yard while looking for some other place. After all, it was late and a lot of these old farm homes looked alike. But he'd watched the retreating men until they'd disappeared into the night. He'd heard the sound of a car starting up just out of sight.

"Nothing to worry about," he'd said.

But he doubts either woman believed him. And he heard Audrey lock and bolt the door as he left.

In spite of himself, and although the idea seems wrong, he wonders if the two overweight shadows have anything to do with the now defunct case of Sylvia's disappearance.

Probably not.

He looks up and smiles as Blanche pokes her head into his office.

"Looks like a quiet day," he remarks to her.

Then he notices the expression on her face.

***

Audrey calls Lois at 10:00 a.m. and wakes her up.

"Lois? You can't still be in bed."

"Oh, but I can. And I am."

"Well, I won't ask why you're so tired, but I think you'll want to hear the news."

Audrey can hear a rustling noise as she presumes Lois is sitting up in bed.

"Is Sylvia back home?"

"No. Not that."

"Oh good. I mean, well what is the news then?"

"First off, how well did you know Greg Long?"

"Nice guy. Honor Society. Part of the theater crowd and one of Sylvia's boyfriends. I always thought he might be the one she'd end up with."

"Well I think they did end up together."

"Oh?"

Audrey outlines what she's learned about Greg.

Lois gasps, "He did time for drug offenses? Was he dealing?"

"That's my guess, but he just got out, and right away he heads to Redbud to see Sylvia Ritter, violating his parole."

"No!"

"Yes!"

"So, Sylvia ran away with Greg? I'm confused."

"No. She got away from Greg and was last seen speeding away in a car driven by Thomas Hardin."

"Our old chemistry teacher? He must be eighty. Audrey, slow down. You're not making sense."

Audrey rattles away, talking all the faster as she tries to catch Lois up with all the latest developments.

"And can you believe it? Sylvia and Shirley knew each other in California." She lowers her voice to a whisper, unable to hold it in any longer. "And for a while they both worked in a night club as exotic dancers."

Audrey stops.

"Of course," she shrugs, "who hasn't done that?"

"Audrey? You?"

"Just kidding. But there's more. Let's meet at Bella's tonight. Carl and Bella have decided Tuesday should be the vegetarian night. Let's support them."

Lois flops back onto her pillow after finishing her call.

She didn't say anything about her evening with Carlton.

She sits back up and dials Barbara.

"Barbara. You won't believe what I've just learned."

As she relays the latest gossip, she scoops up the two miniature pinschers on her bed and carries them to the back door for their delayed potty break.

***

Judy looks up as Audrey ends the call with Lois and watches as she immediately dials again.

The people here in Redbud might be secretive and protective of their own privacy, but throw a little gossip in the air and they're as excited as a Labrador retriever chasing a tennis ball.

Judy also has a phone to her ear. She's on hold, waiting for the police officer who'd called them about Birdy.

"Hello? This is Officer Butler. I understand you have some questions about that Chihuahua my wife brought your way."

Judy snaps to attention.

"Not so much about the dog. I was actually interested in the case. The Chihuahua's owner was murdered, I understand. Have you arrested anyone? It might be important."

Judy can almost hear the officer thinking that one over. Important?

"Well," he hesitates. "Well, no. We're still investigating, but so far, we have only dead ends. It's a strange case when you think about it. The victim was an ordinary, middle-aged woman living in a virtually crime-free town in a small house without a lot of valuables. Not a logical target for a burglary, but that is what it looked like—a botched burglary. She tried to scare them away with a handgun she kept next to her bed, but ended up in a struggle for the gun that left her dead."

"Could the motive have been something other than burglary? Could she have had enemies? How many middle-aged women keep handguns next to their beds?"

"In Missouri? Quite a few. You'd be surprised. We might not have a lot of violent crime here, but we have plenty of little old ladies who think we do. And not just the old ladies either. Young ones and men too seem always to be watching the shadows and buying guns."

"Hmm." Judy considers that. "How sad. Sad that so many people are so afraid. Also sad that this one woman was right to be afraid. But could there have been another motive? Did anyone benefit from her death?"

"Not that I can see. She has a son in Kansas City, who isn't interested in the house and wants it sold cheap and fast. He'll inherit about enough to bury his mother and pay off any outstanding bills. Not exactly a haul. He could have taken the Chihuahua. He gave her the dog as a birthday present a few months ago, found her in a Kansas City shelter, he said, but he wasn't interested in giving the little dog a home."

Judy senses that Officer Butler doesn't think much of the murdered woman's son.

"Well, you were a good person to get that little dog to us."

Judy tells the young officer about the Chihuahua's latest experiences and Chief Sorensen's jokes about the dog being at the center of a crime wave. She's about to thank the officer for his time when she remembers to ask if anyone has provided a description of the burglar.

"Burglars. Two of them. When the gun went off and the dog started barking, people began waking up. Several neighbors looked out their windows and saw two overweight men practically knocking each other over as they stumbled toward their car."

Judy drops her phone.

When she has it back against her ear, she takes a deep breath before she speaks.

"Two old, fat men? I may have seen them here last night."

***

After Judy finishes telling Audrey about the conversation with Officer Butler, both worry about Daisy.

Is she safe?

They reach the same conclusion as Officer Butler. The men are after the Chihuahua. Failing to capture it in Missouri, they've tracked the little dog to the Redbud Area Dog Rescue.

Did they also try to capture the dog from Sylvia? Are they why Sylvia is running? And how long before they figure out that Birdy is the new constant companion of a young, nearly teenaged girl?

Judy speaks first, "We've got to tell Chief Sorensen."

"You're right. I'll call Randy now."

Judy looks outside at the dogs playing there.

"While you're calling, I'll start returning dogs to their kennels. We've got to head to the Jensens' right away. Dear God. What if Daisy's all alone?!"

A few minutes later, as the two women storm out of the house, Audrey is still trying to reach Chief Sorensen. Finally, Audrey closes her cellphone.

"Something's happening. Blanche wouldn't put me through to him. I gave her the message instead. Let's hurry."

"What in the world makes that Chihuahua so important that someone would kill for it?"

Judy barely makes it to the passenger seat before Audrey pulls away from the house, leaving the passenger door still open and one of Judy's legs dangling outside. As the door flies back, Judy yanks her leg inside, grabs the door handle and pulls it shut.

"Here we go again," Judy whispers, pressing one hand against the side of her head, the side that a bullet had grazed less than a year ago.

***

Mort and Mel scowl into their coffee at Bella's.

"We must be the dumbest thugs left in Chicago," Mort growls.

"And the oldest."

Mel looks up with something that's almost a smile.

"Considering our chosen career, we can't be that dumb. We're still alive and not in jail."

Mort refuses to be amused.

"We failed to snatch that Chihuahua in Missouri and ended up with another murder notched on our belts. We also earned the fury of someone who scares me more than the police. Just when I was thinking we could enjoy our golden years and leave the past behind, be a little respectable even, maybe move to Florida and move into one of those retirement villages, flirt with the rich old ladies. I'm worried our luck might be running out. Damn. Why now?"

Mel rearranges his face into a more solemn expression.

"Why, after all these years, did Beluga hire us again?"

In their younger years, the two men had worked for a crime family in Chicago as muscle, thugs by their own description, tough guys who took on many a messy job. They'd done so many stints in prison that they figured they've spent a third of their lives inside.

In time, the Chicago family extended tentacles throughout the country, sucking in profits from the blossoming drug traffic. With the greater money came greater violence, the kind of warfare that needed men like Mort and Mel.

One day they'd received a call about doing some work for a drug lord known by the code name Beluga. They'd last worked for Beluga more than fifteen years back. They'd never met Beluga, but the name scared them then and continued scaring them long after they stopped hearing the name. Assignments from Beluga usually came to them from operatives two and three levels below the top. The assignments came with high demands and even higher rewards. Then one day, Beluga simply disappeared, or at least disappeared from the lives of Mort and Mel.

Up until a few months ago, Mort and Mel were more or less retired from crime. But they weren't living that well. Then they'd received the call that brought them to Missouri and, next, to Nebraska in search of a Chihuahua. One job. One simple job. The money would promise them a much better retirement than the one they'd been enjoying, or rather not enjoying that much.

Then they botched it in Missouri.

They didn't expect the woman would pull a gun on them. They never wanted what happened. But now the woman was dead, and they were in as much trouble as if they'd gone there to kill her instead of just snatch a dog.

And they were in even bigger trouble with Beluga. Their contact with Beluga exploded after they messed up in Missouri. The contact reamed them out good and told them they'd never see a dime for their work. They were fools, losers, idiots who wouldn't live long enough to regret what they'd done. Most of all, they were fired, no longer needed. They should just get lost.

But Mel and Mort have their own ideas. They aren't going to take it anymore. For some reason, this Beluga wants this Chihuahua. It's valuable for some unknown reason.

Mel and Mort made the decision to capture the damn little Chihuahua. If this dog is worth so much, Beluga will pay plenty to get it back. Now all they need is to actually find the dog.

Tracking the Chihuahua from Missouri to Nebraska had been easy. Mort had called the police saying he was interested in giving the poor orphaned dog a good home. A secretary at the police station told him the dog had gone to a rescue group in Redbud, Nebraska.

That had brought them to this ridiculous little town. The chatty woman at the B&B had told them all about the lady who'd disappeared after adopting a Chihuahua, leaving the little dog behind. They figured the dog must have gone back to the Redbud Rescue group, but an ill-timed visit there the night before had been one more embarrassing disaster.

"We need to drive through the area where the lady lived, the one who had the dog. Maybe the dog is still there. We should check out the house. We should have checked there first."

Mel mutters his thoughts as Mort slurps his coffee. They both wonder if Beluga has hired their replacement and if the replacement has failed miserably too, capturing the woman but not the target.

The two men pay their bill and leave the café. And if the Chihuahua affair doesn't prove profitable, they have a backup plan that might bring them the wealth they need, thanks to their visit to the small-town news hub. Rubies.

Bella, who has just finished a phone call from Audrey, follows the men out of the café. She narrows her eyes and grips her nervous hands together in front of her. Stepping out into the thick August heat, she follows the two men until she sees their car. Reaching into her apron pocket, she pulls out her cellphone and snaps a picture. She hurries back inside and dials Chief Sorensen.

Blanche answers the call and tells Bella she can't bother the chief.

"He's out at an accident scene," she whispers. "A suspicious accident."

Bella hesitates, "Tell him it's important. I have some important information for him."

Bella feels Carl's presence even before she sees him standing next to her, his eyes seeking out hers. But her eyes remain focused beyond the door. She tucks her phone back into her apron pocket and speaks softly while continuing to look beyond the café.

"Those men. The two fat men. They might be murderers."

She quickly tells Carl what she's learned from Audrey.

"They're after the Chihuahua!" Carl raises his voice and then abruptly lowers it, looking around to see if anyone else is listening.

"They checked out this morning. Oh, dear. They were asking a lot of questions about Redbud, and I'm afraid I told them about Sylvia's disappearance the day after adopting Birdy the Chihuahua."

Carl reflexively grabs one of Bella's hands and strokes it slowly, a trick he'd learned that helps Bella stay calm and enables her to talk without waving her hands about. As he reflects on what Bella has just told him, he realizes he saw the two men yesterday after he and Martin returned from the old farm site. He and Martin sat not two tables away from the pair of rotund men, older men, rough looking. They had been discussing the possibility of finding rubies buried on the Jensen farm when Carl noticed the two men looking their way.

What had they overheard?

"They also asked about the old Jensen place, said they'd heard stories about buried treasure there," Bella frets.

"What?"

"Yes. I told them we'd already found all the gold coins. Our discovery of the coins had been all over the news last year, so they must have learned about it that way. I didn't see any metal detectors with them, but they both seemed pretty curious, enough so to ask for directions."

"Oh dear," Carl breathes.

"Oh dear?" Bella turns and studies Carl's eyes.

***

Daisy can't believe what she's seeing. Even though she had stopped her regular surveillance of the Ritters' home, she can't help an occasional peek. Her parents have left to visit the college where they'll be teaching in the fall. Daisy had promised to stay inside and continue unpacking her boxes. She'd put away a few favorite books and a tennis racket when she stepped over to her window and lifted the binoculars to her eyes.

She sees a car pull into the Ritters' driveway. Two men hoist themselves out of the car and walk to the door, knocking several times. When no one answers, they circle the house, peeking in windows. Finally, they return to the front. A few minutes later, Daisy can see one of the men inside the house.

"They broke in!" Daisy addresses her alarm to Birdy.

Daisy puts down the binoculars and wonders what she should do next. She's watched enough police shows on television to know she should call 911 and report a break in in progress.

But what if the men are just friends of Carlton and Sylvia who have the key and have come by to check on something or other?

That doesn't sound right, but Daisy figures there's more than one reason the two men could be at the Ritters' home.

Maybe I'll just take a closer look and maybe call Chief Sorensen. I don't want the whole town laughing at me. How will I ever make new friends in Redbud, then?

Daisy leashes up Birdy and hurries out the front door. The two speed-walk around the corner and toward the Ritters' street. They don't slow down until they are only a couple of houses away from the Ritters. Daisy feels for her cellphone and checks to make sure it's ready to take a few fast pictures. The man in the car seems not to notice her as she walks past the car and sneaks a quick shot of the license plate. She and Birdy are on their way down the block and picking up speed when the second man comes out of the house and notices them.

"Hey!" he shouts. "Look!"

The man behind the wheel leaves the car and both men begin running after girl and dog. Well, Daisy isn't sure she would call it running.

They'll never catch us. They're old and fat, and they can't run.

Daisy picks up Birdy and races between two houses and through the tall grass dividing this block from the block with her home. She leaps over bushes and a pile of kindling. She's almost home when she lands wrong and falls to her knees. Birdy flies out of her arms.

I'm dead. They'll grab me now.

She expects to feel arms yanking her to her feet, but instead the two men charge past her and one of them grabs Birdy. Huffing loudly, the men turn around and lumber toward their car.

"Give me back my dog! Give me back my dog!"

Daisy runs after them, furious. She hopes her screams will bring a few neighbors outside. With a few long strides, she catches up with the closest man and hammers his back with her fists. He turns and grabs both her arms.

"Well hello to you, too. I guess you want to go with us."

"No kids!" shouts the other man who has Birdy tucked under one arm.

"But she's seen us! She's seen our car. We can't leave her behind."

"No kids!"

"We can dump her later, after we're safely away."

"No kids!"

But Mel pitches her into the back seat of the old maroon clunker along with the Chihuahua. Mort stuffs Birdy into a dog-carrying case and places the case on the seat. Somehow, he avoids another bite.

As they rattle out of Redbud, the two old thugs chortle and grin, imagining the money that will soon be coming their way. Maybe they aren't the most ignorant old thugs left on earth. Maybe they've pulled off the big one. In spite of all their missteps, they now have the dog.

Mel rubs his hands together.

"We'll be celebrating in the south of France. How much should we ask?"

"At least double what we were offered at first, I think," suggests Mort.

Mel checks the road behind them.

"Nobody behind us. I think we got away without notice."

Daisy pops up from the back seat and puts her head between both men, looking from one to the other.

"Have you forgotten about me? Don't you think they'll be looking for me? Kidnapping is a federal offense, you know. You'll have the feds after you."

"She's right, you know." Mort scowls at Mel. "I said no kids. What are we going to do with the kid?"

Daisy's comments bring the men back to earth and sour their mood.

"We are in so much trouble," mutters Mort.

"But we have the Chihuahua. Remember that. We have that blessed Chihuahua, and that little dog will make us so rich. We have the damn dog and we're holding it for ransom."

"And we have a kid jumping around in the back seat who'll be yelling at every car we pass."

"We can fix that. We can tie her up. Just let me put a few miles behind us first."

Daisy pats her back pocket, feeling her cellphone. Without pulling it out, she sets it to vibrate.

These guys are so old they probably don't know police can trace me to my cellphone. I just hope someone reports me missing soon.

Daisy leans back and smiles. She opens the pet carrier and lets Daisy crawl out and onto her lap.

"We're going to be okay," she whispers to the Chihuahua.

"Keep your head down, kid, if you know what's good for you."

CHAPTER 15

Ten minutes later, Audrey and Judy pull into the Jensens' driveway and sprint to the front door, which they find ajar. Audrey taps on the door and it yawns open. The two women step inside and stare into the silent space.

"Anybody home? Daisy, are you here?"

They know they're talking to an empty house.

"No Chihuahua, either."

"Do you think Daisy is with her parents?" Judy asks.

"Would her parents have left in a hurry without closing the door completely?"

They look around to see if Daisy left a note anywhere, saying she's gone somewhere and will be back soon. No note.

"I don't like this. I don't like this at all," Audrey murmurs.

"What do we do now?"

"I'll try to reach Randy again. You call out to the college and see if you can find Daisy's parents. And while we're here, we should see if any of the neighbors saw or heard anything."

***

Chief Sorensen pulls a handkerchief out of his pocket and covers his nose. The stench of burning gasoline, metal and human flesh assaults his senses. Turning his back on the scene discovered here just outside of Redbud, he coughs several times and blinks away the mist in his eyes.

He'd received the call just past 8:00 a.m. from a farmer who'd found a car smoldering in a ditch off a private road on the north end of his property. The farmer stands apart from the small circle of officers at the scene, waiting for confirmation that he can leave. Noticing the man's discomfort, the chief blots his own face several times with his handkerchief and steps toward the farmer.

"Not the way anyone wants to start the day," the chief laments.

"Can't even figure out how anyone found this road. You almost have to know it's here. I don't even get this way too often."

"And you didn't notice anything unusual until you found this? Hear anything? See anything?"

The man shakes his head slowly, then looks up at the sky as if he might read a better answer there.

"Someone's in there, right? How could someone have an accident here? There's no traffic, nothing to run into, no way to pick up any speed."

The chief doesn't answer, knowing that this is no accident.

Someone has driven the car to this out of the way location and set it on fire.

And that person is not the crispy corpse the emergency workers are extracting from the car, a long, low vehicle Chief Sorensen suspects was the Jaguar owned by Greg Long.

And that means Greg is no longer missing.

And Chief Sorensen's dream of a quiet day is now dead. He's now investigating a possible murder that has a likely connection to Sylvia's disappearance. That means he is also back to investigating why Sylvia left town in a car with a retired chemistry teacher. Which reminds him that Mr. Hardin hasn't returned his call to tell him all is well.

Chief Sorensen thanks the farmer and tells him he's free to leave.

The farmer doesn't need to hear more. He trots back to his truck in a hurry.

The chief puts a little more distance between himself and the smoldering vehicle. Turning his back on the scene, he thinks over what he knows and what he doesn't know, all the time rubbing his forehead, working harder than ever to add one more worry line.

He knows he'll need positive identification of Greg Long, but he doesn't expect any surprise there.

So what is this all about?

He ticks off what he knows or suspects.

Greg had met up with Sylvia on Sunday evening, either accidentally or on purpose. She left with him, perhaps willingly, perhaps not, but she left the Chihuahua she was walking at the time behind. Sometime that night or the next morning, Greg and Sylvia parted company. Sylvia had somehow ended up with Thomas Hardin, her former chemistry teacher. The two left town together in Mr. Hardin's car. Sylvia's husband, Carlton, seems unconcerned about her disappearance. He asked to end the investigation. That's not going to happen now. Does Carlton know more than he is revealing? Did he follow Sylvia and Greg?

The chief has learned a few things about the husband that raises several questions about Carlton's innocence.

Then again, maybe someone else joined the party Sunday night?

The chief recalls the two men he'd shouted away from Audrey's property last night.

What do they have to do with this? Are they the suspects in the Missouri murder? And what are they doing here? And how can a four-pound Chihuahua be involved in all this? Or is it? I have plenty of suspects now, but am I missing the real one?

He considers what he knows about Sylvia, about Carlton, even about Mr. Hardin. He wonders about the two suspects in the Missouri case.

Where were they Saturday night?

He is playing with a number of possible scenarios when one of the officers on the scene shouts at him. The chief turns to see the officer pointing at something on the ground about twenty feet from the car.

"Cellphone ringing. It might belong to the victim."

The chief reaches the phone in four long strides and marvels that Greg or someone else had managed to throw the phone from the car. Although the phone feels warm, obviously it's still working.

"Hello?"

A gruff voice responds, "We've got the dog. How badly does your boss want it?"

The caller laughs.

"Who is this?" the chief asks.

"You know who it is. We don't like being tossed aside. Now we're in charge of this escapade. You want the dog, you pay."

The chief looks at the number for the caller.

"This is Randy Sorensen, police chief in Redbud, Nebraska. Who might you be?"

The line goes dead. The chief pockets the phone and then grabs his own ringing cellphone.

"Chief? We've got real trouble here," Blanche sounds out of breath. "The little Jensen girl is missing along with the Chihuahua.

Audrey's been trying to reach you. She said to tell you those two men from last night probably took both Daisy and the little dog. Oh, and Bella Warner called too—also about the two men you seem to know all about. Oh, and she said she has their license plate number."

Damn! Things are moving fast. The chief spits out the cellphone number of the caller.

"We need to put a trace on that phone. We can hope it's still with the caller and not in a trash can somewhere."

He can almost hear Blanche scratching out the numbers. Thank God for Blanche. She knows what to do.

"And get ahold of Daisy's parents. I'll meet them at their place. I need to know if Daisy has a cellphone. If she does, I need that number too. Maybe we'll get lucky."

The chief yanks open the door to his cruiser and turns on the lights and siren.

As he pulls away, he continues talking, "Ask Bella for the plate number and get it to me. We need a bulletin out right away."

Blanche interrupts him, "Audrey's over at the Jensens' place now. She and Judy have found a neighbor who saw the men snatch Daisy."

"Blanche? Blanche? Call back when you have anything new."

The chief snaps his phone closed and concentrates on his driving. As he shoots past the wildlife sanctuary, he wonders again why Mr. Hardin hasn't called back. Within ten minutes, he pulls up in front of the Jensens' home just as Martin and Margaret turn into the driveway. He hurries up to the couple who stand before him stunned, unmoving.

"Why? Why Daisy?" Margaret chokes out the words.

"We don't think Daisy is what they came for. We think they wanted the Chihuahua."

The couple stare back at him.

He says something he hopes will be the truth.

"We'll get her back. We'll get both of them back."

Out of the corner of one eye, he sees Audrey and Judy hustling his way. His phone rings again with Blanche reporting the plate number and the fact that she's notified, as she put it, "everyone in six states, and I can do more."

He takes a deep breath and directs everyone inside.

***

After several minutes of cursing, Mort pulls off the highway onto a gravel road, a spray of rocks bouncing behind the car. He brakes suddenly and stomps twenty feet into an empty field. Mel follows him cautiously, not sure he wants to step too close to Mort, who appears to be exploding in place.

"Is something wrong?" he asks softly from a safe distance.

"IS SOMETHING WRONG? YES, SOMETHING IS WRONG!"

Mel holds his hands prayerfully in front of his chest. "Oh?"

Mort stomps in a tight circle but says nothing.

Mel looks behind at the car and sees the kid looking back at him, her eyes wide, face pressing against the pane. The Chihuahua bounces into view every couple of seconds.

Mort steps toward Mel.

"Something's wrong. Something's very wrong," he shouts. "I called our contact to tell him how much we'd take for the Chihuahua, and a cop answered."

"A cop?!"

"Not just any cop. He said he was the police chief."

Mort doesn't need to explain the significance of a police chief answering their employer's phone. But Mel spends a little time scratching his head, as if trying to come up with a solution.

Finally, he speaks, "Can't we go directly to Beluga?"

"You idiot! We don't know how to reach Beluga! We don't even know Beluga's real name! We don't even know anyone else who knows Beluga. As far as we know, Beluga doesn't exist. Maybe the guy who contacted us is the only one interested in that Chihuahua, and now he's, shall we say, INDISPOSED."

"So what do we do?"

"We do the only thing we can do. We sneak back to Chicago and spend the rest of our miserable lives hiding out and hoping no one connects us with that dead woman in Missouri."

Mel is grasping for hope, "Maybe Beluga will find us if we keep the Chihuahua. Maybe we should just wait longer and see what happens."

"Beluga delegates all the small stuff—like murders and dog snatchings. It's always been like that. Even you should remember that. Beluga never wanted to know who was doing the job."

"So what do we do with the kid and the Chihuahua?"

Mort considers their options, brushing one foot against the ground.

Both men stand side by side, looking back at the car, watching the young face and the bouncing Chihuahua.

"They're of no use to us now."

***

Shirley gently swipes a sample of brownish goo from the ear of a senior beagle.

"Oh, ouch. Poor baby."

The Redbud veterinarian looks across the exam table at Buddy's owner.

"I'll look at this under the microscope to see what kind of germs we have at work. But this is certain: Buddy has a nasty ear infection. No wonder he's been pawing away at his head. It's a good thing you brought him in."

Shirley avoids criticizing her clients, but she nearly does so in this case. Buddy's ear problems aren't anything new. He's probably lost hearing and has been suffering for some time. But instead of scolding Buddy's owner, she praises the owner for bringing the dog in at all.

She outlines the treatment plan.

"You'll need to leave Buddy with me. I'll clean his ears out under anesthesia tomorrow. When you pick him up tomorrow afternoon, I'll send you home with medication you'll need to put in his ears twice a day. He won't like you doing anything around his ears because they're pretty painful right now. Can you handle that?"

Buddy's owner nods and assures Dr. Thomas that she's up to the challenge.

"He's a wiggler, but he won't bite me."

"Your problem will be holding on to him long enough to squirt the liquid into his ears."

Dr. Thomas smiles and scratches Buddy under his chins.

"I'll draft my husband to hold onto him."

"Good idea. He should be ready at about three in the afternoon tomorrow, but call first."

After Buddy's owner hugs him and plants a kiss on his head, Dr. Thomas leads the reluctant beagle into a room where he joins several other dogs awaiting surgery or other treatment.

Realizing she has a break before her next client, she steps into her backyard and sits in the lawn chair by the door.

Did I talk too much or too little? And how much more do I know, really, about Sylvia's secret life? I know Chief Sorensen will be looking for me soon. What will I say? I don't want to lie. Not even for Sylvia. But will the truth get me in trouble?

Shirley realizes that she doesn't know everything about Sylvia, but she does know a few things Sylvia wanted kept secret. The veterinarian has secrets of her own she'd rather not share. And Sylvia knows all of them.

Is that why she encouraged me to come here? So she could keep an eye on me?

They'd been so young when they'd worked at the nightclub in California. All they had in common then was good looks, cute bodies and several years of dance training. Of course, ballet and tap lessons hadn't entirely prepared them for gracefully removing their clothes in front of a roomful of drunk and leering men.

We were too good for them, all of them.

Just Little Shirl then, she had arrived in California after running away from her home in North Dakota when she was just seventeen. Home was impossible. Shirl had been a top student in spite of her home life, but that home life had touched bottom the day her parents skipped her high school graduation. When a disappointed Shirl marched home to hear their excuses, she found both parents naked and asleep on the living room floor, wine bottles scattered throughout the room. Without waking them, Shirl packed a bag, stole whatever money she could find in the house and hitchhiked to the closest bus station. Her plan was to take the next bus out of town.

The next bus was bound for California. Shirl wondered for years if her parents ever tried to find her. During her first weeks in California, she lived in a cheap motel and applied for minimum wage jobs. She'd also shown up for a few cattle calls at talent agencies. She was almost out of money with no place to stay when she ran into Sylvia and her friend Greg.

And that's when everything changed.

Shirley smiles, remembering that day.

She had taken a bus to the beach, determined to enjoy a sunny California day before deciding what to do next. Would she return home? Terrible thought. Would she live on the streets? Also bad. She carried everything she owned in her backpack, except for the bright pink bikini she wore under her jeans and t-shirt.

After jumping lightly off the bus and following signs to the beach, she found a spot close to shore and undressed down to her bikini. Stretching out in the sun, she twisted her toes in the sand. She didn't even own a beach towel, but she loved the warmth of the sand, the smell, even the gritty spray that settled on her lips. She felt pretty and young in a way she knew she might never feel again. She let herself enjoy the sensations. Closing her eyes, she listened to the ocean, its distant roar, its nearby whispers, its bold fingers rushing onto land toward her.

Finally, she sighed, got to her feet and raced to the shore. Splashing into the ocean, she screamed with a joy known only to a North Dakota girl cavorting in the ocean for the first time.

When she returned to her spot on the sand, the future Redbud veterinarian huddled with arms wrapped about her, shivering as she waited for the sun to warm her. She watched the shorebirds chasing the ocean as it pulled away and then changing direction as the waters chased them back to dry sand. She barely noticed the tears now rolling down her checks.

But she did notice the young couple who appeared suddenly, sitting down on either side of her.

"I'm sure I'm not the first to tell you you're pretty in pink," said the young man.

"And why so sad?" asked the young woman, who smiled and reached over to wipe away a tear.

"Here," Sylvia said. "You need some suntan lotion. You don't need tears."

***

"I don't believe it. This can't be possible."

Chief Sorensen looks at the note Audrey holds in front of his face.

"The car that took Daisy is registered to this man," Audrey repeats.

"Mel Grabowski! I thought he was dead. He and his brother Mort haven't been active in years."

He frowns as he remembers the two Chicago thugs. In their day, the two Grabowski bothers were a force to fear. Although they had connections to a Chicago crime family, law enforcement knew the two would work for anyone with the money and the need. The chief had arrested them several times, helped send them away more than once.

"After all these years, they take on a job and end up in my town. I can't believe it," he says again.

The chief studies the growing crowd in the Jensens' living room. Several FBI agents from the Omaha office had arrived so quickly that the chief thought they might have grown wings. Several neighbors brought over sandwiches as the noon hour arrived.

Audrey and Judy are circling around the distraught parents, doing their best to reassure them. One of Chief Sorensen's officers is out knocking on doors, looking for anyone who might have seen the men grab Daisy and the Chihuahua.

"Hey chief," calls Officer Smith. He introduces one of the neighborhood teenagers, "Douglas here says he not only saw what happened, he tried to chase the car."

The teen had indeed hopped into his parents' car and followed the fleeing car to the outskirts of town. He gives the chief the details he witnessed, including the direction the car traveled. He is also the second person to provide a license plate number.

This shouldn't take long. We've got half of law enforcement looking for the car. And we have the added advantage of dealing with two of the dumbest bad guys I've ever known.

That's the optimistic side of him thinking. The pessimistic side remembers the potential brutality of the two men. But to the best of the chief's knowledge, Mel and Mort have no history of violence toward children.

But desperate men do desperate things. They're probably hoping for a big reward that will make their senior years more comfortable.

Instead, they're running from a murder and a kidnapping. They're wanted in two states and running toward a hometown where trouble is waiting. And they aren't very bright.

The chief remembers the time Mel had bitten into a block of cheese at a crime scene and then left the rest of the cheese behind. His dental impression placed him at the scene and assured a conviction.

Mort once stole a car for a joyride. He actually returned it but forgot his jacket in the back seat—the jacket with his name stitched across the back.

Cops in Chicago loved to tell Mel and Mort stories. But that was many years ago, and Chief Sorensen remembers that Mel and Mort stories are not always funny.

And why now? Why this Chihuahua?

The most obvious explanation is that Greg called on Mel and Mort because he'd known them before he went to prison. He needed someone to steal this Chihuahua and he turned to the two Chicago thugs from the old days.

Why did Greg arrange for the kidnap of a tiny dog? Why did he come to Redbud to meet Sylvia? And what happened when they met?

A cheer from across the room interrupts the chief's thoughts.

"We've got them!" One of the FBI agents pumps a fist in the air. "Iowa Highway Patrol stopped their car just outside of Council Bluffs. Took them into custody without incident."

Everyone in the room rises to their feet as if summoned to do so. The room explodes with dueling conversations.

"But what about Daisy?" Margaret's voice rises above the others.

All conversations end as if sucked out of the room. Eyes turn to the agent who is still on the phone. He stands facing a wall, his back to the others in the room. As he talks into the phone, he waves a finger as if scolding a misbehaving child. When he puts down the phone, he turns around and catches Chief Sorensen's eye. He shakes his head slowly.

"NO!" Margaret screams.

She turns and buries her head in the shoulder of her sobbing husband.

***

Mel and Mort aren't talking. They know better. Long experience has taught them this much. Once in the presence of cops, shut up. Mel glares at Mort to make sure he understands.

"What happened to the little girl?" The officer sprays spit with his shouting.

Mel and Mort say nothing. They stand silently next to their car.

"What happened to the dog?"

Mel and Mort say nothing.

At one point, Mort believes they might have the Iowa cops fooled.

"Can we go now? As you can see, we're just a couple of harmless old farts out for a ride."

He smiles with what he figures is a harmless-old-fart smile.

Mel chimes in, "Obviously, this was all a mistake. We don't know anything about a little girl or a dog. We'd really like to be on our way."

"Not gonna happen," the officer steps closer to both men. "You two are quite the popular gents today. You have invitations to parties in both Nebraska and Missouri. You'll be coming with us."

He nods at the other officer who is looking in the backseat window.

"Ready, Joe?"

Officer Joe straightens up and ambles over, grinning.

"I'm betting we'll find evidence that a little girl and her dog spent some time in your car."

"Now, where are they?" The first officer shouts again.

Mel and Mort say nothing.

***

Margaret and Martin sit side by side on the sofa, holding on to hope that Daisy is alive and will soon be home.

After their initial misinterpretation of the FBI agent's shaking head, they'd learned that Daisy and Birdy were missing, just missing. They were no longer with the two men who had taken them. That might even be a good thing.

But where were they?

Chief Sorensen told them about the men requesting ransom for the Chihuahua but not for Daisy.

"After that, they probably just wanted to get away. I'm guessing they just left both of them by the side of the road. We should be hearing something soon."

He hopes that's the case. He is waiting for a trace on Daisy's phone. He already has an officer on the way to the area where Mel and Mort must have ditched their phone. They've been able to trace that phone but are still waiting for a call back on Daisy's number

Maybe her phone is off. Maybe the phone's signal is too weak. And if Daisy is no longer a hostage, why isn't she calling home?

That's what worries him.

The chief looks around the room. He asks Audrey and Judy to head back home. He also clears the room of concerned neighbors.

The FBI agent is on the phone calling in extra support.

***

Judy spots it first.

"Audrey, stop. There's a little dog close to the road."

Audrey slows to a stop, looking in the direction Judy is pointing.

"Hand me that bag of treats. We can't just leave a little dog out here in the middle of nowhere."

In this case, the middle of nowhere is about five miles from Audrey's home and the headquarters of Redbud Area Dog Rescue. It's also about ten miles outside of Redbud.

Both women grab handfuls of dog treats and step from the van. Audrey approaches from the dog's left, Judy from its right. The dog runs barking toward them, then turns and races away.

"Damn. A scared dog. Now our work is cut out for us."

Audrey tries sitting in the field and throwing a treat in the dog's direction. Judy backs away and tries for a wide circle that will take her to the dog's other side.

Well-socialized dogs will usually run up to rescuers, happy to accept food and assistance. If they could talk, they'd say something like "I seem to be lost. Could you help me find my way home?"

Scared dogs, on the other hand, run away from rescuers. Judy remembers how she helped trap Blue Lady, a frightened puppy mill dog who'd escaped from her people last year. Not again, Judy sighs.

Judy looks over and sees Audrey standing and shading her eyes with one hand.

Suddenly, Audrey runs toward the dog and calls over to Judy.

"That's not a scared dog. That's Birdy! She wants us to follow her."

Judy catches the significance without asking for explanation. Raised on Lassie movies, she's seen dogs lead the way to missing children many times. But the dog had never been a four-pound Chihuahua.

Birdy is racing ahead of them, tail held high.

Judy spots Daisy first and slides to a stop next to the prone girl. She quickly realizes that Daisy is alive but unconscious, one side of her head bloody and resting against a jagged rock.

Audrey arrives huffing and panting, not far behind Birdy. The tiny heroine leaps onto Daisy's back and begins licking Daisy's ear. Daisy moans and starts to wake up.

"Daisy!" Both women say at once.

Daisy pushes herself up to sit but then groans and lies back down, touching the side of her head. She smiles up at Audrey and Judy.

"Birdy saved my life."

CHAPTER 16

A festive mood fills Bella's. Even those who prefer meat dishes find time to celebrate at the newly designated Tuesday vegetarian night.

The guest of honor and her parents keep saying they can't stay long, but people keep stopping by their table to say hello. Daisy's bandaged head embarrasses her, but she loves praise for her bravery. She tells everyone that Chief Sorensen is knitting a special hat for her.

Daisy recounts the story of her capture up to the moment when the two "fat, old men" yanked her out of the car and pitched her into the field,

After that, everything went dark, she informs her listeners, ending with a dramatic pause. The fall against a jagged rock had knocked her out.

In great detail, most of it made up, Daisy, skinny arms waving as she talks, explains how Birdy had gone for help and led Judy and Audrey back to the spot where she was lying unconscious.

"Birdy should be here. She's the best dog in the world! She saved me!"

Birdy may be absent, but she clearly hasn't been forgotten. Since making the evening newscasts, Birdy has received a mounting supply of toys and treats. Diners have been coming to Bella's to drop off gifts for the four-pound heroine. Other gifts have piled up in front of the Jensens' home.

And yes, some of the gifts are for Daisy, who wonders what she'll do with all the stuffed animals, which she really doesn't need since she has a Chihuahua.

Daisy's medical checkup had gone well, although the doctor checking her out and bandaging her head frowned at the news that she had lost consciousness. He suggested that Daisy spend the night in the hospital. Finally, he approved sending her home after Margaret and Martin swore they'd take turns sitting next to her bed all night and waking her up every few hours.

Of course, Daisy is too excited to even think about sleep.

As Bella drops off menus, Audrey sifts through the dog toys lined up on the table in front of Daisy. Audrey picks up one toy and then another, studying them as a jeweler might study pearls and sapphires. When the accumulating toys and treats leave no more room for plates, Bella produces a collection box and sets it near the café's door.

"Dinner's on me," Bella insists to the Jensens. "It's never too soon to let children know that they can enjoy a meal that doesn't involve hamburgers and fries."

They all laugh, and Audrey says it was a good thing Randy isn't here because he might argue in favor of burgers and fries.

Chief Sorensen is on his way to Iowa to pick up the two men who'd abducted Daisy and Birdy. The chief had left Redbud as soon as he was sure Daisy and Birdy were safe and reunited with Margaret and Martin Jensen.

The chief has a lot of questions for Mel and Mort. They obviously know Greg. They'd called his phone with their ransom request for the Chihuahua. Greg's cellphone records showed several calls between Greg and Mel.

The chief hopes the two old thugs might also help solve the mystery of Sylvia's disappearance. He plans to question Mel and Mort at length before turning them over to Missouri authorities. Federal authorities also are interested in the two. Mel and Mort were never this popular in the old days.

The Jensens and Bella's customers also have plenty of questions for Audrey and Judy, who'd spotted Birdy by the side of the road and followed her to Daisy.

Both women acknowledge that this was a day and an experience neither will ever forget. It might go down as one of their happiest moments.

"How many people have a story like this? And what are the odds that we would be the ones to spot Birdy and then to follow her to Daisy?" Audrey asks.

"And what if we hadn't been driving down the road at that exact moment?"

For Judy, this has been a day when everything turns out right.

"I'll never forget how I felt when Daisy opened her eyes and tried to sit up."

Judy presses both hands against her heart and looks up at a couple standing by the table.

"I'll remember this all my life."

Audrey pats Judy's arms. Audrey knows how important it is for Judy to collect memories like the one from today. Everyone needs to balance the painful memories with heart healing ones.

After Bella drops off the vegetarian menu, the Jensens again order the vegetable lasagna and say they'll share theirs with Daisy.

"You'll love it, Daisy," Margaret assures her.

Daisy tilts her head as if to say "are you sure?"

Audrey again orders "Bella's Surprise," and Judy asks for the same. Bella has just started to leave for the kitchen when Shirley slips into a chair next to Judy and thumbs through the menu for a few seconds before selecting a spinach salad with artichokes and cashews.

"I heard the news," Shirley says, nodding at the Jensens and handing Daisy a bag of dental chews for dogs. "This is good for the teeth."

"Leave it to a veterinarian to give Birdy something that's good for her," Audrey laughs.

While Daisy repeats her story for Shirley, Barbara drags a chair from another table and tucks herself between Shirley and Judy, who waves an arm to attract Bella.

"Don't bother," Barbara whispers. "I called in my order. You can do that, you know."

Not wanting to interfere with Daisy's monologue, Judy whispers back, "Is Lois coming?"

Barbara shrugs and lifts both palms in the air.

"Who knows? I think she's adopted Carlton as her latest rescue. She says he's a lot more upset than he looks. She's probably with him right now, being her helpful old self."

Audrey leans over toward Judy, and continues the whispering, "I hope she knows what she's doing. How do we even know Carlton is all that innocent? He's got to be a suspect in the death of Greg Long."

"Greg Long is dead!?" Shirley and Barbara say in unison, both equally startled by the news.

Daisy stops talking to ask, "Who's dead?"

Margaret and Martin both warn away discussion of dead people, pointing fingers at Daisy's back as if to say "there's an impressionable child here."

"Oh, just something that happened in one of our favorite television programs," Barbara lies, composing her face with what she presumes is a reassuring smile.

Daisy crosses her arms over her chest and stares back at Barbara.

"Which television show?"

When neither Barbara nor Shirley responds fast enough, Daisy turns her stare into a glare. She leans forward, waving the bag of dental chews.

"You're lying. You think because I'm a kid, I can't handle the truth. Well, I can."

The entire table quiets as each person waits for someone else to respond.

Bella saves the day by arriving with dinner.

"Enjoy, everyone. Enjoy," she chirps.

One thing about the food at Bella's is that it can stop conversation. The tantalizing aroma arrives ahead of the dishes. Daisy loses interest in challenging the adults. She picks up a fork and beats her parents to the vegetable lasagna. The adults approach their meals with slightly more decorum but can't help a few undignified yelps of pleasure.

"I think vegetarian night is going to be a big success," Audrey murmurs.

Judy looks around the room. "Look. Most of the people here have stopped talking and are just eating. I guess you *can* sell vegetarian meals to Nebraskans."

"Randy will be the test. If he starts ordering vegetarian when meat is on the menu too, then it'll be time to call a press conference."

Audrey chuckles as she turns back to her dinner.

Until Daisy and her parents leave for home, the table conversation centers exclusively on rice, nuts, artichokes, peas and other vegetables. But as soon as the door closes behind the happy family, Barbara and Shirley echo their earlier question.

"Greg is dead? How? When?" Shirley sputters.

"And where? And where's he been all these years?" Barbara asks. She turns to Shirley and asks another question.

"And how do you know Greg? I went to school with him. Where did you meet him?"

Audrey relays what she's learned from Randy.

"He was at the scene when he learned about Daisy's abduction. A farmer discovered the burned-out car with the body inside on his property."

"Oh, poor Greg," Barbara mutters.

Shirley says nothing, but her eyes study the ceiling as she remembers the years so long ago when she, Sylvia and Greg had all been friends.

"Where had Greg been all these years?" Barbara asks. "I last saw him at graduation. Everyone said he and Sylvia left together to become Hollywood stars."

"Randy knows something about that, but he wouldn't tell me," Audrey huffs a bit.

Judy adds that Chief Sorensen did say that Greg was probably the person who picked up Sylvia on Sunday night as she was out walking her new Chihuahua.

"But what happened next? That's where things get fuzzy. Sylvia leaves with Greg, willingly or unwillingly. We don't know. Later, Greg is dead and Sylvia is on the run with her old chemistry teacher."

Audrey adds, "And we also know that Greg had talked to the two old crooks that abducted Daisy and Birdy."

"And we really don't know where Carlton was when all this was going on," Judy acknowledges.

"Or how and why Sylvia ended up with Thomas Hardin?"

Barbara looks up, startled. "Who would want to kill Greg? Not Sylvia!"

164

Barbara, Judy and Audrey all turn to look at Shirley, who is sitting quietly.

"Sylvia would never hurt Greg. She loved him. I know she did."

Audrey speaks softly. "Shirley, I think it's time for you to tell us more about your friendship with Sylvia. This is no time for secrets."

Shirley smiles sadly, "I've always believed in secrets. It's what we don't know about others that make them interesting. Maybe that's why for so long I thought Sylvia was the most interesting person I'd ever met."

The three other women remain silent, waiting for the town veterinarian to begin her story.

***

"Before I knew it, I had a place to live and a job. And two friends who promised they'd take care of me."

Shirley describes meeting Sylvia and Greg on a southern California beach.

"If they hadn't sat down next to me, I don't know what would have happened. I was alone, broke and afraid."

She sighs, remembering her first impressions of Sylvia and Greg.

"They were both so fearless. They expected success. They expected wealth. Hollywood didn't scare them. California didn't scare them. Nobody scared them. Nothing scared them. But sometimes they scared me. They loved danger. Today we would call them thrill seekers. What I never understood was why they adopted me. I was like a puppy they found wandering alone and decided to take home with them. But why me? I was just clueless little Shirl Thomas."

165

Audrey fidgets with the long silk scarf she's looped around her neck. As a natural skeptic, she would have found Sylvia and Greg too good to be true.

Why wasn't the young Shirl more suspicious?

Audrey tries to imagine Shirley as a teenaged runaway. As she does so, the mature veterinarian seems to change before her eyes. Pretty. Naïve. Fresh from North Dakota.

As Shirley tells her story, her listeners no longer hear the town veterinarian, but the lost girl trying to find herself.

Shirl went home with her two rescuers and moved into the spare bedroom, promising to pay rent as soon as she found a job.

"Not a problem," Sylvia said. "We can help you with that."

At the time, both Sylvia and Greg were working as deckhands on a whale-watching boat. They found Shirl a job selling snacks on the boat. Shirl loved all animals, including whales. But with Sylvia and Greg, the whales were part of something more. They loved the action, adored the whales and tolerated the tourists. They were happiest when waves tossed the boat, when the whales breached and slammed back into the ocean close enough to alarm the passengers. A good day was a day when most of the whale watchers vowed never to come back.

"I was just a little girl from North Dakota, impressed with my two rescuers and wishing I could be more like them. But not completely like them."

She pauses and looks at her listeners.

"They wanted more than thrills. What they wanted most was danger. Dangerous places. Dangerous times."

Her face darkens as she pauses and then whispers, "Dangerous people."

166

She repeats the words "dangerous people" again, with a firmer voice, and then looks silently at the three listening women leaning forward, waiting to hear what comes next.

For several minutes, what comes next is silence.

The women see Shirley struggling with her memories and tucking her younger self safely behind her.

Finally, Judy prompts her.

"What scared you? Was it the exotic dancing? Did Sylvia force you to work in a strip club?"

Audrey kicks Judy under the table, and Judy bounces upward, stifling a yelp, and hisses a few words for Audrey's ears only.

"You've already told half the town."

"Exotic dancing? Strip club?" Barbara hasn't heard this part. Her questions bring a second demonstration of Audrey's kicking ability.

But Shirley seems comfortable, even eager, to talk about the dancing.

"The dancing came later, but not much later."

Shirley looks at the others with a shy schoolgirl smile. She strokes the tabletop as if comforting a nervous puppy.

"The truth is, I didn't mind the dancing that much. Sometimes I hated the leers, but I was a good dancer, and it paid great. With good money coming in, I felt like my life belonged to me. I could use the money I made to go to college. I hoped to eventually get into veterinarian school."

She lifts both arms and points back at herself.

"And here I am. The best veterinarian in Redbud, Nebraska."

They all laugh together at that.

Audrey stops laughing long enough to ask about Sylvia's work at the nightclub.

"Was Sylvia dancing there when you started?"

"Yes, Sylvia had met the nightclub owner on the whale-watching boat who turned out to own a fleet of whale-watching boats. I remember thinking how funny it was that this sleazy nightclub owner would be such an avid whale watcher."

"So Sylvia suggested you could make good money at the nightclub? Right?" Audrey prompts.

"She said that with my sweet, innocent face, the men would all love me."

In a hushed tone, Barbara ventures, "Did she suggest you might do more than just dance?"

She shifts her posture, as if the mature Shirley is stepping protectively in front of the young Shirl.

"Oh, no. I would never do that! And Sylvia never suggested it."

As the women listen to the story, they can imagine Shirl trailing after the always adventurous Sylvia and Greg. They can imagine her dancing night after night while watching her savings grow.

Judy asks about Sylvia.

"Did Sylvia hate the dancing? She wasn't saving up for an education. She wanted to be a star. I would imagine her turning bitter."

"Bitter? Sylvia? If she was, she was good at not showing it. But I guess I wasn't clear. I was her replacement. Once I started dancing, she quit. She spent more time trying to break into the movies. She stayed with the whale-watching job, but that didn't pay much. And yet both she and Greg seemed to have plenty of cash all the time."

Audrey grows impatient.

"That must have made you suspicious. Both of them attracted to danger and dangerous people. Both of them with plenty of money.

Did Sylvia really have a sugar daddy? Or had she found some other way of making money? And what was Greg doing? Besides working on the whale-watching boat, that is."

"Did I say Sylvia had a sugar daddy? It was all so long ago. I think that was what she told me when I asked her one day about all the money she seemed to have. But she might have been kidding me. She was good at that."

Shirley studies her hands before she looks up.

"There's more, of course. There were days when I wished I'd never met those two. And then the next day I'd be back to thinking how fortunate I was. What if I hadn't gone to the beach that day? Where would I be now?"

"Probably not in Nebraska," Audrey bursts out.

"Or maybe yes." Shirley smiles as she stands up "I like Redbud."

She looks at the three women.

"Thank you for listening. I haven't talked about my life to anyone in a long time. Maybe it's about time."

"But you said there's more," Judy contends.

"Yes, there's more. But I'd like to talk to Chief Sorensen first. And right now, I need to return to the clinic to check on a couple of patients."

She nods and walks briskly out of the café.

Judy breaks the silence that follows.

"Were you really an exotic dancer yourself, Audrey? When Shirley first told us she'd worked in a strip club, you said 'Well, who hasn't?'"

Audrey laughs as she gets to her feet and curves one arm over her head.

"Would you like a demonstration?"

"No!"

Both Judy and Barbara shout, horror on their faces.

***

"Another successful vegetarian night, don't you think?" Audrey asks as she and Judy leave for home.

"A successful night, and quite a day, I'd say," Judy yawns.

The two chat about the events of the day: their hurried and too-late trip to the Jensens' home after learning that Daisy might be in danger, learning about the murder of Greg Long, spotting the Chihuahua by the side of the road and following it to Daisy, celebrating at Bella's, listening to Shirley's story.

"But there's so much we don't know," Audrey complains, reminding Judy that Shirley hasn't said anything that would explain Greg's murder or Sylvia's disappearance. "I think she stopped short of the important stuff."

"And we still have no idea why Birdy was so important. So important that someone hired a couple of Chicago hit men to snatch her. And it looks like that person was Greg or someone he worked for."

Judy looks out the side window, studying a field of grazing cattle.

"I'm wondering if Sylvia came to our adoption event specifically to find and adopt that one particular dog."

"I was thinking the same thing. It can't be a coincidence that Greg drove into Redbud the same day Sylvia adopted that particular Chihuahua from Redbud Area Dog Rescue."

"If it was so important, maybe even worth killing for, why did Sylvia leave the dog behind?"

***

Lois tiptoes out of the Ritters' home, leaving Carlton asleep on the sofa.

Poor man. He's so exhausted and upset.

As she closes the door behind her, she stops to reconsider. Something isn't right. Maybe she doesn't understand Carlton's emotions at all. He was so eager to talk, so willing to explain himself to her. He'd talked about his life before his family moved to Redbud.

Oh my God. Oh my God.

She doesn't know what to do with what she's learned about Carlton, what he's told her. How can she reconcile her new knowledge of Carlton with the Carlton she thought she knew, a man almost pathologically silent and unadventurous? Silent and unadventurous. Those adjectives no longer fit.

Who are you, Carlton? Who are you really? And who are you, Sylvia?

***

With Birdy the Chihuahua curled against her neck, Daisy smiles, knowing she is safe.

Martin sits in a chair near Daisy's bed, his laptop on her desk. When he isn't studying his daughter's face, he's searching the internet for information on rubies and metal detectors.

"Dad?"

Martin looks up from the computer to see his daughter gently stroking the little dog.

"Birdy has a little lump here on her shoulder."

Daisy twists her head to look at the dog. She rubs the spot.

"We'll have it checked out tomorrow. I was surprised she made it through the day without at least one bruise. Don't worry about it. I'll call Dr. Thomas in the morning."

Daisy smiles and closes her eyes, but she continues circling the lump with her finger.

"You're such a brave little dog. And so smart."

Birdy looks up at Daisy.

"Go to sleep, both of you." Martin scolds softly.

He doesn't need to say more. Martin watches as both girl and dog yawn in unison and reposition themselves in the canopy-topped bed. Within minutes, Martin notices the slow, sweet sounds of a sleeping child, a child he knows won't be a child much longer.

She's twelve already, but today she's still our baby. And she's safe. Thank God. She's safe.

***

Chief Sorensen knows the moment that they gave up.

Driving them back to Redbud from just outside of Council Bluffs, Iowa, he does most of the talking. He reminds them of their earlier encounters years ago in Chicago.

They grunt in reply.

"Remember when everyone called you the 'cheese-bite burglar?'"

Mort growls.

"Boy, that was funny. Didn't one of you even call 911 after the safe you were cracking fell on you? Good thing you could reach a phone. We all laughed about that for weeks."

Nobody in the back seat makes a sound.

The chief remains silent for almost ten minutes before speaking again.

"At one time you were both just a pair of laughable young punks. You might have grown up and lived straight."

Someone in the back seat mutters "ha."

"Instead you sank into violent crime for hire. Cold violent business. How much time did you two do?"

No answer from the back seat.

"I'll answer for you. Not enough. Too bad you aren't still on the inside. You wouldn't have been available to take the call from Greg Long that brought you out of retirement? You were retired, weren't you? If you'd stayed retired, a lady in Missouri would still be alive."

The chief thinks he hears a sob coming from one of the passengers.

They stay silent while he pulls up in front of his Redbud office. One of the night officers comes out to help escort Mel and Mort inside.

A department as small as the Redbud Police Department doesn't have a separate interview room, so Chief Sorensen invites Mel, Mort and Officer Ryan into his office.

And there he tells them that he recovered a blood sample at the crime scene in Missouri. DNA from the sample is a perfect match for Mort.

That's when Chief Sorensen sees both men deflate. That's the moment they surrender. They may not be the brightest thugs out there, but they know the score.

Mel, more than Mort, understands the situation. He sifts through his memory, hoping he can come up with information he can trade for a more lenient outcome. Unfortunately, he fails to understand that the police, even police chiefs, can't promise you anything. But maybe he just feels like talking, shifting the blame where he figures it more rightly belonged.

When Chief Sorensen realizes Mel's tongue is loosening, the chief lifts up one hand, asking for a pause. He reaches below his desk and pulls out his knitting project.

Mel and Mort drop their jaws. Officer Ryan rolls his eyes.

"Go ahead," He pushes the button on the recorder. "Who hired you for this job?"

Mel, with occasional grunts of agreement from Mort, explains that the two of them had stayed clean for close to twenty years, mainly because no one wanted to hire a couple of out-of-shape brothers when they could hire a young bodybuilder with attitude. But then out of nowhere they receive a call from Greg Long, although they don't know his name at the time.

"He wanted us to do one last job for Beluga. Now that was a blast from the past. I hadn't heard that name in years. Didn't know Beluga was still active or even alive."

The chief winds a strand of yard around his right needle and pulls it through a loop on the left needle.

He stops to look up and ask, "Is that beluga as in the caviar or beluga as in the white whale?"

The brothers look as if they don't understand. The chief recalls photographs of whales in the Ritters' family room. Is one of them of a beluga?

"OK. Let's try this. Who is Beluga?"

"Never knew a name. It was always just Beluga, head of a California operation, mainly drugs. Said to be one scary customer, someone you didn't want to cross."

"Hmm" The chief fiddles with his knitting and appears deep in thought. Two lines appear between his eyes as he squints at Mel and Mort.

"And why was this Chihuahua so important?"

Mel and Mort say nothing. They only shrug. Finally, Mel volunteers that they thought it best not to ask questions where Beluga was involved.

"How did you end up here in Redbud?"

Mel looks at his hands as he answers the question.

"When we messed up in Missouri, we were fired and threatened. We decided to find this dog and hold it for ransom."

He looks up and the chief notes the sad, defeated expression on Mel's face. In any other situation, the chief might have felt sorry for the man.

Mel continues, "Then it all fell apart."

He points at Mort

"Dummy here grabbed the kid. Then someone killed the only contact we had."

"Bummer," Mel mumbles.

"Bummer, indeed," intones the chief, "if that's all you know. What else can you tell me? For example, who do you think killed Greg Long?"

Mel and Mort look at each other, and each rubs his chin thoughtfully. They scratch their heads in unison.

"Probably Beluga," Mel squeaks out the words.

CHAPTER 17

"I might as well arrest Eunida Heppelwhite. She's the only one mean enough to kill one person and scare a couple of others enough that they leave town."

Chief Sorensen greets Blanche, who rolls her eyes back at him.

"Making jokes this early in the morning? You must not have had your coffee. Thought you'd want to know you have a couple of prisoners talking about police cruelty because they're still waiting for breakfast."

"They can wait a little longer. In fact, they can wait until lunchtime. That's when the Missouri officer will be here to pick them up. Save Redbud the cost of feeding them. They're too fat anyway."

"If you say so."

Blanche is still looking over messages left by the night crew.

"Oh, and here's an important message for you. Thomas Hardin called."

The chief snatches the pink slip from Blanche and looks it over.

"Well that answers one question. He says both he and Sylvia are fine. So at least we know Sylvia didn't force him to drive her out of town. He doesn't say where they are, though, or when they'll be back. He asks that we let his sister know he's okay. Could you take care of that, Blanche?"

He drops the note back on Blanche's desk and turns toward his office.

"That might be more than I can do," Blanche answers quickly.

The chief turns to look at her, "Why's that?"

"His only sister died two years ago. I remember he went to the funeral in Syracuse, New York."

"So, maybe everything's not okay."

The chief sits at his desk and ruminates for a while.

He might be telling us they're in Syracuse, NY. That would make sense. But is that their destination or are they still on the road. Where are they heading?

He looks at the globe he keeps on his desk, a reminder of the travels he hopes to accomplish someday. He finds Syracuse and moves his finger in several directions, but only one makes sense.

Canada? Why Canada? What's in Canada? Who's in Canada?

He calls Greg's parole officer in California to tell him about Greg's death. Since the parole officer isn't in yet, the chief leaves a message, also asking him if he knows anything about Greg's other associates during his drug dealing days. Does the name Beluga ring a bell?

Then he calls Carlton, who is on his way to work.

"Turn around. You're staying home today. We need to talk."

***

Judy waits in front of the home her family once owned, now the future headquarters for Redbud Area Dog Rescue. She pulls out her cellphone to check the time. The contractor is on his way to discuss modifications to the house and construction of several separate dog kennels.

Would I enjoy living here? Am I ready to live on my own instead of down the hall from Audrey?

A year earlier, she'd arrived in Redbud with a photo of this house, a picture her grandmother had given her. She'd pulled into town planning to research her family history and possibly purchase this home

Then she'd found a dead body in the doorway of this same home and had become embroiled in the terror that followed as Dog Ladies, women who ran dog rescue groups, were dying from lethal overdoses of phenobarbital.

Judy walks toward the lake, not much more than a pond, and remembers the day she'd found a gold coin near the water's edge. Later, she'd been there to help find gold coins worth several million dollars. Her great-great-grandfather had hidden the coins. Now the money from those coins was making several things possible, including developing the site as a new headquarters for Redbud Area Dog Rescue.

Audrey had suggested that Judy might want to live here eventually. *I could try writing murder mysteries.*

She knows just the room she'll use for an office, one with a window overlooking the lake. She loves watching the ducks and geese racing across the water to lift off and fly in ever widening circles before disappearing into the horizon. She loves ice-skating poorly on the pond in the winter.

I think I could live here. I could be happy here.

"Hello. Sorry I'm late."

A deep voice interrupts her thoughts. Startled, she turns suddenly and stumbles. The man reaches out to grab her arm.

"I'm sorry, again. I didn't mean to sneak up on you."

Judy looks up, way up, into the smiling face of a man with hazel eyes and thick brown hair that blows recklessly across his forehead.

"Bob Jenner," he announces, "and you must be…"

He looks down at the thick red folder he pulls out from under one arm. She can see the words "Jenner Construction" emblazoned across the front.

"Judy Barnes."

He looks at her and smiles again.

In spite of her every intention to remain professional and in charge, she smiles back.

"How about we look around."

It isn't a question. He leads the way to the spots where several kennels will go. Bob walks the yard, pointing to perimeters for the fencing.

"You'll need several separate areas, considering you have dogs of all sizes and might want to keep some separate."

As they walk, Judy catches herself studying the contractor's face a little too closely. She even does the unforgiveable and seeks out his ring finger. No ring.

Why am I smiling?

She replaces her smile with a thoughtful frown, nodding each time he points at another important location

"Let's take a look at the plans for the house, should we? Is there a table inside?"

Judy nods and pulls the key out of her pocket. Minutes later, with architectural plans spread out on the dining room table, they lean over to study the details, their heads almost touching. After pointing out several things on the paper, the contractor walks her around the house, showing her what the plans mean to every room in the house.

"This wall will go," he declares, thumping his hand against one wall. "That'll give you more open space."

He frowns at the holes in one of the kitchen walls but says the damage just leaves a little less for him to pull away.

"A nice way of putting it," Judy laughs, a happy, rumbling laugh.

He stops and faces her after they reach the second floor.

"Who's going to live here? How many people, I mean."

"Me, for one. Maybe only me. But we'll need a couple of rooms for people who might want to stay and help for short periods."

"Lucky you. How about we turn two of these bedrooms into a single, large one with its own bath?"

Judy likes the idea.

"That'll leave you with two extra bedrooms that are roomy enough for short term visitors. They can share the other upstairs bathroom. I'll put a half bath downstairs. So, when do I start?"

"Start?"

Judy stops daydreaming about her possible new home long enough to smile at Bob.

"Whenever Audrey gives you the go ahead. If it's okay with you, I'll report back to her and call you with a start date."

"Perfect."

As they close the house and walk side by side to their cars, the two talk amiably about recent happenings in Redbud. Bob, who lives a couple of towns away, has plenty of questions.

"I'll be the most popular guy in town if I come home with some inside poop on all the Redbud happenings."

He looks at the sky for a while and kicks the rocks on the driveway.

"Usually I only get to Redbud when my dog needs to see Dr. Thomas."

"She's your vet?"

"Yes, I talked to her yesterday to make an appointment for Heathcliff. She said she'd squeeze me in tomorrow because she might need to go out of town in a couple of days."

"That's funny," Judy remarks, sliding into her car. "I saw her last night, and she never said anything about leaving town."

Judy wonders where Shirley might be heading and if it has anything to do with Sylvia. As she returns Bob's parting salute and backs out of the driveway, her next thought sends heat up her neck and over her face. She realizes this is the first time since losing her husband and child that she's looked at a man and felt… well, felt something.

Judy arrives back home to find Audrey waiting by the door, ready to pounce.

"What did you think of Bob Jenner?"

"He seemed nice. Why? Do you know him?"

"Just nice?" Audrey puts her hands on her hips as if she expects to hear more.

Judy avoids eye contact and instead leans down to ruffle the fur around Buster's neck.

With her back to Audrey, Judy murmurs, "He wants to know when he should start work."

***

Everything about the Carlton Ritter who opened the door surprises Chief Sorensen. The man holding the door half-open isn't the same man the chief had visited two days earlier. That Carlton Ritter apologized excessively for his shortcomings, his disinterest in adventure. That Carlton Ritter struggled with words, with even the necessity for conversation. That Carlton Ritter slouched and lowered his head rather than look anyone in the eye. That Carlton Ritter adored his wife and praised her every action.

But the Carlton Ritter standing erect in the doorway leans closer and glares directly into the chief's eyes.

"We are done. I don't have anything more to say. I told you Sylvia left on her own accord. Can't you just leave me alone?"

The chief steps around Carlton and leads the way into the family room. Without a word, he points at a chair. Carlton waits just long enough to express some displeasure, then walks to the chair and sits stiffly near the edge of the seat. He crosses his arms over his chest.

The chief selects a nearby chair and turns it so he faces Carlton.

The two men scope each other out in a game most men understand. Only one can be in charge. Who's it going to be? Finally, Carlton drops his arms to his knees and speaks with a lowered voice. Subtly, he cedes the leadership role to Chief Sorensen, but just barely.

"What is it you want?" Carlton asks.

"I want your help."

The question surprises Carlton.

"My help?" He snorts. "How can I possibly help you? More than that, why should I?"

The chief speaks slowly and cautiously.

"I'll forget you said that. You will help because it's your responsibility to help in a murder investigation. You'll help because your wife may be in trouble."

"Ha! Sylvia can take care of herself. Don't worry about her."

"What about Thomas Hardin, the man she's traveling with? He's almost eighty. Can he take care of himself? He's contacted me with what I think is a coded message letting me know he needs help. Maybe they both need help."

Carlton listens without comment as the chief explains the message's request to contact his sister who is dead and buried in Syracuse, New York.

"Syracuse, you say?"

"Does that mean something to you?"

Carlton looks around the room, studying some of Sylvia's framed photographs of whales.

"She sometimes stayed in Syracuse when she drove to Quebec. She went there every August for whale watching on the St. Lawrence River. I can't tell you much more than that because I never went along."

He raises his voice and spits out, "That was one of many things she did without me."

"I thought you preferred not to go with her."

"And you believed me?"

He's beginning to sound like an angry husband. Am I looking at the real Carlton Ritter? Did he create his forgettable persona to hide what he really was? Anything but forgettable? Will the real Carlton Ritter please step this way.

"Did you know about Greg Long? Did you know she was the love of his life?"

Carlton glares at Chief Sorensen.

"And then you found out Greg was coming to see her. Something woke you up Sunday night and you walked downstairs and onto your deck. You saw them, maybe an embrace. I can imagine how you felt."

184

Carlton continues to glare, saying nothing in response.

"You saw her get into the car. Maybe she shoved the Chihuahua in the back door first. You held your breath, backed away from the railing and hoped he wouldn't notice you on the deck."

The chief watches Carlton's face, watching for the telltale twitch, the eyes moving to one side.

"You decided to follow. On your way out, the dog escaped back outside. Maybe it was an accident. Maybe you kicked the dog out of your way."

"I didn't kick the dog."

Chief Sorensen decides to strike. He slams one hand on the coffee table and leans closer to Carlton.

"Did you kill Greg Long?"

***

Daisy wakes up to see her mother standing by her bedside.

"How about pancakes?" Margaret asks.

"Pancakes!" Daisy sits up and pulls Birdy onto her lap. "You only fix pancakes on special days."

"This is a special day."

"Will you make blueberry pancakes?" Daisy asks as she steps out of bed, Birdy in her arms. "I'll get dressed and take Birdy outside. Then I'll be ready for breakfast."

Margaret wishes happiness could always be as easy as making pancakes. She smiles to herself.

"And Birdy needs to see Dr. Thomas about the bump on her shoulder."

"She already has an appointment at one p.m."

It is a good start to what Margaret hopes will be a wonderful, peaceful day, a day when no one disappears, no one finds a murdered body, and no one kidnaps a dog and a little girl.

But she can't help worrying. She and Martin have vowed to keep Daisy always in their sights.

I know those men are in custody, but what if someone else is looking for Birdy the Chihuahua? Why is that dog so valuable?

As she pulls out a frying pan, she reconsiders the tiny dog her daughter loves so much.

Why is that dog so dangerous?

***

Carlton's mouth drops open.

"Me? You think I killed Greg?"

Chief Sorensen watches the transformation. He's looking at the old Carlton, the forgettable, cautious, unadventurous man.

"I know what you're capable of. I know why your family moved to Redbud. They were running from your shame, hoping to give you a new start."

Carlton's face blooms red. In anger? In shame? Chief Sorensen frowns, trying to take a measure of the man he faced.

Carlton bows his head, then looks up with head still bent.

"I was thirteen. It was an accident."

"You killed someone. You killed a classmate."

"He was a bully. He was tormenting George." He pauses, swallows hard as if remembering the past. "George was always a little

186

different, awkward. He stumbled when he walked. He had a bad overbite and wasn't too bright. I felt sorry for him."

Both men sit silently for a moment, Chief Sorensen waiting for Carlton to continue speaking, Carlton not wanting to finish his story. But finally, he does.

"Our school was next to a park. One day I walked home through the park. So did George. And so that day did the class bully. He spotted George and began teasing him, grabbing his books, getting in his face. Finally, I couldn't take it anymore. I got between them and started pushing the bully away. George ran off, so he was safe, but I didn't back off. I couldn't cool down. I kept on pushing the bully. Pushing escalated into fighting."

The chief doubts his story.

"You killed him with a punch? You, a thirteen-year-old kid?"

"We were on a bridge. I shoved him and he flipped over the railing and fell onto the sidewalk below. The fall killed him, but I shoved him. I made it happen."

Chief Sorensen adds what he knows, "They charged you with manslaughter. Fortunately, you had a good lawyer. You ended up with six months in juvenile hall. Then you and your family moved to Redbud, where you continued your probation. You knew you needed to stay out of trouble."

"My parents told me not to call attention to myself. And I was successful in that. As I'm sure you remember."

Chief Sorensen smiles, "But you still ended up with the most popular girl in the class."

"But did I, really?"

Carlton stands up and walks out onto the deck.

Chief Sorensen follows him.

Carlton points to an area near the Jensens' home and describes what he'd seen there Saturday night. Yes. He saw them together. He saw Greg step from his car and approach her. She looked at him, backed away as if to run, then stopped as if recognizing him. They embraced. Moments later, Sylvia tramped through the tall grass, shoved the Chihuahua in the kitchen door and hurried back to the man standing by his car. When the car pulled away, Sylvia was in the passenger seat.

"I didn't follow them. I didn't kill him."

"But you knew about him, didn't you? She told you about Greg? You must have remembered him from high school."

Carlton shakes his head.

"She never told me. She never told me much about her life in California. She said we should live in the present. To me, that was enough."

The chief studies Carlton, wondering how he had survived so many years hiding behind a bland personality that didn't fit him at all.

"How much did you tell her about your past?"

Carlton smiles, a sad smile.

"Did I tell her I killed someone? Did I tell her I had a history of violence? No. Of course not. She wanted to marry the Carlton she remembered from high school, the safe, quiet man. I loved her and decided to be that man for her."

To Chief Sorensen, those words are among the saddest he's ever heard. And yet he understands Carlton's desire to give Sylvia what she needed.

Couples remake themselves all the time to better fit their partners' images of them. But could Carlton and Sylvia have been happy with so much unspoken, so much unknown?

"I wish I could have gone with her on some of her vacations. Believe it or not, I've always wanted to travel. But any sense of adventure didn't fit the Carlton that Sylvia had married."

The chief replies, "She might have welcomed a few changes to your personality. Did you ever suggest traveling somewhere as a couple?"

Carlton remembers that once he had suggested he might come with her on vacation, but Sylvia had talked him out of it.

"She thought it would be too stressful for me."

The chief rubs a finger across his forehead, wondering where to take the discussion next.

Do I really believe what Carlton is saying? Is Carlton innocent of any wrongdoing? Or is Carlton pulling some sort of elaborate con?

"You're saying you never knew about Sylvia's other friends, the ones she traveled with, camped with, watched whales with?"

Carlton shakes his head again, slowly.

"I made it a point not to. They made her happy. That was what was important."

Does he really expect me to believe anyone is that selfless? Or that foolish? I can see his anger? He's really to explode. Do I trust anything he says?

"Let's change the subject a bit. Why did Sylvia adopt the little dog? You'd never had a dog here before. Why now?"

Carlton appears completely bewildered.

"I never knew she even liked dogs. Then Saturday morning she rushed out of the house saying she was off to look at some dogs. Later she called me because she said I needed to agree that I wanted to adopt a dog too."

"You didn't notice anything unusual? Either before or after she brought home the dog? More calls? More emails? Unusual behavior?"

"No. No." Carlton shakes his head. "I just don't know."

He looks up

"Sylvia is chatty with everyone in town. You know that. She talks to Dr. Thomas sometimes. They knew each other in California. Not many people know that. Sylvia talked Dr. Thomas into setting up her practice here."

He looks at the ceiling for a while, as if looking for cracks.

He adds, "But Sylvia never invited Dr. Thomas over here. I never got to know her."

Chief Sorensen leans in with the questions rising to the top in his mind.

"Where do you think she is now?"

He pauses and raises his voice.

"Why did she run?"

He raises his voice a little more.

"And why is she with Thomas Hardin, her high school chemistry teacher?"

***

"Show me a person with high self-esteem and I'll show you someone who can't be trusted."

Judy looks up from her laptop to watch Audrey pacing around the living room.

"You're upset about people with high self-esteem? Why?"

Sometimes Audrey's philosophical lectures amuse Judy. Other times they surprise her. But usually they make sense, eventually.

"But isn't high self-esteem a good thing? Shouldn't we feel good about ourselves?"

"I think it's better to feel okay about ourselves while realizing we could do better. We can always do better. People who talk about self-esteem want something for nothing. They want an excuse for not changing anything about themselves."

"And?"

"If we aren't always changing, or trying to change, we aren't really living."

Judy considers that.

Audrey drops into a chair next to Judy.

"Too much self-esteem shuts everything down," she snorts.

Judy laughs, "My head is spinning. But everyone talks about the need for high self-esteem and the problems with people who have low self-esteem. Isn't low self-esteem a bad thing?"

"Not as bad as unwarranted high self-esteem."

Audrey stands up and looks out the window at several dogs that are playing leapfrog over bushes.

"When low self-esteem keeps a person trapped in a gloomy place, then it's bad. Someone needs to help kick such people free by showing them how to do something that will boost their self-esteem. Everyone earns their own self-esteem. No one can give it to them."

Judy smiles, "Ah. So now we're back to 'Take care of the dogs and everything will be okay.'"

Audrey laughs, then continues, "When you're taking care of the dogs, you're doing a good thing, something that involves hard work."

"So what brought his on? Why the sudden rant about people with too much self-esteem?"

Audrey sighs, "I've been thinking about Sylvia. From everything I've heard about her, she had plenty of self-esteem. Being pretty and popular in high school isn't always a good thing. She could have charged out into the world with the idea that she was perfect and could do no wrong. Maybe her elevated self-esteem got her into trouble."

Judy isn't ready to completely accept Audrey's theory, but she remembers Shirley's memories about the young Sylvia as someone who was fearless and attracted to danger.

"If you're right, Sylvia's elevated self-esteem led her to more danger than she could handle. I'm guessing it all came crashing down on her when Greg was arrested."

Audrey nods, "She escaped back to Redbud and married someone safe and reliable."

"And arranged to bring Shirley here too. That's another mystery."

"Were they both hiding out?"

The two women review what they know from their own investigations. They've located a few of Carlton's coworkers, who described him as outgoing, hard driving, even ruthless. Those are not words anyone in Redbud might have used to describe Sylvia's husband.

Judy had searched online for any clues to the former lives of both Sylvia and Shirley in California and had found nothing useful.

"Shirley knows something she's holding back," Judy insists. "I don't think we can trust her completely."

The two have also failed to learn much more about Birdy. They know the little dog had been in a Kansas City shelter and then adopted by a man who'd given the dog to his mother in a small Missouri town.

But why was the dog so important?

"She's too small to be transporting drugs of any sort, but I'd bet everything I have that drugs are part of the story."

Judy adds, "Chihuahuas aren't good at passing on secrets."

Audrey stands up and snaps her fingers.

"That's it! She delivered a message, a secret message!"

CHAPTER 18

Chief Sorensen walks into his headquarters, head bowed as he reviews his visit with Carlton. He barely notices his office manager waving a note his way.

"Chief! Chief!" Blanche shouts, and he finally looks up. "A couple of calls from California. Thought they might be important."

He snatches the messages from Blanche's outstretched hand, walks into his office and pulls out his chair. For a few minutes, he sits silently, writing a few notes on a yellow pad. When he isn't writing, he massages his head just above his ears. Thinking.

I can't rule Carlton out. He could have caught up with Sylvia and Greg and killed Greg in a jealous rage. Then again, Carlton's story rings true. He might be innocent of any wrongdoing other than falling for the wrong woman. But is she the wrong woman? Maybe she's the right woman, in love with the man Carlton pretended to be. Maybe Carlton deliberately tried to turn my attention to someone other than himself. Could Sylvia have killed the man she waited fifteen years to see again? Had she ever visited Greg in prison? Does she still love him? And if not Sylvia or Carlton, who else? Certainly not Mr. Hardin. Or is he the kind of chemistry teacher who might be supplementing his income by cooking meth?

Now I'm getting ridiculous. Or am I?

He shakes his head as if clearing the cobwebs away and picks up the two notes. One is from Greg's parole officer. The other is from a retired detective. The chief dials the parole officer first.

"I see a few things in his file that might be important," the man reveals, his voice bouncing with obvious excitement.

"Go ahead."

"I wondered about the length of his sentence. I found out he could have received a shorter sentence or even walked away if he'd cooperated with the prosecutors. They wanted him to name names. Point to those he worked for. But he wouldn't do it."

"He was either very loyal or very afraid."

"Or maybe both. It's sad in a way. He was pretty low on the totem pole, and he paid a mighty high price."

"The highest," Chief Sorensen adds. "The highest."

"I hope that helps. It isn't much, I know, but I thought you might want to know."

The chief thanks the parole officer and recalls the stage-struck classmate he'd known. Just a regular Nebraska kid. How sad to end up the way he did.

He dials the second number and is about to hang up when someone pants into the phone and gasps out a hello.

"Sorry. Sorry."

The chief imagines the man on the other end of the line, struggling to catch his breath.

"Sorry. I was out back weeding the garden and almost didn't hear the phone ring. This is Sam Crawford."

"Would that be Detective Crawford?"

"Retired Detective Crawford. Is this Chief Sorensen in Nebraska? I've been expecting your call."

"I'm hoping you can help me."

196

The chief briefly reviews the recent activities in Redbud, from Sylvia's disappearance to Greg's death, as well as the appearance of the two old thugs who are now on their way to Missouri to face murder charges. With some embarrassment, he also includes the role of a four-pound Chihuahua.

Crawford laughs, "That's a first. A Chihuahua connection. I probably can't say much about that. But I remember Greg. I followed him for several months. Him and his girlfriend. We knew they were part of a big operation that reached beyond California and most likely into Canada and maybe even overseas. When we caught him, he had a trunk full of heroin. We figured we were about to shut down one of the biggest operations in the country. Didn't happen, though. He clammed up immediately. We couldn't get anything out of him."

Chief Sorensen sits up straighter in his chair.

"His girlfriend? Do you have a name for the girlfriend?"

"We never talked to her. She disappeared about the same time. But her name was, let's see, something with an 'S'. Samantha? Shirley? Sharon? Sylvia? Sadie? I'm not sure. My memory isn't what it used to be. But we weren't that interested in her. We were aiming for the top, for the mysterious figure running the operation. Our only clue was the code name Beluga."

There it is again. The name Beluga.

"Beluga as in the caviar or beluga as in the whale?"

Crawford laughs again, "We ran down a lot of blind alleys after Beluga. I'd like to say we snacked on a lot of caviar, but it would be more accurate to say that the white whale tried to snack on us."

The retired detective laughs again at his own stab at a joke.

"I'm guessing you had someone in mind? Your educated guess?"

Crawford sighs, "It's one of those cases I couldn't put down. Drugs were ruining a lot of people then, destroying families, spreading violence and death. For a long time, I had my eye on a nightclub owner who also owned a few whale-watching boats. Sam Abelov. Now, there was a piece of work."

The chief is furiously jotting notes. He's circled two of the possible girlfriend names: Sylvia, of course, but also Shirley. Now he writes down Sam Abelov.

"Very secretive. Stayed hidden. We didn't even have a description. We were hoping Greg would lead us to Sam, but that didn't happen. Then again, maybe I was wrong about Abelov being Beluga. What I do remember is that the Beluga organization slowed down to nothing and disappeared from our radar not long after Greg went to prison."

"And this Sam Abelov? What happened to him?"

If a shrug made a sound, Chief Sorensen hears a shrug.

"I'm guessing he's dead. If not, he's pretty old. Maybe eighty or more. I don't think we need to worry about him anymore."

The chief thanks the former detective and ends the call.

Then he sits for a long while, doing nothing but staring at the paper where he's written several notes. He is drumming his fingers across the page when Blanche buzzes to tell him the county coroner is on the line.

The chief picks up and hears the gruff voice of Dr. Harold Ames, a man whose high forehead and buggy eyes are enough to frighten some people even before they learn he spent most of his workday with dead bodies.

Dr. Ames starts, "This body from the burned-out car?"

198

He clears his throat several times.

"Yes?" the chief encourages him.

"I have something for you. The victim was shot several times in the back. I'm guessing he was running away from the shooter. Then the shooter must have dragged him back to the car, arranged him in the driver's seat and set the whole thing on fire."

He was running away.

***

Dr. Thomas rubs her skilled fingers over the small lump on the little Chihuahua's shoulder. She looks over at Daisy, who is searching the veterinarian's face for some sign of concern.

"Is it something serious?" Daisy asks. "Did she hurt herself rescuing me?"

Daisy's mother places a hand on her daughter's back, just enough of a touch to let the anxious girl know she's not alone.

Dr. Thomas smiles, "Birdy looks like a healthy dog to me, so I'm not too worried. But I'd like to know what this is."

She smiles as she softly pinches the lump.

"Let's see what an x-ray shows us."

A few minutes later, Dr. Thomas places the x-ray on a light board and steps back to analyze what she sees. It's an object, metal—like a microchip—but shaped differently. She guesses the object shifted closer to the skin yesterday, becoming obvious to the touch. This is no tumor, no twisted muscle, no evidence of disease, no swallowed object. Someone injected this piece of metal in this dog.

So, little Birdy. You are the messenger. The carrier pigeon. The carrier Chihuahua.

She recalls the day she'd arrived in Kansas City too late to pick up this same Chihuahua. Sylvia had been furious, screaming over the phone about how Shirley might have ruined everything. Shirley had asked why the dog was so important, and Sylvia had hung up on her.

Now she understands.

She reaches into a drawer and pulls out the scanner she uses to check dogs for microchips. As she passes it over Birdy's shoulders, nine numbers appear on the scanner's display. These are the numbers for the microchip Dr. Thomas herself had injected into Birdy when she carried the name Mia.

She lowers the scanner to pass it back and forth over the lump on Birdy's shoulder. Nothing happens. Dr. Thomas frowns. With Birdy tucked under one arm, she searches through another drawer until she finds an older model scanner she'd brought with her from California.

This time the scanner pings loudly as she moves it across the lump. A series of letters and numbers appear on the scanner's display. She hurriedly jots them down.

Does Sylvia have a scanner like this? Does she have these numbers and letters with her now and know what they mean?

Dr. Thomas knows what she's seeing. A code known by only a handful of people.

And she is one of them.

***

Audrey pulls up in front of the Redbud Animal Hospital in time to see a smiling Daisy leaving with her mother and Birdy.

"Is Birdy okay?" Audrey asks.

"She's just fine," beams Daisy, smiling broadly. "She has a little bump, but the doctor says it's nothing to worry about. She took an x-ray and everything. See her bump?"

Daisy holds up Birdy and points to the bump that Audrey dutifully fondles, frowning only slightly.

"She's a very special girl, that's for sure," She affirms to Daisy and, turning to Margaret, "and so is your daughter."

Audrey looks up to see Shirley standing in the doorway. She walks toward her and steps inside, closing the door behind her.

"Did you find the message?"

Shirley gasps, "How did you know?"

"A lucky guess. I knew someone thought that dog was pretty important. Why would that be? I was joking that a four-pound dog was too small to transport drugs, but then I realized she wasn't too small to carry a message as long as it was encrypted in a microchip."

Shirley nods, "I had no idea until Daisy showed me the lump. It felt like a microchip that might have slipped out of position, but it wasn't the chip I'd injected."

She explains how she'd scanned Birdy's shoulder and read the message, a series of letters and numbers, too long to be an identification chip number. The numbers and letters also make no sense as they are.

"But I know the code," she sighs. "I can figure it out."

She turns and looks out the lobby window.

"In California, we needed a way to pass private messages; we developed a code."

"We?"

"Sylvia, Greg, me, a couple of others. But eventually coded messages weren't enough. We couldn't write anything down. Too dangerous. That's when... well, that's when Nebraska started sounding like the place to be."

Audrey furrows her brow. She isn't sure what Shirley is hinting at. But she does remember the other question she'd come to ask.

"I understand you told someone you might be going out of town in a few days."

Shirley turns away from the window but doesn't explain.

Instead, she looks at the clock on the wall and announces, "I have a break before my next appointments. Maybe we should walk over to Chief Sorensen's office."

***

Blanche stands up to greet Audrey and Shirley.

"He's not here. He just left for the coroner's office."

She looks at the two other women, twisting a handkerchief between her fingers.

She lowers her breath, "He told me not to say anything."

"Blanche," Audrey asks, "do you know when he'll be back?"

Blanche presses her lips together as if holding back news she'd love to spread. She slowly shakes her head.

"OK." Audrey sighs. "Ask him to meet us at Bella's tonight. About 6:30. Tell him it's important."

"It always is," Blanche whispers.

"And tell him we'll be waiting for his news, and we might share a few surprises of our own."

***

Judy sits at her laptop, writing about an eight-year-old shih tzu that she's just named Sophia. Outside, the Nebraska sky fills most of the horizon with a cloudless blue.

Sophia is looking at me now, wondering what plans I might have for her. She's on my lap but I feel her shivering in fear. She has no reason to believe her life is about to get better.

A breeder brought her to us. She said she'd just taken in all the dogs from a puppy mill operator who was shutting down. Sophia was too old to breed, so the breeder didn't need her. If we wanted, we could have her. Otherwise, she'd have her put her to sleep.

We took her and soon found out that Sophia was not only too old, she had extensive physical damage. Her age was the least of her problems.

First, her mouth. The first thing we noticed was what looked like a misaligned tooth sticking out of the bottom center of her mouth. The truth was much worse. Our vet was horrified to see that the problem was a fractured jaw and that what we saw sticking out was not a tooth but a piece of the jaw. Next, the vet realized her jaw had completely deteriorated and was beyond repair. The vet pulled out the loose fragments and pulled the rest of Sophia's teeth. Around the molars, the vet found pus pockets eating away at her mouth.

But the worst was yet to come. The vet figured the spay surgery would be easy. It wasn't. Someone (either the puppy miller or an incompetent vet) had done a C-section on the little dog and in the process had sutured the uterus to the bladder. The vet worked to separate the uterus from the bladder, clearing away black infection in the process. Finally, the vet completed the surgery.

Sophia survived and is now on the way to recovery.

It's horrifying to imagine how much the little dog suffered to make money for her puppy mill breeder.

We're making Sophia a promise. Only the best ahead from now on. Only the best.

Judy posts her blog, along with Sophia's picture, and shuts down her computer. She strokes Sophia and then closes her eyes.

I understand wanting money. I understand wanting to live well. But when making money means hurting others? Humans or dogs? That is wrong, so wrong.

Judy and Audrey both reserve the term puppy mill for the worst of the commercial breeders; Sophia had certainly come from one of the worst. Judy continues stroking the little dog.

Her mind drifts to the woman in Missouri who died when the two old thugs broke into her home to snatch a Chihuahua. For them, it was money; for the Missouri woman, it was everything. Her thoughts move to Sylvia, Greg and Shirley.

Was their California story about money? And had they hurt people? Or maybe many people?

She opens her eyes and looks out the window. The blue Nebraska sky is as bright as her thoughts are dark.

Is everything always about money or the lack of it? The worst dog breeders neglect and abuse helpless animals in their drive to make money. Drug dealers become wealthy while destroying other lives. And what about those who conduct legal businesses but increase their personal wealth through practices harmful to both their employees and their customers?

Judy sighs and stands up, trying to shake off her gloomy thoughts. She wonders when Audrey will be back home from visiting Shirley.

Minutes later, as if she has summoned her, she sees Audrey pull into the driveway.

Audrey has barely walked in the door before she begins a breathy explosion of news.

"Hurry," she adds. "We've got to feed dogs, clean up, and get to Bella's by 6:30."

CHAPTER 19

Audrey bursts into Bella's, a long silk scarf looped around her neck and trailing behind. She is a woman on a mission. Her sleeveless sundress swirls around her legs as she stops suddenly, scanning the café. In a far corner, Randy sits next to Shirley, her head bent, the chief leaning back slightly in his chair.

Audrey fairly sprints toward them with Judy hurrying to keep up. Judy has changed into orange pants and a short-sleeved white shirt. Her change of clothes has brightened her outlook, but she worries about what she might soon learn. She tucks a loose hair behind one ear as she slides into a chair.

"How much have you told him?" Audrey asks Shirley, possibly a little annoyed that they'd started talking without her presence.

Randy sits up straighter and pats one of the hands Audrey has placed, palms down, on the table.

"Some things are for my ears only, Audrey."

But he turns to Shirley and asks how much she wants to repeat for Audrey and Judy.

Shirley seems to swallow hard before beginning to speak.

"I'm not proud of what I did in California. I know it was wrong, but at the time it seemed like the answer to all my problems." She looks up and scans their faces as if looking for understanding, friendly nods.

"You'll remember I replaced Sylvia as an exotic dancer at the nightclub. I wasn't sure what Sylvia and Greg were up to at first, but eventually I started to suspect they were involved with drug trafficking. I asked them about it."

Ellen Carlsen

"What made you suspect drugs?" Judy asks, remembering her earlier musings about how often people hurt others in their search for wealth.

"All the whispering. The late night calls. The money. A lot of money. Finally, I asked them straight out what it was all about."

"And they told you?" Audrey leans toward Shirley, then looks up and sideways to check out the somber expression on Randy's face.

"Not only did they tell me, they invited me to be a part of their business. And they made it sound so easy. We would just do a few more jobs and we'd have all the money we needed. Then we'd quit. That was the plan."

Audrey looks again at Randy before turning to Shirley with her next question.

"But how did you even know how? Where do two Nebraska kids and a teenaged runaway from North Dakota make the contacts to import and distribute drugs?"

"The owner of the nightclub was a player in the drug world. That's how it all began—with a simple offer to Greg and Sylvia. All they had to do was pick up a package from someone at a bus station. For that, they earned more money than they could in a year. And about then, they really needed money."

She pauses. "They really wanted money. Remember? I told you they had big dreams."

Shirley looks from Audrey to Judy.

Judy jumps in, "I thought Sylvia had a sugar daddy, and that was where she got her money."

"That wasn't quite the case. Sylvia had help—from the nightclub owner. But…"

She looks at Chief Sorensen. "I guess I can tell them this?"

208

The chief nods. Knitting in hand, he is connecting a new color to the expanding sweater on his lap.

Shirley smiles, as if amused by what she's about to say. "There was no sugar daddy."

Audrey pats one side of her head, causing her corkscrew curls to spring out from her face and back. It's a nervous habit.

"No sugar daddy? Just someone who offered her—all of you—a way to wealth? Who was this man?"

"Not a man. A woman. A very smart, very mean woman."

"What about the police? How could they not know about her?" Audrey asks.

She looks briefly at Randy again and sees his smile.

He nods at Shirley, letting her know she may go on.

"They knew they had a big drug operation headquartered in their territory. But they were always looking for a man. They watched the nightclub for a while but finally moved their investigation elsewhere."

"Then what?" Audrey asks.

"By the time Greg was arrested, we'd been on our own for a long time. I was completely out of it, working as a newly minted veterinarian. Sylvia owned her own travel agency but still made money with drugs. But Sam Abelov wouldn't leave us alone. She never let us forget what she'd done for us, or maybe I should say to us," Shirley whispers.

"Police caught Greg with a trunk full of heroin. We hoped he would finger Sam and get off with a short sentence or even probation. He never would have betrayed Sylvia or me, but he would have happily given them Sam."

"Why didn't he?" Judy asks. "He could have saved himself a long sentence."

"That evil woman somehow got a message to him in jail. She told him Sylvia and I would die if he said a word about her."

One tear trembles on the lip of Shirley's left eye, gradually slipping off to slide down her cheek.

Judy, who has no sympathy for drug traffickers, does admire courage and sacrifice, and she recognizes that in Greg's actions.

"That's so sad," she sympathizes, then presses further, "but it's not the entire story, is it?"

Shirley shakes her head.

"You're right. That's only part of it. And I'd rather Chief Sorensen tells you the rest, or whatever he decides he should. I'm a little wasted right now and need to get back to a couple of patients at the clinic."

She stands up and walks quickly out of the café, just as Bella and Carl show up at the table, ready to take orders."

"I have a vegetarian pizza to die for," Bella crows, and then suddenly covers her mouth. "Oops. Wrong word. Sorry about die."

She describes a pizza with fresh mozzarella, red onions, spinach and tomato sauce with just enough honey, pepper and lemon to make it interesting.

"Oh, and we also have steak and baked potatoes," she directs this to Randy.

She takes an order for one veggie pizza that Audrey and Judy will share and one steak and potatoes meal for the chief.

While Bella takes the orders and tries to pry loose some news from Randy, Carl steps behind Judy and asks if she can come by tomorrow sometime. He wants to ask her a few questions about Martin's stories.

"Let me guess," she concludes, "you and Martin are on a search for rubies."

"Guilty," he admits, laughing. "Maybe a little brainstorming will lead us in the right direction."

"Let's try lunch," she teases.

After the couple return to the kitchen, Judy and Audrey turn to Randy.

"Well?" Audrey asks. "Why did you visit the coroner today?"

* *|*

I only told one lie. Well, maybe two.

Shirley reaches into a cage to pull out a Maltese recovering from surgery for a broken leg. A three-year-old girl had dropped the white lapdog while carrying it down the stairs.

How many times have I warned people about small children and small dogs? If people with small children also want small dogs, they need to train the children first.

She sighs and strokes the dog while checking the cast. She prepares an injection for pain. When she's done with the Maltese, she takes a chocolate Lab outside for a quick bathroom visit. The Lab will go home tomorrow. This dog had required surgery for removal of a pair of socks.

Labs will eat anything.

She shakes her head, smiling, remembering the annual contest among veterinarians for the most unusual x-ray of an ingested article. Labs always win, she remembers. Labs always win.

With her patients bedded down, she reviews her conversations with Chief Sorensen and, minutes ago, with Audrey and Judy.

I'll straighten everything out soon. I'll tell the whole truth, the rest of the story.

She looks around the clinic before locking up, checking for anything out of place. Satisfied that all is well, she leaves for her car.

Tomorrow I'll find someone who can cover for me.

She'd told Chief Sorensen about the message encrypted in a microchip inside Birdy. But she'd lied when she told him she couldn't break the code. She'd done that easily.

Not a serious lie at all. More like a delay.

But there's no way she can justify the other lie, except to say that she just isn't ready to address that part of the story.

She hasn't told him about Beluga.

***

At Bella's, the night is just beginning. The little Redbud café attracts diners from Omaha and other nearby towns. Laughter and conversation bubbles upward and spreads like smoke through the comfortable room. But at a back corner table, the three occupants keep their voices low and their heads bent, occasionally looking around to make sure no one is near enough to listen to them.

"Why did you visit the coroner?" Audrey repeats when Randy doesn't answer fast enough. "Blanche wouldn't tell us anything, but she said it was something big."

"Well maybe not big, but certainly important."

He stops to finish off the last bite of steak.

Wiping his mouth with his napkin, he continues, "The body in the car was definitely Greg. The California prison system's dental records for Greg matched what the coroner found. I was expecting that, but the rest was a surprise. He died from gunshot wounds to the back."

Both Audrey and Judy gasp.

Audrey asks, "Does that change anything?"

"Well, we know for sure it wasn't an accident," the chief confirms.

He yanks at his knitting, pulling loose a couple of stitches. "Damn."

He pulls the knitting closer to his eyes to repair the damage, his lips pursed and brows furrowed.

Is he upset with his knitting? Or is he turning over something in his head, something he knows now that he hadn't known before?

Both women wonder the same thing as they wait for him to finish.

He sighs and puts down the knitting.

"We also have bullets from the weapon used. That will be important when and if we recover the gun."

Audrey drums her fingers on the table.

"So who do you think killed Greg?" Audrey leans closer to the chief. "And that brings us back to the old question of why Sylvia ran. Did she think she was next?"

"Or did Sylvia kill Greg?" Judy interjects.

The chief shrugs. Audrey and Judy can speculate all they want; he has no more to say.

Judy finishes the last of the vegetarian pizza and wipes off her fingers. Looking from Audrey to Randy.

"So all we know for sure is that Sylvia is traveling somewhere with Thomas Hardin. Right?"

"Only half right," answers Audrey, pointing to the man entering Bella's.

A very rumpled and weary Thomas scans the room and shuffles toward the table at the back of the room. Randy stands up to meet him.

Less than a minute after Thomas enters Bella's, an elderly woman scowls her way in the door on the arm of a handsome man. Bob Jenner, the contractor Judy had met to discuss construction and remodeling at the old Jensen farm, moves slowly toward the back table, grinning all the way.

He smiles at Judy and explains, "I thought that as long as I was in Redbud, I should visit my great aunt Eunida and take her out to dinner."

An obviously pleased Audrey wiggles in her chair and invites Bob and Eunida to join them.

Randy returns and greets the new arrivals and excuses himself, saying he will see Mr. Hardin home.

Judy tries not to blush.

Eunida complains about the lighting. "It's not bright enough in here. How am I supposed to read the menu?"

Then she stretches her head, tortoise-like, toward the woman with the corkscrew curls and the flapping scarf, the woman demanding her attention.

"Eunida, I'm Audrey Nevins. I've been meaning to stop by. Have you ever thought of adopting a dog? I have one special senior dog looking for someone to love. What do you think?"

Both Judy and Bob laugh.

But Eunida tilts her head, as if thinking it over.

***

"Of course, if you end up with this guy, you'll also end up with his crabby great aunt Eunida."

Audrey spreads her lips in a somewhat creepy clown smile as she looks over at Judy in the passenger seat.

"Audrey! No!"

Judy concentrates on the farmland they're passing on their way home.

"Why not? He obviously has his eye on you. He's handsome. He has a job. He knows how to use pronouns correctly. And he doesn't listen to hate radio."

"How do you know that?"

"Know what?"

"That he doesn't listen to hate radio."

Judy leans back in her seat and closes her eyes.

"I'm tired," she mutters.

"Well, you'd better wake up or you'll miss a great opportunity, a great man."

"How do you know he doesn't listen to hate radio?"

Audrey huffs, "Didn't you hear him mention the author he heard interviewed on NPR? See! Another good thing. He reads!"

"Audrey, please."

Judy keeps her eyes closed.

"I'm not ready. I'm so not ready I could win a contest for most not ready to meet a man."

Audrey lowers her voice, "I'm sorry, Judy. I just don't think you should spend the rest of your life with a bunch of old women twice your age."

"You're not old."

"Borrow my bones sometime and you might reconsider that statement."

Judy smiles and opens her eyes. She looks over at Audrey, who appears to be forcing herself to remain silent.

"You set this up, didn't you? Of all the contractors in the state, you just happened to know one who was handsome, single and apparently a nice guy. Right?"

"Guilty. But that doesn't make me a bad person."

"No. It just makes you a meddlesome old woman."

"I'm not old."

"Ha! You just said you were. Make up your mind."

Audrey suggests changing the subject.

There is so much we don't know. For example, what will Chief Sorensen learn from Thomas Hardin? Where is Sylvia? What is Shirley not telling us?

Then there's the Chihuahua affair.

Audrey describes what she'd learned from Shirley. The Chihuahua carried a message so important its sender didn't want it in writing.

What is in that message? And if Sylvia should have received the message, how did it end up with a woman in a small Missouri town? And how did Sylvia know which dog was meant for her?

"My head is spinning again," Judy groans as they pull into the driveway.

A chorus of barks erupts from inside the house.

"Mine too," Audrey agrees, slapping her forehead with one hand.

Stepping on the porch, she stops for a moment before pulling out a key.

"Time to take care of the dogs."

216

She opens the door and steps aside to wave Judy inside ahead of her.

"And tomorrow I'm taking Ruby the Pekingese over to meet Eunida Heppelwhite. They're perfect for each other."

***

"Do you have a passport?" Lois asks Carlton.

"No. I never thought I'd need one."

"Then you obviously won't be going to Quebec to look for Sylvia."

They sit side by side on the sofa, Carlton with his hands pinched between his knees.

"But I want to know the truth. I want to know if she's gone forever or if she plans to return," he pleads.

Lois says nothing, thinking the answer is obvious.

When Carlton remains quiet, she asks, "How do you even know she's in Quebec?"

"I'm not sure, but she's been going to Quebec every August since we were married. She says it's the best time for whale watching on the St. Lawrence."

He tells her what he'd learned from Chief Sorensen about the call from Thomas Hardin that might have come from Syracuse, NY.

"She often stopped there on the way north."

"I have a passport, if I can remember where I put it," Lois concedes.

***

Elsewhere that night, several others are pulling out their passports. Shirley slips her passport into her purse. Randy removes his from a locked box and taps it thoughtfully on his thigh.

Judy pulls open her bedside table, looking for a tissue, and notices her passport nestled under a pile of clutter. She looks through the pages, remembering times she'd traveled with her husband.

Those were good times. France. Switzerland, Costa Rica. New Zealand. I wonder if I'll ever travel again. I enjoyed those vacations so much. Each page of this little blue book, each stamp, brings back memories.

She feels a tear slip down one cheek.

Is it time to move on?

She touches the picture on her nightstand of the family that is no more. Her husband. Her baby. Their deaths crippled her in many ways.

Will they understand? What if I'm not the most unready woman in the world, unready for romance, unready for anything but helping dogs, unready to be anything but a Dog Lady in a small Nebraska town?

She decides she is too tired to write in the journal she's recently started keeping. Instead, she crawls into bed and pats the space beside her. Three dogs respond by jumping onto the bed. Shenzi the chocolate Lab places her blocky head on Judy's shoulder.

"Shenzi, are you going to snore all night again?"

***

Randy pulls into Thomas' driveway after spending more than an hour listening to what the man has to say. Making sure the elderly man is comfortable, he leaves to sort through all that he hadn't known a day ago, less than a day ago.

He has to admire the old man, although the chief has trouble thinking of Mr. Hardin as elderly. His grandfather, who'd died at age 110, was his idea of elderly. Mr. Hardin is a whole other category.

Thomas had told the chief how Sylvia had come stumbling into the wildlife sanctuary just as he was about to unlock the door to the visitors' center. She'd insisted that he help her.

"Really insisted. Quite strongly. And if you know anything about Sylvia, she doesn't take no for an answer."

The chief doesn't know that much about Sylvia and is wondering if any of what he knows is accurate, but he accepts Mr. Hardin's words.

Thomas explained how he'd taken Sylvia to her home where she picked up a suitcase.

"First she had me drive around the block to make sure Carlton's car was gone. She was in and out of the house in a hurry. Then she pointed the way out of town. She didn't tell me where we were going and ignored all my questions about what was going on. She said it was better I didn't know. I know she's in some kind of trouble. I just don't know why."

Thomas had reminisced about Sylvia from the days when she was one of his favorite students, how smart she was, how likely to succeed.

"I wonder what went wrong. She cried part of the way and swore quite a bit. I never knew that about her, the mouth on her, that is. But I always liked her. I thought Sylvia and Carlton made a good couple. I thought they were good for each other. But when I mentioned Carlton, she told me to just shut the f up. She said she needed to think."

The chief had patted the distraught man on his back, tut-tutting a bit about the experience he'd just been through. He praised Thomas's willingness to help a former student. Then he'd asked if Sylvia had said anything about where she was going.

"She didn't say, but I'm pretty sure she was heading to the Canadian border. I saw her checking her passports. And in Syracuse, she rented a car and thanked me for the ride. Just like that. Like it was nothing unusual at all. She thanked me and waved as she drove away. So I turned around and headed home."

The chief felt like tucking the poor, tired man into bed. He elected not to upset him further with what had been happening in Redbud while he was away.

Mr. Hardin needs a good night's sleep. And so do I. A bourbon would be nice, too.

Back home, the chief sighs as he drops heavily into his favorite chair. He knows it's too late to stop Sylvia at the border. He considers his next move.

Meanwhile, his knitting project rests on the floor next to him, but he no longer feels like picking it up. Maybe he'll start on a hat for Daisy. But he doesn't feel like that either.

He needs a drink.

For a long time he sits, silently going over what he knows, putting the separate pieces together into a picture that makes sense.

He imagines Sylvia, Shirley and Greg, three young people struggling to get by in California. Suddenly the strip club owner offers them a change to make a lot of money. Easy money. They understand the risks. But they'd only do it once. One pick up. One delivery. That would give them all the money they needed. The chief has heard that story before.

A great opportunity to make good money. The chance of a lifetime. One risky venture and they'll be on their way. Who could it harm? Only people who make their own stupid choices. One time. But one time leads to one more time. And one more time. Were they just innocent kids who foolishly decided to work with an obviously disreputable strip club owner? Or were they not so innocent after all? Why in real life is everything so complicated, so gray? Why is it only in the movies that you can easily tell the good guys from the bad?

Shirley had divulged quite a bit about her California days. She told him about the ruthless Sam (Samantha) Abelov. Shirley had danced in Abelov's club for a while. She had learned of the older woman's drug operation. She'd helped Sylvia and Greg when they first began working for Abelov and later when they ran their own business.

He remembers Shirley's hushed description of those times:

"It was so exhilarating at first. The money poured in like water from a broken faucet."

Her face had darkened then as she described the escalating danger, their plunge into a world of danger and crime.

"We never thought we were hurting anyone," she'd said, begging for understanding. "I pulled back, telling them to leave me out of what they were doing. I had all the money I needed. And I was terrified. I thought that at any moment we'd be caught either by the police or by others in the drug world, those who thought we were cutting into their wealth."

The chief leans back in his chair, trying to imagine these three staying a few steps ahead of some very dangerous people, people who killed easily and often.

Shirley had put a hand over her heart when she talked about Sylvia's bravado.

"She did a good job of acting very tough. She even kept a list of bad guys for hire, the type who took care of messy problems."

She'd looked up with a stunned expression on her face as if just realizing how extraordinary her story must sound.

"But then things became very dangerous. We'd already developed a code we used with any written communications. But eventually even that wasn't enough. We were literally packed and ready to run when Greg was arrested."

The chief had asked about the money they'd made. What had happened to that?

"Greg had hid it away before he was arrested. We couldn't get the information from him because if we visited him in jail, they'd arrest us. If he wrote to us, the police would know how to find us. So we moved to Redbud and waited."

An extraordinary story, indeed. It's easy to put together. Greg remained silent and the two women escaped to the tranquility of a small town in Nebraska where Shirley became Dr. Thomas and Sylvia became the wife of Carlton Ritter. If Sam Abelov was still alive, she might have been waiting for the day Greg left prison to shake him down for money she thought belonged to her. Then what? What happened that night when Greg picked up Sylvia while she was walking her newly adopted dog?

Shirley admitted that she and Sylvia both knew Greg was out of prison and heading this way. She didn't know anything about Sam Abelov, whether she was dead or alive or still capable of doing them any harm.

But what about the Chihuahua? If Greg or someone else had shipped a dog with an implanted message, how did it end up in Missouri, and how did the little dog end up finally in Sylvia's arms? Why didn't it go directly to Sylvia? What went wrong? And why was it necessary to send a coded message under the skin of a dog when Greg was coming to Redbud?

Finally, an excuse to call Audrey, as if he needs one.

He picks up his phone and is relieved to find Audrey still awake and reading in bed.

He intends to probe her thoughts on how the little dog with a secret message finally made it to Sylvia. Instead, he looks at his shaking hands and imagines how they'd feel holding a glass of bourbon, the way he'd let the first gulp slide easily down his throat, the delicious shudder after that first swallow, the warmth spreading through his veins, the glorious relief.

"I need some company," he confesses, without mention of the little dog.

She doesn't need to ask why or when.

"I'll be right over."

CHAPTER 20

Audrey is nowhere to be found.

Judy wakes later than usual, wondering why Audrey isn't already clattering away in the kitchen. Remembering the horrible day she'd found Audrey unconscious in the living room a year ago, Judy steps into her slippers and pads down the hall to peek at Audrey's favorite recliner. No Audrey. She walks through the kitchen to make sure Audrey isn't being extra quiet for some peculiar reason. No Audrey. Next, the yard. No Audrey. Now really concerned, Judy hurries to Audrey's bedroom door, which she finds half-open. No Audrey.

Damn! Where is she? I am feeling a mild panic coming on, if there is such a thing as a mild panic.

A look out the front door reveals no Redbud Area Dog Rescue van in the driveway. Judy calls Audrey's cellphone and hears it ringing down the hall.

She must have left in a hurry, but where did she go?

Sensing restless dogs around her, Judy begins letting dogs outside. Then she calls Chief Sorensen, who answers on the first ring.

"Audrey's missing!" she calls into the phone.

"Hold on," he responds.

The next voice Judy hears is Audrey's.

"I'm fine, Judy. Just start feeding the dogs. I'll be there soon."

Judy smiles to herself, relieved.

Oh, of course!

"You're sounding pretty chipper this morning," Judy teases.

"Just feed the dogs." Audrey laughs.

"Audrey?"

"Yes?"

"It's about time," Judy whispers into the phone. She chuckles and raises her voice slightly, "Say hi to the chief. Oh, and no hurry. I've got it covered here."

***

Lois promises Carlton she'll find out the truth about Sylvia, even if she has to run her down. Carlton suggests Sylvia might be in Canada, at her favorite whale-watching spot in Quebec—the village of Tadoussac. He knows the places she usually stays and even the names of a few restaurants.

"It's a small place. If you can't find her at the hotel, watch as the whale-watching boats come and go."

He disappears into his home office and returns with several postcards.

"She sent these to me last year."

Lois studies the cards and tucks them into her purse.

"I'll do my best," she promises, hoping that her best won't involve Sylvia returning to this poor man she has so misused.

"I'll find out where her head is now. I promise that."

I might be falling in love with this man. What will I do if Sylvia comes home? What will he do?

She always liked Carlton, even when she knew him only as Sylvia's quiet husband, the forgettable boy from high school. Now that she knows how unforgettable he actually is, she struggles to pound down complex emotions. She reminds herself that she'd been

Sylvia's friend too—or at least a friendly acquaintance. She sees now that she never knew Sylvia that well. Oh yes, she always understood that Sylvia kept a lot to herself, but Lois figures she came as close to being a friend to Sylvia as anyone in Redbud.

But do I really know him at all? Which Carlton is the real Carlton? For that matter, who is Sylvia? What do I really know about her? And why is Carlton asking me, of all people, to search for his wife?

Carlton signs on to his laptop, arranging an airline ticket to Montreal.

"Would you like to rent a car in Montreal or take a second flight to Quebec City and rent a car there?"

Lois balances her choices for only a few seconds. She likes driving more than she likes waiting in airports. She'll have enough of that when she changes planes in Chicago.

"Montreal."

"OK," Carlton confirms, and reads off the details of her Friday morning flight.

Lois stands up, realizing how much she needs to do. First off, she needs to drop her foster dogs off with Audrey and Judy. Then pack, of course, and make sure the bank knows she'll be out of the country and will honor her debit and credit cards in Quebec.

"I'll do my best," she repeats again, "I'll do my best."

This is so silly, the girlish way I feel about Carlton. It's almost as jolly as the idea of Randy and Audrey falling in love, as if either of them will even acknowledge their feelings for each other.

She wonders how she'll react when she catches up with Sylvia.

Who's to say I won't turn into a mean girl and make sure Sylvia stays away from Redbud?

She sighs, knowing she just doesn't have a mean girl inside her.

***

Audrey sails through the front door at about 10:30 a.m. shouting for Judy, who looks up from her laptop.

"Hurry! We've got some sleuthing to do!"

"We've got some what to do?"

"Sleuthing. You know. Solving mysteries."

Judy considers crossing the room to hug Audrey, then reconsiders and holds back, then reconsiders again and actually does.

Mid-hug, she plants a kiss on Audrey's cheek and whispers, "Did you sleep well?"

Judy giggles.

Audrey extracts herself from the hug and turns away, just enough to hide her own smile.

"We have an assignment. We need to find out how Birdy ended up in Missouri. We need to find out what went wrong. If Greg shipped the little dog to Sylvia, how did the little dog end up in Missouri?"

They divide up chores. Audrey calls the police officer in the small Missouri town where the Chicago thugs broke into the home to kidnap the dog, and ended up murdering the dog's owner.

Judy begins calling shelters in Kansas City and searching for any stories online about missing dogs in the Kansas City area. On a hunch, she also calls a pilots' group that specializes in transporting animals.

Within minutes, they've put together a likely scenario.

Pilots4UrPets had picked up Birdy and several other dogs in California to fly them to Kansas City. Greg had delivered the dog and the transportation fee to get the dog to Kansas City. A local shelter picked up all the dogs, not realizing that one of the dogs was destined not for a shelter but for an individual, a woman who'd arrived an hour too late. The enraged woman wasn't able to find the dog or the pilots, who had already taken off for their next destination.

"We can only guess what happened next. Sylvia probably reached someone from Pilots4UrPets later that day. By then, several people were searching for Birdy."

Audrey tracks down the shelter that had picked up the planeload of dogs.

"I talked to the shelter director who remembered a lot of interest in that four-pound Chihuahua. She looked up her records and found the name of the man who adopted the dog. That would be the son of the woman in Missouri."

Judy nods, "And we know how Birdy ended up with us, and how Mel and Mort tracked her to us. We can also guess that Sylvia went through the same process, locating the dog in Missouri, and then making discreet inquiries to find out the dog had come here."

"Imagine her surprise to find out Birdy was here in Redbud," Audrey remarks.

Judy is silent for a couple of minutes, staring at her computer screen.

"There's only one problem," she looks up, "according to Pilots4UrPets, the person who was late to pick up Birdy wasn't Sylvia."

"Oh?" Judy looks at Audrey and can see her wheels turning.

Both women speak at the same time.

"Shirley."

Audrey quietly repeats, "Dr. Shirley Thomas."

***

Blanche looks up as Chief Sorensen strolls into the police station, whistling.

"Whistling? Really?" The office manager tilts her head and studies her boss. "What put you in a good mood this morning?"

Chief Sorensen doesn't answer, but Blanche detects a slight reddening about his neck.

"Maybe I should be asking *who* put you in a good mood."

Since she has a pretty good idea of what and who is responsible for his mood, she says no more and ducks her head toward the pile of papers on her desk.

The chief turns with one hand on his office door.

"Blanche? Could you call over to the animal hospital and see if Dr. Thomas can make time for me today?"

He pauses before adding, "And make sure her answer is yes."

He drops lightly into his chair and drums his fingers on the top of his desk, reviewing what he still doesn't know about the cast of characters in the drama playing out before him. His right hand drops down toward the floor before he realizes he hasn't brought his knitting along this morning.

No problem. Don't need it. I'll finish that sweater eventually and knit a hat for Daisy, but I don't need yarn and knitting needles next to me all the time.

The evening before, he'd felt overwhelmed, tormented by his growing knowledge that some otherwise good people had fallen into bad ways.

Youthful indiscretions? Or more? The line between good and evil blurs so often and in so many strange ways.

He remembers a book he'd read once about a lawyer who was involved in a series of nefarious deals that included bribing judges. The author of that book had accomplished the impossible, the chief thought, by making the crooked lawyer the one character the reader cared about the most, and for all the right reasons. The lawyer was the only character in the book who actually loved other people and went out of his way to help them.

I keep wishing things could be just black-or-white, good or bad, easy or hard. Instead, I see gray. The truth about anyone hides inside an emotional tornado. Our secrets define us.

Blanche interrupts his thoughts, cracking his door open enough to poke her head inside.

"She's gone. I called over to the animal hospital, and a Dr. Sullivan answered. He said he was filling in for a while."

"I don't suppose he knew how to reach her? Or where she'd gone?"

Blanche shakes her head.

The chief has a pretty good idea.

***

Chief Sorensen isn't the only one calling the animal hospital. No sooner had Dr. Sullivan hung up after Blanche's call when the phone rings again. This time a very excited woman starts talking before he can introduce himself.

"Who is this?" Audrey asks, once she realizes she's talking to a man and not to Shirley.

Dr. Sullivan explains who he is, why he's there and what he knows about Shirley's absence: Nothing.

"She asked me to fill in for a while. I retired last year, but I fill in for vacationing veterinarians. She didn't say where she was going. She just said something had come up."

Back at Redbud Area Dog Rescue, Audrey relays the news to Judy.

"Is she running away? Or is she running after Sylvia? Are they joining forces? Have they been working together all along? Or? Oh, I don't know."

Audrey paces across the room, stopping only long enough to shush Cleo, a black Lab mix who's started barking incessantly.

Judy looks toward the door. "Someone's here."

"Open up," calls the voice. "It's me. Lois. I need your help for a few days."

Judy holds back Cleo and a couple of other dogs so Lois can slip in without any of them escaping to the outside. In each arm, Lois carries a miniature pinscher.

Judy and Audrey each scoop up a dog from Lois and motion her toward the sofa.

"What's up?" Audrey asks while snuggling the little dog in her arms.

"I need to be gone for a few days, so I'm hoping you'll make room for Nigel and Amy."

"Well, of course, but where are you going?" Judy probes.

Lois quickly outlines her plan to visit Quebec and track down Sylvia to find out if she's gone forever or planning to return to Carlton.

"I'm doing this as a favor to Carlton. He needs to know where he stands."

Both Audrey and Judy nod and look at each other. As if the same thought has occurred to both of them at the same time, they blurt out together, "But you can't go alone!"

Lois speaks slowly, smiling as she does.

"Who could go with me?"

She pretty much knows the answer to that one.

"But we can't all go," Lois objects, "someone has to take care of the dogs."

Audrey disappears down the hall as Judy and Lois continue talking about the logistics of getting to the village of Tadoussac along the St. Lawrence River.

An agonized scream erupts from down the hall. Judy bolts toward the sound only to run into Audrey, who is waving a passport in front of her.

"It's out of date. I forgot to apply for a new one."

"I guess we know who'll be taking care of the dogs."

Judy puts an arm around Audrey's slumped shoulders.

"Harrumph."

The phone rings at the same time Cleo the black Lab mix barks an alarm, followed by a soft knocking at the door. A thick red folder bearing the Jenner Construction logo leads the way inside the door, held at the end of Bob's outstretched arm.

"Hello? I thought we might discuss—"

He stops.

"What's going on? Did I step into the middle of an uprising?"

Audrey, not noticing the new arrival, calls over to Judy with her phone still in her hand.

"And now Randy says he's going to Quebec."

"Chief Sorensen is going to Quebec?" Judy repeats.

"And I can't go," Audrey pouts.

Bob puts his folder down on the table.

"What's this all about?"

And they bring him up to speed, as best they can when three people are talking at the same time and one is also talking on the phone.

He asks, "How are you getting there? It's a long drive."

Lois jumps in, "I already have my plane ticket. I'm flying as far as Montreal and driving the rest of the way."

"And I'm making arrangements right now," affirms Judy, poking away at her handheld.

Bob waves his arms, trying to get everyone's attention at once. "Wait! Stop! I'm a pilot and I have access to a plane. I can fly you there."

Audrey turns back to her phone conversation and relays the offer. She nods back enthusiastically.

"The chief thanks you and can be ready when you say so."

Judy puts away her phone.

Lois picks hers up to begin cancelling her arrangements.

Bob gets on his phone, arranging to have his plane ready as soon as possible.

All explore their own thoughts as their travel plans take form. Lois reflects on Carlton and his request that she go to Quebec to locate Sylvia and find out her plans. Bob is looking forward to this opportunity to get to know Judy better. Judy mulls over Bob and his willingness to help, whale watching and the mystery they hope to solve.

Across town, Chief Sorensen hopes that in Tadoussac he'll find the answers to the rest of his questions.

***

A disappointed Carl decides to invite Martin out to the old Jensen farm where they can try out the new metal detector he bought online.

Judy cancelled their lunch plans. He had hoped she might remember something from her genealogical research that might point them in the right direction. So far, the only person aware of the possibility of rubies at the old Jensen farm is Martin, who heard the stories from his grandfather.

Had the old man been confused? Probably, we've found all the buried treasure a person could hope for already. Why be so greedy?

He smiles to himself. "Ah, but it's so much fun."

"Carl, where are you?" Bella calls from the kitchen. "We need to get ready for the lunch crowd."

Carl looks around the café, checking the tables, spotting a few dislocated chairs and tucking them into proper positions.

We can't help it, I guess. It's part of the human condition, this thirst for treasure, this hunger for sudden, easy wealth. Or maybe it's just the quest we need, the search, the journey.

He sighs and pulls his phone from his pocket to call Martin.

Who knows? Maybe we'll stumble over something. Maybe it'll rain rubies.

***

"Where is the gun?"

Chief Sorensen leans back in his chair and looks at Officer Ryan.

"We need the gun," Officer Ryan agrees, "if we're to match the bullets with one particular gun."

Chief Sorensen talks through the possibilities, sharing his thoughts with his officer. One, of course, is Greg himself. As an ex-con, he can't legally purchase a gun, but he may have had one stashed away or obtained one from someone who didn't care about the laws regarding gun sales. Plenty of people like that around. Greg could have lost control of the gun during a struggle.

"He might have lost the gun in a struggle, but that wasn't how he was shot. The coroner thinks he was running and was shot several times in the back."

"So if Sylvia didn't shoot him, someone else was involved," Officer Ryan concludes.

The chief has a few ideas who else might have been there, but he waits to hear his young officer's thoughts. The chief has been careful to keep his young officers abreast of all new developments in the case.

Officer Andy Ryan, who to Chief Sorensen looks like a recent high school graduate, sits at the edge of his chair, thrilled to provide his opinion.

"Beluga?" the officer suggests. "The mysterious Beluga? Who might be Sam or Samantha Abelov? She would have the motive. Sylvia and Greg had cut into her business. They might have considerable profits hidden away, money she wanted back."

The chief rubs his forehead, still trying to insert one more worry line.

"Maybe. But Sam Abelov would be pretty old to be chasing down those who had cheated her. Not impossible, though. We need to check into her whereabouts. And if we like the idea of octogenarian murderers, what about Mr. Hardin? Maybe he isn't the honest retired chemistry teacher we all think he is."

"And what about Eunida Heppelwhite?" Officer Ryan quips.

They both explode with laughter.

The chief wipes away a few tears and reigns in his hoots before he's able to catch his breath enough to talk.

"As long as we're throwing out such a wide net, can we really rule out Mel and Mort, the Chicago thugs? Maybe they're capable of being in two places at the same time."

They both laugh again so loudly that Blanche sticks her head in the office just to see if they're okay. They assure her they're just letting off a little steam while trying to solve a murder.

Blanche disapproves of the levity. They can tell by the way she slams the door shut behind her.

"Does Sylvia Ritter own a gun?" asks Officer Ryan.

"If she does own one, would she really have it with her while out walking the dog?"

Officer Ryan points one finger at the ceiling as if to make a point.

"She might, if she knew she was about the find herself in a potentially dangerous situation."

"Meeting an old lover? How dangerous can that be?"

The words have no sooner left his lips that he realizes how ridiculous they sound. Meeting an old love is one of those encounters pumped full of danger to the point of bursting.

"What about a stranger? A coincidence? They just happen to run into someone on a lonely Nebraska road. Maybe it was a farmer who doesn't like trespassers on his property."

Chief Sorensen discards the stranger possibility but gives his officer credit for coming up with the angry property owner scenario. Without trying too hard, the chief throws out a few more possibilities, some more likely than others. The chief feels things are coming to a head, either in Redbud, Nebraska, or in Canada somewhere along the St. Lawrence River.

Is going to Quebec the right thing to do? Or should he stay behind in Redbud?

Where is the gun? Where is the gun?

***

While others pack for a quick trip to Quebec, Audrey scoops up a grumpy red Pekingese and stalks out to the Redbud Area Dog Rescue van. If she can't go to Quebec, she can at least match a grumpy dog with a grumpy old lady.

Audrey has other reasons for her bad mood. Her morning included several calls about dogs in need of rescue:

One found tied to a vacant trailer, thirteen years old and not in the best shape. Could Redbud Rescue take her?

Another left alone in the backyard without food or water while his owner traveled, sometimes for five or more days at a time. Toby is about ten years old and has a heartworm infection. Neighbors finally talked Toby's owner into giving him up. Could Redbud Rescue take him?

Finally, a frantic woman called about a border collie that has lived at the end of a chain for almost ten years. Its owners are moving and threatening to have the dog put to sleep. Could Redbud Rescue take this dog?

What's wrong with people? How can anyone think it's okay to treat dogs this way? God, I hope they don't have children. Give me a grumpy old lady anytime.

As Audrey pulls up to Eunida's home, she remembers being told that Sylvia had grown up next door and that Eunida has nothing pleasant to say about Sylvia. Audrey closes her eyes for a moment trying to imagine growing up on this small-town block with a snoopy, crabby neighbor. She marches up to the front door, hoping for magic.

When the old lady opens the door, her face actually brightens at the sight of the red, frowning Pekingese in Audrey's arms.

"Come in. Come in."

Eunida shuffles aside with her walker to make room for Audrey. Once both are sitting, Audrey drops Ruby the Pekingese onto the floor. The dog sniffs around the living room, then disappears into the kitchen for a few minutes, finally returning to look out the sliding glass door to the backyard.

"I think she likes it here," Audrey concedes, gritting her teeth.

Come on, Ruby. You're supposed to be selling yourself, not ignoring both of us.

Audrey tries to send mental messages to the orange Pekingese rapidly waddling back and forth in front of the sliding door.

"Maybe she needs to go outside," suggests Eunida.

Audrey pushes herself out of her chair and walks over to slide open the door.

Ruby prances outside and circles the entire yard before returning to request reentry. The dog looks up at Audrey and snorts, then turns away and trots quickly over to Eunida. The dog jumps easily onto her lap and gazes upward at the surprised old woman's face.

Audrey claps her hands.

"She likes you. She really likes you."

The dog then closes the deal by placing her front paws on Eunida's shoulders and licking her chin.

The old woman giggles.

The Pekingese doesn't actually smile, but its perpetual frown takes on a more benign appearance.

Audrey breathes, and puts her hand over her heart as if pledging allegiance to the flag. If this isn't a match made in heaven, it's at the very least a very good match.

So what if I'm staying in Redbud while Judy, Lois, Randy and the handsome contractor are all leaving for Quebec, and Shirley is on her way to who-knows-where. I'm having a good day, and last night was more than just good.

She smiles most of the way home, until the driver behind her blasts his horn several times and then accelerates past her.

Someone's in a hurry to get out of town. Before long, I'll be the only one left behind.

***

Chief Sorensen ends his phone call to Missouri with a sigh. He wishes he could answer the question of the day, but he doesn't know the answer. He doesn't yet know Beluga's actual identity.

Missouri has all the evidence they need to convict the two old Chicago thugs, but prosecutors also want the person who hired them in the first place. That's the person who set in motion the events that led to the death of an innocent woman.

A callback from California will tell him what he needs to know about Samantha Abelov, the woman who owned a nightclub and a fleet of whale-watching boats while also running a drug operation.

Is she the real Beluga?

He rubs his forehead again.

Who is responsible for the death in Missouri?

He drums his fingers on his desk.

Who killed Greg Long?

He can feel the answers rushing toward him. Part of him wishes he could just get out of the way. He calls Officer Ryan and gives him several specific instructions for the next few days. The chief already arranged for some extra help from the county police.

"You may be the one with all the action," the chief cautions, standing up and stepping away from behind his desk to reach out and shake his officer's hand.

His cellphone sings out. He smiles as Audrey invites him over for a leaving-for-Quebec-tomorrow dinner.

He returns to his chair just as the phone rings again with a callback from California.

He has one of the answers he needs.

***

Shirley chews on a fingernail, a habit she had beat many years ago, but now she gnaws away like a hamster as she waits in line for a rental car. Her flight to Montreal was uneventful except for the mad rush through Chicago's O'Hare terminal to catch her international flight. She envisions what awaits her in Tadoussac.

"Madame?"

Shirley looks up at the counter attendant and wonders if she should stumble through her slight French vocabulary. She decides instead to beg for mercy.

"English?" she pleads.

The girl at the counter smiles and switches seamlessly to her second language.

They must think all Americans are stupid or at least selfish to be fluent in only one language.

A few minutes later, she buckles into her rental car and winds out onto the highway east toward Quebec City. She'd been this way only once before—the one time Sylvia invited her along for her annual whale-watching trip on the St. Lawrence River.

She smiles, remembering the Zodiac boat they climbed aboard every day of their vacation. Sylvia had chatted and charmed the other passengers with her vast knowledge of the whales they were seeing. The boat's captain had simply given up and turned the narrating over to Sylvia.

It was fun. It was really fun. But this year is different.

She wonders what's happening back in Redbud.

Does everyone know by now that I'm gone? Probably. Where do they think I've gone? Will they figure it out? Does Chief Sorensen see me as a criminal? Am I a criminal? In my mind, not at all. But, I know it looks bad. I lied and ran. Two things guilty people do.

Questions keep running through her head.

Greg is dead! Who killed Greg? Does anyone suspect me? I met up with Sylvia and Greg that night. Did I leave some sign behind?

They'd discussed the Chihuahua affair. That's what they'd called it. Greg had done his part in California. After getting out of prison, he'd found a prison contact who encrypted a code onto a metal chip which another contact (a vet who'd done time for tax fraud) implanted in the Chihuahua that Greg had received as a gift. They didn't want to leave a trail anyone could follow. No emails. No letters. The implanted chip contained half of the information they needed to recover their money from a Swiss account. Sylvia had hidden the rest of the information in a painting she'd donated to the Hotel Tadoussac, along with an annual donation sufficient to keep the watercolor of beluga whales up on a lobby wall.

They had put their plans on hold when the police arrested Greg. Sylvia and Shirley couldn't approach Greg for his half of the information without risking their own freedom. So they'd waited for Greg's release. Shirley wonders if Sylvia was trying to shut her out. Sylvia hadn't told Shirley about the importance of the Chihuahua, hadn't explained that it was delivering an important message.

Should I have figured it out earlier? Why didn't I just ask? Something about best laid plans. How could things go so terribly wrong? Sylvia and I have lived respectable lives for so long. We're good people. So is Greg. So was Greg. He suffered to protect us.

She remembers her panic when the Chihuahua wasn't waiting for her in Kansas City. One little mistake. A traffic delay. And what followed changed everything.

She follows the signs pointing west to Quebec City and beyond.

I wonder if I'll ever see Redbud again.

***

Back in Redbud, Audrey decides to cancel the dog adoption event scheduled for the next day. She notifies the store, updates the website and sends out a mass email to people who may have planned to attend. She can't handle such an event on her own.

Meanwhile, she isn't completely unhappy about not going to Quebec. She welcomes a few days alone with her thoughts, time to relive the awakening of emotions between her and Randy.

Ridiculous. Ridiculous. I'm past sixty and he's getting there. We should be rocking and knitting. Well, he is knitting.

She smiles to herself. Minutes earlier, she'd kissed him goodnight as he returned home to pack before the early flight to Quebec. Judy had stayed out of the way, swimming with Shenzi the Labrador retriever after dinner, then hiding in her room while she packed for tomorrow.

She's the one who should be smooching with a new fella. I hope something sparks between Judy and that nice contractor—even if he is related to Eunida Heppelwhite.

She laughs at that thought. Maybe Eunida isn't so bad after all. She just needs something to love.

For a change, she doesn't waste a single thought on Sylvia or Carlton, Shirley, Greg, Mel and Mort or even Birdy the Chihuahua.

She'll get back to that tomorrow.

CHAPTER 21

"Look at the waterfall!"

After landing in Quebec City, they duck into a waiting rental car and soon find themselves arguing among each other about whether *est* means east or if *ouest* mean east. Lois had forgotten that French was the language of Quebec.

"That last sign said *est*. We need to go east, but what if we put a 'w' in front of *est*? Wouldn't that mean we are going the wrong way?" Lois asks. "And *ouest* could be pronounced 'east,' which could mean we're going the wrong way."

Randy sighs and wonders how he'll ever survive the next 130 miles to Tadoussac.

"*Est* is definitely east," Judy confirms, finally settling the argument.

She looks up from her smartphone and hands it to Lois.

"See. We're going the right direction."

She looks out the car window in time to insist that they all stop to see the waterfall.

Bob agrees to allow twenty minutes at the waterfall. He pulls into the parking lot and they all read the posted information about the waterfall that plunges 272 feet in a thunderous spray. They climb up to a viewing station where, looking north, they can see the broad waterfall and feel it on their faces. Turning their backs, they look out over a spectacular view of the St. Lawrence River.

"I wish we were just here for a vacation," Judy whispers.

"Me too," Bob replies.

He also enjoys the view before beginning to round up his passengers.

"We want to arrive before dinner," he encourages.

As they continue east, Bob refuses any more stops, not even to see the Sainte Anne de Beaupre shrine or to shop in any of the pretty little towns nestled in the Charlevoix hills.

"Look at that sign!" Judy points. "That's not a deer on that sign."

Randy looks, "No, it's a moose."

"Something you really don't want to run into," Bob assures.

A few miles down the road, high fencing appears on both sides.

"That's to keep the moose off the road," the chief informs. "They were having too many moose/auto accidents, with casualties for both people and moose."

The fencing holds back the woods for much of their trip until a sign warns them that the fencing has ended.

"They're reminding us to keep our eyes open now," Bob instructs.

And all three passengers start peering into the woods on both sides of the road, watching for any emerging antlers. As they draw closer to their destination, they stop briefly several times to admire stunning panoramic views of the St. Lawrence. Finally, they roll onto a ferry that crosses over the Saguenay River to deposit them in Tadoussac. They find their two-bedroom rental unit above the Restaurant Le Bateau. After dropping off their luggage, they head down to the restaurant where they find a table that looks out over the St. Lawrence.

"Oh, I wish Carlton could see this," Lois sighs.

Randy doesn't say anything, but his thoughts return to Carlton.

How can I possibly understand a man who can so easily hide his true self and play the role he needs to play?

He looks away from the St. Lawrence to watch tourists ambling through the village.

Will we find Sylvia soon? Is Shirley also here?

He studies his menu awhile and notices Judy and Bob leaning head-to-head over a single menu. They look over toward the buffet and leave the table together. The chief smiles, wondering if a romance might blossom. He turns to make polite conversation with Lois while continuing to watch the parade of people outside. Later, he'll check in with Officer Ryan. He'll also need to make a courtesy call to the local police.

Lois is talking about Carlton again, chattering away about how different Carlton is once you get to know him.

She sounds like a woman in love. Carlton seems to be a different person for different people. Can she ever really know him? How could he have so easily won the heart of this woman, who is at an age when most women approach suitors with considerable caution? Is she just lonely? Is that what makes her so vulnerable?

He can't think of any way things will work out for Lois and Carlton, and that makes him uncomfortable.

"Should we try the buffet?" Lois's question draws Randy back to earth.

***

"What are we going to do now?" Shirley asks Sylvia.

Shirley found Sylvia on the lawn in front of the Hotel Tadoussac, where she was perched at the edge of a low-slung wooden lawn chair, binoculars held against her eyes and aimed out beyond the beach.

"I can see part of the beluga colony from here," Sylvia announces, as Shirley drags a chair over and collapses into it.

From where she sits and without binoculars, Shirley sees a few white spots, like flags waving in and out of the water.

She repeats her question, "What are we going to do now?"

Sylvia sets the binoculars in her lap and turns toward Shirley.

"Oh, Sylvia," Shirley whispers as she looks at Sylvia's red-rimmed eyes and the dark circles smudging her still-lovely face.

She reaches over to clutch the other woman's hand.

Sylvia smiles.

"This was supposed to be such a lovely day. The three of us were going to celebrate and plan our future lives. Finally, we'd claim the wages of those few sinful years of our youth."

She laughs at her words. They'd joked so often about the wages of their sins. Pretty good wages, too, for a few misspent years. Now Sylvia considers the biblical interpretation of the wages of sin.

Shirley interrupts her thoughts, "And now what? Can we still do that—just us two? Can this still turn out good for us?"

"Without Greg? He waited so long for this. He suffered so much for this."

Shirley adds, "He changed so much. He wasn't the same. Prison changed him."

"He just needed time. He and I, we belonged together. We could have been happy again."

"Maybe," Shirley shrugs, remembering the dullness in Greg's eyes, the flatness in his speech when they'd all met that night outside of Redbud. "So what do we do now?"

Sylvia lifts the binoculars to her eyes again and moves them slowly from left to right.

"I had to run. You know that. It wasn't safe for me. I knew you'd be okay and you'd know how to find me."

Shirley nods.

Sylvia continues, "The money is all still safe and there's plenty of it, more than I ever imaged. It has grown since Greg first deposited it. We are rich beyond our wildest dreams, Shirley."

"But?"

Sylvia knows what Shirley is asking. They sit in silence while Sylvia continues studying movements in the waves.

After a thoughtful pause, Sylvia resumes, "If it were just about the drug trafficking, we'd be okay. No one is interested in crimes that old. We're way beyond the statute of limitations."

Sylvia leans forward as if she's spotted something in the distance.

Without taking her eyes off the water, she speaks more softly, "But that woman in Missouri. That's a different matter—for me, anyway. I hired Mel and Mort to recover the Chihuahua. They were the only ones I could think of for the job and by some miracle we were able to contact them after all these years."

"I never told anyone about you," Shirley professes. "No one knows you were the one in charge."

"No one knows?"

Sylvia pushes herself out of the low-slung chair and turns to offer a helping hand to Shirley.

Once they're both standing, Sylvia looks straight into Shirley's eyes, warning her, "Chief Sorensen may sit around knitting like an old woman, but I'm betting he has it all figured out. He may even be here in Tadoussac right now. In fact, I hope he is. He needs to know the truth."

"But, Sylvia!" Shirley feels confused, uncertain of where to turn.

She and Sylvia have a long history, but they've never been that close.

Can I drop everything and tie my future and safety onto Sylvia's wild wings?

Sylvia turns and smiles, "If we hurry, we can go out on one of the last whale-watching boats of the day. And tomorrow, we'll try the first boat out."

***

Back in Redbud, Daisy picks up her own binoculars and aims them at the Ritters' home, which has been dark and quiet all day. She sees several people moving through the home and a couple of police cars parked out front.

"What's going on?! Mom! Dad!" she yells from her scouting post in front of her bedroom window.

Both of her parents appear in her doorway and position themselves behind her.

"I'll bet they're searching for something," Daisy insists, picking up Birdy just to make sure the little dog is safely in her arms.

"A search warrant, maybe?" Martin suggests.

"But what would they be searching for?" wonders Margaret.

In her most hushed and mysterious tone, Daisy suggests, "Maybe they're looking for a dead body. Or a weapon. Maybe they're looking for a murder weapon. That's what they're always looking for in the television shows."

The three of them form a tight triangle with Daisy in the front and take turns peering through the binoculars.

"Redbud certainly is a lot more exciting that I thought it'd be," Margaret mutters.

"Where's Carlton?" Martin wonders.

After staring out the window for a while, he picks up his cellphone to call his new friend and fellow treasure seeker, Carl.

"You won't believe what's happening over at the Ritters' place. The police are there searching the house."

After he ends his call, Carl tells Bella, who calls Audrey, who calls several others…

***

Alone at home with most of the dogs bedded down for the night, Audrey practices an old dance step in the living room. Her corkscrew curls bounce about her face, and she laughs to herself.

I feel young again. Well, younger. Maybe ten years younger. Maybe fifteen years younger.

She is barefoot and braless, dressed in a baggy shirt and loose sweatpants. When you're alone, you can relax, she figures. You can dress as you please and sing as loudly as you wish. She doesn't want to be alone forever, but she loves this evening alone.

She begins singing an old Carly Simon song, something from the days when she really was young.

Randy had called earlier from Quebec, checking in to make sure she's okay. The chief didn't say much about his trip and simply asked about her day.

How sweet of the old boy. Actually, maybe I shouldn't call him an old boy. He's younger than I am. A younger man. Ha!

"I'm seeing a younger man."

She practices the way she might say that to a stranger, someone who just happened to start up a conversation with her and just happens to ask her about her love life.

"I'm seeing a younger man," she might say, with a sly smile.

The chief warned her to keep the door locked and to not let anyone in.

Who is he worried about?

She wonders if he's worrying about her in a police chief sort of way.

Or is he just worried about me? Or is he worried about some specific villain who might be knocking on my door?

After Bella calls with her report about something happening at the Ritters' home, Audrey makes a few calls herself. The small-town way, faster than any other means of communication, except for maybe texting, which she's never grown used to.

Has something happened to Carlton? What could they be looking for at the Ritters' home? I wonder if the Redbud travelers have caught up with Sylvia yet. I wonder if Shirley is also in Quebec. Is Lois really falling in love with Carlton? How could that not turn out disastrous?

And then she remembers a few tap steps from when she was about six years old. She begins stomping and spinning around the room. Finally, out of breath, she drops into her favorite recliner and turns on the television. She picks up the waiting glass of red wine, smiles, stretches her legs and wiggles her toes.

A little later, she suspects she hears someone tapping on the front door. Several dogs wake up, howling. She's about to get to her feet when she remembers Randy's warning.

"Thank you, Randy," she breathes. "I don't feel like solving anyone's problems tonight."

Instead, she calls Officer Ryan to tell him someone is prowling around outside her house.

How's that for being a good girl.

Then she dances off to bed.

***

In Quebec, the Redbud travelers return to their two-bedroom condo after an evening of walking through the charming village. They'd watched the sunset from the boardwalk overlooking the St. Lawrence. Several dogs run about the beach below, and Randy wonders if Audrey would have paid them a visit.

The tired travelers, though, all elect to sit quietly for a while. They had not seen either Sylvia or Shirley, but they haven't tried that hard either. They're leaving that encounter for tomorrow. The chief is pretty sure they'll find them at the Hotel Tadoussac, the stately 1970s hotel overlooking the St. Lawrence. In the meantime, he wants to collect his thoughts.

Officer Ryan reported back about what they'd found at the Ritters' home. One more piece of the puzzle falls into place. The chief doesn't like the emerging picture.

He looks around and sees Lois anxiously ringing her hands, perhaps rehearsing what she'll say when they find Sylvia.

Is she wondering if Sylvia will say she's returning to Redbud and Carlton? That poor woman might be in for an unhappy discovery or two before long. She's a survivor, though, and she has good friends. She'll be fine.

Randy looks at the next bench where Judy and Bob sit side by side.

They seem comfortable together, but their body language stops short of being what you might expect of romantic partners. And yet, they might be moving in that direction. Judy, with her history of loss, will proceed cautiously, even fearfully.

He hopes Bob is the patient type.

And what about me? What's ahead for me?

He smiles as thoughts turn to Audrey.

Are we both just a couple of old fools? Maybe, but who really cares? Whatever is happening sure feels fine.

Other tourists walk past him, speaking French in what sounds to Randy like the songs of exotic birds. He'd talked to the local police earlier, explaining his presence and purpose here. They'd offered any assistance he needed but reminded him that he's no longer in the United States. He's in a foreign country. He has limited powers here. Very limited.

Randy gets to his feet and stretches.

"Maybe we should get on back," he recommends. "We have a big day ahead."

He doesn't mention it, but he also wants to get back to his knitting.

***

"Why exactly are we here?" Bob looks up from the English-language program they'd found on the television in their Tadoussac rental. Bob knows about some of the recent happenings in Redbud—the kidnapping, the body in the burned car—but he isn't sure how all that led to this spontaneous trip to Quebec.

Judy and Lois try to update him, but he throws up his arms when they start talking about the role of a small Chihuahua currently in the care of a child detective.

"Stop!" he laughs. "Enough! You lost me at the Chihuahua."

Judy laughs with him, but adds, "Maybe it's not as complicated as it seems. At least our reasons for being here are pretty straightforward. I'm here to help Lois."

Lois looks over at Bob.

"And I'm here to find out if Sylvia plans to return to Redbud and to her husband. Carlton asked me to find out for him."

"That seems like an unusual request. Couldn't he find out for himself?" Bob asks.

Lois starts to explain Carlton's lack of a passport but then wonders herself why he couldn't just make a few calls to the hotel where he thought Sylvia was staying. She looks over at Chief Sorensen as if he can sort it all out.

"I'm here to ask Sylvia who killed Greg Long. She was there. She either saw the shooter or was the shooter."

"Now that makes sense." Bob nods as he plays with the remote control, running through other options on the television. "But I'm guessing you already know which it is."

Chief Sorensen nods.

Judy and Lois both sit up straighter.

"Who?" they ask in unison.

Ignoring them, he concentrates on his knitting. After a few stitches, he looks up.

"And I need to know the real identity of Beluga. The Missouri authorities want the person who hired Mel and Mort, even if that person only wanted them to collect the Chihuahua and not kill anyone."

"But I thought Shirley told you about Beluga," Judy remarks.

The chief nods but says nothing.

They all look up at the sound of someone knocking on the door.

"Who could that be?" Bob asks as he walks over to peek outside and open the door wide.

Sylvia and Shirley step inside.

***

Chief Sorensen pushes himself out of his chair. He merely nods at the two arrivals and points to a table they can sit around.

"You must promise me one thing," Sylvia requests as she pulls out a chair and sits down. "Promise me we'll all make it onto the first whale-watching boat tomorrow. That's all I ask. For that, I'll tell you everything. You'll close your case. Everyone will be happy."

The chief has to correct her, "I don't think anyone will be happy."

"Sorry. Bad choice of words."

As Shirley sits, silently staring at her hands, Sylvia tells her story. She divulges their youthful exposure to a drug-infused world and the money they'd made dabbling in that world.

"We left the nightclub and Sam Abelov behind after a few years. I opened my travel agency. Shirley finished school and joined a veterinary practice. Greg worked with me at the agency and led many tours, often transporting drugs to and from foreign locations at the same time. It was a natural fit."

She looks around at her listeners and attempts a slight smile.

"What about Shirley?" Judy asks.

"Shirley?" Sylvia turns to look at her friend. "Shirley was involved in the early days, but she stepped back after she earned her veterinary degree. She said she didn't want any part of it anymore."

Shirley nods without looking up.

"Then what?" the chief prompts.

Sylvia shrugs.

"It was a once-a-year adventure. Sometimes twice a year. Greg and I would use the contacts we'd made earlier and arrange everything. God damn, it could be such a rush."

Judy notices Shirley slowly shaking her head as if to say "but not for me."

"As I said, Shirley had pretty much dropped out, but Greg and I still saw her as part of the team. So we planned one exit adventure. One big deal. Big risks. Big money. Then it would be over. And we'd split a big payout—all of us."

She looks over at Shirley.

"And that's when everything fell apart?" the chief figures, and Sylvia nods.

Sylvia describes an increasingly dangerous world. They realized that the authorities and the competition were both closing in on them.

"A roller coaster ride is a great, screaming adventure until you're flying off the rails. And we were flying off the rails. We started communicating in code only and decided to run for cover."

"To Redbud," Judy concludes. "To the safety of Redbud."

"Yes. But we didn't move fast enough for Greg, as you know."

Her last remark drops a blanket of silence over the room. Finally, the chief asks his two main questions.

"Who is Beluga?"

"Why, I am, of course." Sylvia smiles, a slight expression of pride on her face. "But you knew that, didn't you?"

"And who killed Greg?"

Sylvia pauses for a moment, always the dramatic schoolgirl playing a role.

"You know what I'm going to say, don't you, Chief Sorensen. Who killed Greg? Why, the best actor of us all: Carlton Ritter."

Lois screams.

***

Audrey is still reading in bed when she hears the pounding at her door, followed quickly by a rising cacophony of barking and howling.

"Ms. Nevins! Ms. Nevins! This is Officer Ryan. Are you okay?" The young officer successfully outshouts the dogs.

He must be using a megaphone, she quips to herself, as she steps into her slippers and reaches for her robe. She pads to the door and opens it to see Officer Ryan and another officer on the other side. The red and blue lights on their cruiser pulse, boldly streaking the yard and porch.

"I'm okay. What about you?" she asks, looking around the yard.

"You called earlier about a prowler. I drove by and didn't spot anything, but we decided to take another swing by." He points toward the pool. "Whose car is that?"

Audrey spots a car partially hidden by the fence on the far side of the pool.

"Not mine."

SPLASH!

The officers take off toward the pool. Audrey shuffles along a respectable distance behind them. As she arrives at the pool, Audrey watches the two officers pull a fully clothed man out of the pool. Stepping closer, she recognizes Carlton.

"What's this all about?" she demands. "You fell in, obviously, but…"

Suddenly in no more than ten seconds, she slips together the last pieces of the mystery and beholds the whole picture of events that answers her question.

"It was the husband all along. Just like it usually is."

Do I sound a little disappointed at the banality of it all?

Water streams down Carlton's face as he stands bracketed by the two officers, each gripping a soggy arm.

"I was going to turn myself in. I thought I might find the chief here," he confesses.

"Or maybe you thought you'd find a place to hide and a hostage," suggests Officer Ryan.

Audrey pulls her robe about her tighter, although the night temperature hasn't dropped much from the scorching highs of the daytime.

"You have the right to remain silent." Audrey hears Officer Ryan begin the oft-heard Miranda warning. She follows them to the patrol car and watches as an officer places a hand on Carlton's head, easing him into the backseat.

"I'll let Chief Sorensen know you're okay."

"Don't bother. I can do it myself."

CHAPTER 22

Chief Sorensen keeps his word. The next morning all the Redbud visitors, including Sylvia and Shirley, line up for the orange or yellow padded overalls and hooded jackets they'll wear on the Zodiac boat that will take them out on the St. Lawrence.

"We should be easy to spot if the boat overturns," the chief mumbles. "I wonder if we'll float."

He also wonders if this all might be a mistake—both going on the whale-watching trip and granting Sylvia her request. Both Sylvia and Shirley had promised to return to Redbud. It seems fair. He has trouble thinking of Sylvia as the fearsome Beluga of past years. Or either of them as people who would know anything about drug trafficking.

And yet. And yet. Sylvia is a special case. As is Carlton. As is their marriage. Redbud citizens have always gossiped about the Ritters, always wondered how the most popular girl in her high school class had ended up with the most forgettable boy.

As the chief steps into his orange suit, he laughs with the others about their new Doughboy physiques. If only this were just an ordinary vacation, an experience to share with friends.

He looks over at Sylvia, whose mind seems elsewhere, her face set in a determined mask.

Masks. That's what Sylvia and Carlton have in common. They both clothe themselves in personalities of their own creation. They both know how to play roles so well, to be what circumstances require. To fool the world. To fool even each other. To fool even themselves.

"Hey, chief. We're heading to the wharf. Wake up."

Judy punches his arm and they all join a line of people waddling toward the boats, laughing about their getups, bubbly about the two hours ahead of them. Judy has been reading brochures about the whales they might see and is trying to cheer up Lois, who's been morbidly silent since learning the truth about Carlton. She'd tried to beg off the whale-watching trip, but Judy talked her into coming along.

Randy looks over at Judy and Lois.

Lois will get over this. She'll be fine.

He isn't so sure about Sylvia or Shirley. Although Greg had actually hired Mort and Mel to recover the Chihuahua, Sylvia had told him what to do and who to hire. She had confessed to being Beluga. She would need to answer to Missouri authorities.

Shirley probably won't face prosecution. Sylvia signed a statement saying that Shirley had nothing to do with hiring the two Chicago thugs. Sylvia asked Shirley to pick up the little dog, but that was the extent of Shirley's involvement. As for Shirley's part in the drug business? Her illegal activities are too far in the past to be of interest to California authorities. She'll suffer only from the opinions of others. Will she stay in Redbud?

The brightly colored lineup of eager whale watchers begin stepping onto the boat, grabbing railings as the boat bounces with each new passenger. The captain directs his passengers to their seats and begins explaining the rules, speaking first in French and then in English.

The boat, with its twenty-four passengers, backs away from the wharf and turns about to begin slapping its way out to the whales.

It doesn't take long. They aren't far from the shore when several white heads pop above the surface. The captain points and the passengers on the wrong side all stand up for a closer look, causing the boat to wobble slightly. A few of the standing passengers drop suddenly to their seats

"Belugas!" someone yells.

No sooner have the watchers admired the round-headed belugas, who are watching them back, than the captain shouts and points in the opposite direction.

"Minkes!"

Heads swing around and the boat dips slightly in the opposite direction as passengers maneuver for better views.

Minkes, Judy explains to those around her, are among the most common and smallest of whales.

"They still look like they could take on this boat and win if they wanted to," the chief comments, shading his eyes for a better view.

He glances briefly at Sylvia and Shirley who are side by side at the front end of the boat. Sylvia has climbed up to sit on the boat's edge with her feet on the seat. She seems to be fussing with her hood, pushing it back off her head. Shirley, by contrast, sits solidly on the seat, hands pressed between her knees, eyes focused more on the boat's floor than the whales in the water.

"Madame! Sit down! On the seat, *s'il vous plait*," the captain calls out to Sylvia.

She instead lifts her binoculars to her eyes and points out beyond the minkes.

"I see a fin whale!" she shouts.

The captain takes a look for himself and turns the boat slightly for a better view. The broad back of the eighty-foot long whale appears as a dark arch above the water, one fin pointing skyward.

"*Oui, Madame! Oui, Madame!* Yes. Yes. This is a treat. We don't see a finback every trip. We are lucky this morning."

Then he turns toward Sylvia, perhaps to smile or thank her. But what he finds instead is Sylvia, now stripped of her bulky orange suit

"Madame, no!"

All heads turn away from the whales to the middle-aged woman perched on the edge of the boat as if on a high-dive board. In the next few seconds, all but one of the whale watchers freeze, and their silence leaves only the sound of water slapping against the rocking boat.

Chief Sorensen stands up and begins edging toward Sylvia. With his eyes on Sylvia, he still registers Shirley huddled with her head in her hands. He reaches too late for Sylvia, who dives off the boat and starts swimming for the pod of belugas.

His empty hand still outstretched, Chief Sorensen watches Sylvia disappear among the whales. Around him, he hears the rising voices of the other passengers and the alarm in the voice of the captain as he screams into his radio for assistance.

CHAPTER 23

EIGHT DAYS LATER

Randy pushes open the door at Bella's and looks around. He is one of the first Sunday breakfasters to arrive.

Good.

He walks over to his favorite corner table and claims a chair where he can sit with his back to the wall and an unobstructed view of the door.

He's had plenty of time during the past week to analyze the "Chihuahua Affair"—the series of incidents that had led to three deaths and one kidnapping. Dead include the Missouri woman, Greg Long and now Sylvia Ritter, presumed drowned in the St. Lawrence River.

In a fair universe, the bad guys would actually look evil, and the good guys wouldn't waiver from their goodness. Drug lords shouldn't look like Nebraska housewives. Murderers shouldn't be quiet, shy and forgettable. Shoot, even Mort and Mel looked more like character actors than thugs for hire.

The chief raises an arm to welcome Audrey and Judy, who hurry single-file across the café to his table.

Audrey slips in next to him and demands that he show her his knitting. He laughs and pulls the sweater-in-progress onto the table's top.

"You've barely made any progress at all. You need to get with it."

"I hope to. I hope to," he laughs and pecks her on the cheek.

Judy notices that the chief also reaches under the table to take Audrey's hand in his.

"So when did you figure out Carlton was the one who had murdered Greg?" Judy asks.

Audrey adds, "And when did you first suspect Sylvia of being Beluga?"

Randy sips his coffee thoughtfully. "At first, I suspected everyone. That's the way it works."

"We know that," Audrey huffs.

The chief nods, "It could have been an unknown outsider. It could have been a known outsider, such as Sam Abelov. It could have been Sylvia herself, Shirley or even Mr. Hardin. Suicide wasn't completely out of the picture."

"And?" Judy prompts him.

"Suicide seemed out of the question since Greg and Sylvia were expecting to live happily and richly ever after. Sam Abelov left the suspect list after I found out she'd died ten years ago. Mr. Hardin had no motive, at least, nothing to gain. I knew Shirley was hiding something, but I guessed she was most likely protecting Sylvia. Sylvia? Only if Greg was double-crossing her. For a while I wondered if Greg and Shirley were the ones planning to drive off into the sunset."

"But you finally settled on Carlton?" Audrey suggests.

The chief explains what he'd learned about Carlton's youth—his history of violence and his responsibility for the death of a classmate. Carlton had explained away the death as an accident but admitted to fighting with the victim. He'd claimed he was protecting someone from a bully. Police reports told a different story—one in which Carlton's intention was to kill or seriously harm the other student.

"Sylvia was right when she said Carlton was the best actor of them all. He was able to hide his true nature all through high school. He later adopted one personality for his wife and home, and a completely

266

different one for his work in Omaha. I saw more than one of his personalities just before we left for Quebec. I think he was starting to fall apart and was unable to hide behind a mask much longer."

Both women nod as if to agree.

"Then two things happened. Carlton asked Lois to go to Quebec to find Sylvia, an odd request. I think he wanted her out of the way so that he could more easily make his escape."

"But that didn't happen," Audrey reminds him. "He never got any farther than my swimming pool."

"That was because of the second thing. He ran out of time. Once Carlton became our prime suspect, we needed to find the murder weapon. Before I left for Quebec, I obtained a search warrant for the Ritters' home so that my officers could search for the murder weapon."

"Which they found," Judy chimes in.

"Which they did indeed find. They found Carlton's fingerprints and no one else's on the gun. And as you know, they picked him up outside your place."

"Thank God you didn't go outside to investigate the noises you heard that night," Judy smiles at Audrey, relieved.

Audrey reassures her, "For once, I thought before I acted. I was already suspecting we had a murderer loose in Redbud, and I had a fair idea of who that might be."

Conversation stops for a moment while Bella brings by a plate loaded high with freshly baked muffins.

"What else?" she asks, while pouring coffee all around.

They place their orders just as several other neighbors stop by with their own questions. After they move on, Audrey asks what Randy knew about the night Carlton shot Greg.

"As Sylvia told us, she and Greg left in his car to an out of the way place to discuss their plans. Shirley joined them briefly and then left for home. Shortly after, Carlton arrived on foot. He must have followed them and then hid his car so he could approach silently. He started shooting, and they both ran. Greg fell; Sylvia kept running and eventually hid in a fallen tree trunk all night. In the morning, she found her way to the nearby wildlife sanctuary and to Mr. Hardin. Apparently, Carlton carried Greg back to the car and set it on fire. He may also have thought he'd killed Sylvia and her body would be found soon."

"He must have been shocked when he found out she was still alive," Judy muses.

Audrey repeats what most people in Redbud had been saying, "I just can't see any of them as criminals."

Judy taps a fist on the table.

"Well, Eunida Heppelwhite can. She's going about saying she was the only one who always knew there was something wrong with Sylvia. She's saying she always wondered about Carlton too."

Audrey grins, "And you know that how?"

Judy blushes, "Bob told me. He's been working every day at the farm site. I've been there… supervising."

Audrey smiles and lifts an eyebrow.

"Does he need a lot of supervising?"

"I'm also there to keep Carl and Martin out of his way. They've been out there every day with their spades and metal detectors, hoping rubies will fall out of the walls or shine out of a shovel full of dirt."

"There's just one thing I still wonder about," Audrey watches Judy's expression and assures her, "No. Nothing about rubies. I wonder if Shirley was supposed to dive off the boat, too."

"Maybe," answers the chief. "But she came back without knowing what she might face here. You have to give her credit for that."

"I'm hoping the town will forgive her," Judy says.

"We have to. She's a good veterinarian and we need her."

"And we like her."

"She did make some serious mistakes," the chief adds.

To which Audrey responds, "Well, who hasn't?"

***

Lois opens her laptop. Two foster dogs look up from their resting spots at her feet to study her face. She pulls up a Facebook page. Pausing only a few seconds, she leaves a message for a man she hasn't seen in thirty years: "Remember me?"

Smiling to herself, Lois finds a dating site for people over fifty.

I was such a fool. But that's me, I guess. I tried to help someone. What's wrong with that? It's who I am. But maybe now I'll start helping myself. Or someone more worth helping.

***

Daisy lounges on the deck, binoculars aimed at the neighbors' birdfeeder.

"Look at that, Birdy," she chirps to the Chihuahua on her lap, "three goldfinches and a white-throated sparrow."

Daisy strokes her little heroine dog. After filling out some paperwork for the Redbud Area Dog Rescue, Daisy has become Birdy's official guardian.

"I think I'm going to have a good year," Daisy tells Birdy. "I've already made a few good friends and I've learned the middle school has a good drama program. They're doing The Lion King this year. I can't wait to try out!"

***

Dr. Thomas peers into the scruffy stray's cloudy eyes and knows the poor thing is at least twelve years old. She finds a yeasty infection in both ears, infected teeth and what looks like mange over most of her body. She runs her hand over the hairless tail and the greasy, reddish rump. All four feet glow a raw red.

She shakes her head.

She's already treated the dog, Millie, for fleas and several intestinal worms. She is the only hospitalized dog this Sunday morning.

"You poor thing. I don't know when I've seen a more neglected dog. You're lucky Redbud Rescue decided to give you a chance."

As she talks to the dog, Dr. Thomas draws blood from one of Millie's skinny legs and begins running a test for heartworms.

"Someone loved you once. You're friendly and housebroken. What happened? How did you end up all alone? You break my heart."

She kisses the top of Millie's head, bringing her nose close to the dog's foul odor.

"A bath, my child, a bath will help you feel better."

She finds the right shampoo and holds her hand under the tap, waiting for the right temperature. She starts wetting down the twenty-pound dog and squirts on the shampoo. Once she has the dog bathed and wrapped in a towel, she checks the results of the heartworm test.

"Positive," she sighs. "As if you needed more trouble."

Dr. Thomas writes down a treatment plan. Millie will need several months before she'll be ready for adoption—maybe half a year, she guesses.

Once she has Millie dry and safely deposited on the softest dog bed she can find, Dr. Thomas looks at her computer. Her curiosity drives her closer to the keyboard.

In Quebec, before that last whale-watching trip, she'd told Sylvia that she didn't want any of the money. She'd rather stay a small-town vet. Sylvia had surprised her then by suggesting that they both take a suicidal dive off a whale-watching boat and swim into eternity. Shirley refused. She wanted to live. She wanted to return to Redbud.

However, she's curious about the money. She pulls up a chair and stares at the screen.

Sylvia made her choice and believed Shirley would follow her lead. That didn't happen.

I could use that money to do good things. I don't need to keep any myself. I'd just like to know how much there is. I'm the only one left who can turn that ill-gotten money into something worthwhile. I have a responsibility.

A few minutes later, she finds the information she wants.

TOTAL FUNDS: **$0.00**

Someone had emptied the account a week ago.

She throws back her head and laughs.

TO READERS:

Thank you for reading *THE CHIHUAHUA AFFAIR*. If you enjoyed this story, I hope you'll write a review and tell others about this book.

This is the second in a series that began with *REDBUD: A DOG LADY MYSTERY*, available on Amazon.com and as an eBook on Kindle.

The Dog Lady Mysteries continue in *THE GHOST OF REDBUD MEADOW*, and *THE REDBUD STRANGLER*.

You can visit http://www.ellencarlsen.com to learn about other books and upcoming projects. Or email me at EllenE9466@aol.com.

Made in the USA
Las Vegas, NV
21 August 2021

28580697R00154